CINDY GERARD

OVER THE LINE

"I'm blown away . . . Cindy Gerard is an absolute standout in the genre."
—JoAnn Ross, *New York Times* bestselling author

"Cindy Gerard's roller coaster ride of action and passion grabs you from page one and doesn't let up until 'The End'."
—Karen Rose, *USA Today* bestselling author

"Gerard's books are sexy and irresistible. You won't be able to stop turning the pages."
—Kat Martin, *New York Times* bestselling author

"Wonderful . . . will leave you sitting on the edge of your seat and gripping the pages. . . . Gerard does a beautiful job penning a spellbinding plot and charismatic characters that will leave you breathless."
—*Romance Junkies*

"A fast-paced thriller of action, adventure, and romance. This is a fantastic book in which to quickly escape the day-to-day routine because of the many twists and turns awaiting the characters."
—*Fresh Fiction*

"Cindy Gerard has a definite winner on her hands with *Over the Line*, the latest in the Bodyguards series. Intrigue, suspense, chemistry, and good old-fashioned romance all combine to keep the pages turning and the reader hooked from page one. If you're looking for a book to tuck in that summer beach bag, this one should be at the top of your list."
—*Writers Unlimited*

MORE . . .

TO THE BRINK

"Pulse-pounding action erupts from the very first page, dragging readers on a thrilling ride through both the past and dangerous present."
—*Romantic Times BOOKreviews*

"Not only does Cindy Gerard create flat-out exciting stories, her heroes are of the extremely macho, extremely virile, extremely sexy variety. . . . This novel is romantic suspense at its best. . . . Slick, edgy, thrilling, skillfully executed with some wonderfully sketched characters and loads of sizzle."
—*Romance Reader at Heart*

"Starts off with a rush and remains at a high excitement level until the final explosive climax. . . . Readers will enjoy the action, but it is the feelings that still exist between the protagonists that make this novel a very special cross-genre treat. Cindy Gerard writes a gripping high-octane romantic suspense." —*The Best Reviews*

"The sexiest and edgiest of the Bodyguards books yet. You'll feel like you're right in the thick of the conflict."
—*Writer's Unlimited*

"An intense escape from cold weather and winter doldrums."
—*Fresh Fiction*

"Spectacular. . . . Gerard's best book yet! A masterpiece of tight scenes, excellent dialogue, steamy sex, and heart-stopping adventure. You'll be thinking of this one long after it's finished."
—*Romance Reader's Connection*

"Moves fast and is both a tightly-woven thriller and a beautiful, sexy romance. . . . Outstanding series." —*Reader to Reader*

"Fantastic story. . . . heart-pounding action." —*Romance Divas*

"Fast-moving story, which has suspense and sexual tension moving in parallel. Characters are extremely well drawn. . . . First-time readers will no doubt start seeking Gerard's prior books in the Bodyguards series, which in reality is one of the greatest tributes to an author. This one is strongly recommended."
—*The Romance Reader*

TO THE LIMIT

"Crackles with sexual tension, dark drama, and thrills."
—*Romantic Times BOOKreviews*

"A super action-packed investigative thriller."
—BarnesandNoble.com

"Gerard has done an excellent job capturing the same blend of action and lust that powered her first book in this series, *To the Edge*. Though reading the books in order is a plus, this is one tale that can stand on its own. The characters are riveting, the action fast-paced, and the storyline superbly created. This is a great tale that lets you appreciate the slower pace of your own life while reveling in the adventures of the heroine."
—*Fresh Fiction*

"This second book in Gerard's the Bodyguards series is even better than the first, *To the Edge* . . . taut, suspenseful . . . filled with action, sizzling sex scenes, and fascinating settings and situations."
—*Romance Reader's Connection*

TO THE EDGE

"Edgy and intense, this tale of romance, danger, and past regrets is a keeper."
—*Romantic Times BOOKreviews*

"A tense, sexy story filled with danger . . . romantic suspense at its best."
—Kay Hooper, *New York Times* bestselling author

"Heart-thumping thrills, sleek sensuality, and unforgettable characters. I have one word for Nolan Garrett. Yum!"
—Vickie Lewis Thompson,
New York Times bestselling author of *Nerds Like it Hot*

INTO THE
DARK

BOOK SIX IN THE BODYGUARDS SERIES

CINDY GERARD

St. Martin's Paperbacks

INTO THE DARK   SEP 07 2007

ISBN: 0-312-98118-X
EAN: 9780312-98118-1

Printed in the United States of America

St. Martin's Paperbacks edition / June 2007

St. Martin's Paperbacks are published by St. Martin's Press, 175 Fifth Avenue, New York, NY 10010.

10 9 8 7 6 5 4 3 2

As always, this book is dedicated to the brave men and women of the U.S. military services who defend, on a daily basis, all that we hold dear. Your sacrifices are many, and we all owe you a huge debt of gratitude.

And to my amazing editor, Monique Patterson, who not only took a chance on me but loved this series from its inception and has championed and cheered it all the way.

ACKNOWLEDGMENTS

As in the writing of every book in this series, I've received generous assistance from many individuals. Without them, this book would not be what it is. In fact, it might not be at all. That said, very special thanks to the following individuals.

First and foremost, mega thanks to Joe Collins, FF/NREMT P, weapons expert extraordinaire and all-around great guy. Joe was my go-to guy for many areas of this book, foremost being weaponry and tactical planning. His generous sharing of information added incomparable depth and color to the story. Thanks, Joe, for everything—including an amazing day shooting.

Jim Connell, my guy in the sky. Again, thanks for your expert assistance on the Piper.

Gail Barrett, from the CNN loop, for once again coming through with her excellent assistance with my Spanish translations. Also thanks to her friends Lino and Miriam Gutierrez for adding the Argentina influence.

Victoria Wasserman, also from the CNN loop, for her assistance with geography and topography of up-state New York.

Glenna McReynolds (aka Tara Janzen), Susan Connell, Leanne Banks, Carol Bryant and Pam Nelson-O'Neil—thank you all for being there for me during the crunch. I couldn't have pulled this one off without you.

As always, any mistakes are mine and mine alone. I was delighted to place a major portion of this story in beautiful Argentina. And while I drew from historical data on ODESSA, the MC6 compound, the people and events that take place are pure fiction.

MARINE MOTTO:
Semper Fidelis—Always Faithful

FORCE RECON MOTTO:
Celer, Silens, Mortalis—Swift, Silent, Deadly

PROLOGUE

Afghanistan—Winter, 2001

It was quiet. Maybe too quiet.

Staff Sergeant Dallas Garrett reined in his mount, lifted his field glasses, and scanned the switchbacks winding down the barren slopes of the mountain range 100 km south of Mazar-e-Sharif.

Thoughtful, he lowered the glasses as an icy wind whistled around the steep shale walls of the pass.

"Yippee ti-yi-yo, get along little Taliban," he muttered with a final glance down the trail and urged the short coupled little gelding forward.

He'd been five years old the first time he'd sat on the back of a horse. The memorable event had taken place back home in West Palm on one of those kiddy pony rides where the bored little critter had slogged around in a circle to the tune of a rotation about every thirty minutes. Hadn't mattered to him. He'd thought he was Roy freaking Rogers. To this day, his brothers and sister still gave him shit about his little red straw cowboy hat, black plastic boots and toy six-shooters that would have made a real cowpoke laugh his ass off.

It had taken the war on terror and twenty some years for Dallas to mount up again. Good thing the horse knew what he was doing. Three days ago when he'd swung into the saddle, he'd still been as green as that five-year-old playing shoot 'em up bang, bang in the wild, wild West. Well he wasn't green now. He was saddle sore and trail weary. And while the terrain he rode was wild, he was halfway to hell and gone from the West he'd dreamed of riding as a boy.

Cold sliced through his bones like a meat cleaver—along with an itchy, niggling feeling that this op was running way too smoothly. The snow that scented the air as his team headed down a large, deep chasm toward the bottom of the Dar-i-suf valley could prove to be their first glitch. Weather was a complication they didn't need—not if they were going to accomplish their recon on the gathering hordes of Taliban-friendly Pashtun fighters who were elements in serious need of attitude adjustments. At the very least they needed to be destabilized to marginalize the classic warlord structure. Enter Dallas and his Force Recon team on a mission usually reserved for the Army's S.F. "A" teams.

Mounted up behind him, Rodriquez, Gates, Stover, and Stalinsky—Ski—swore like the marines they were when the first snowflake fell. Like Dallas, they were running on guts and determination. And like him, by design, they all looked like they'd been born in these godforsaken mountains.

Their faces and hands were baked brown by wind and sun. Their dark beards were rangy and full. To further blend in with the locals, either Lungees or turbans covered their heads; the wind played hell with the flapping fringed tails of the traditional Shemagh wrapped around their necks to keep the headgear from going airborne. Their dull brown-and-blue striped Chapmans were woven from coarse wool and camel hair; the loose-fitting garments smelled like wet dog, scratched like hell and, as an added bonus, did damn little to keep out the cold.

"When in Rome, shit." On a grunt, Dallas sucked it up and didn't think about the fleece jackets they'd had to leave behind so their bulk wouldn't show beneath the Chapmans and give them away. He had everything he needed. His M4A1 carbine and MEU(SOC) .45 pistol were hidden beneath the long, flowing folds of the robe. His team was similarly armed, combat-wise, and ready.

Gates carried an M-14 pimped out for sniping with a Leupold Long Range M3A 3.5-10 power-mounted into a SAGE EBR—a lotta "bang." Rodriguez's M-4A1 was equipped with the "boom" in the form of an M203 grenade launcher. Stover's mount was loaded ass deep in medical supplies. If all went as planned, they wouldn't need any of it. They'd get in, get out, and report their findings back to COC before the bad guys ever got wind that they'd been made. Then the flyboys could start their destabilization efforts in the form of a few tons of JDAMS—smart bombs—and Daisy cutters.

Ooh-rahh!

Ahead of Dallas, Atiqualla, the Jimbush warlord whose friendly political party consisted primarily of ethnic Uzbek Afghans, guided them through the pass.

Atiqualla rode his gray gelding—t'Aragh—like he'd
been born in the saddle. If you could call two pieces
of wood with a thin slice of carpet slapped on top a
saddle. Dallas shifted, gave his ass a rest and wondered if his balls would ever be a color other than
blue again.

Last night he'd dreamed of riding in a Cobra—had
even smelled the exhaust, felt the rumble and shake
of the bird. Hell. If someone had told him four years
ago when he'd survived the rigors of Recon Indoctri-
nation Program—aptly referred to as RIP—and the
mind-fuck of SERE (Survival, Evasion, Resistance
and Escape school) that he'd be leading a Force Recon op on horseback, he'd have told them they were
full of shit. Horse shit, specifically. He was a marine.
He hiked. He jumped. He swam.

And yet today, he rode.

Whatever it took. With luck, they'd be hauling ass
out of here tomorrow, the bad guys marked as targets
for a precision bombing run. Mission accomplished.

Only luck, it seemed, was about to run out.

He saw the initial then the secondary backflash
from the rocket propelled grenade launcher just before Ski called, "RPG nine o'clock!" from their flank.

The first grenade hit an instant later. Then the side
of the mountain exploded and the world blew apart
around them.

CHAPTER ONE

January, six years later
Essex County, New York

The night was crystal clear, vacuum still and brittle with cold. Pale gold rings rimmed an egg-shaped moon floating in a diamond black sky. A killing moon. In a graveyard sky.

With no wind to slap it into thin wisps, smoke from the twin chimneys of the 1800's two-story brick-and-mortar building curled skyward in thick, lazy streams. Snow hung in heavy drifts from north-facing windowsills, on thick concrete eaves and on the winter bare limbs of dormant trees.

"A regular Currier and Ives Christmas card moment." Amy Walker watched her breath crystallize through chattering teeth in the arctic air inside her car.

Yes, it would have been picture-pretty if she hadn't known that Winter Haven was home, mental hospital and sometimes prison to the tortured souls inside.

"G'night, Mom," Amy whispered, looking up toward the third window on the second floor where a faint light burned behind the barred panes. "And good-bye. For now."

Tonight it was particularly hard to control the pain
that always accompanied thoughts of her mother.
Anger followed quickly on its heels.

*Soon, Mom. I'm going to find him. And I'm going
to make him pay for what he's done to you.*

And for what he's done to me.

It was a promise she fully intended to keep. It was
a payment she fully intended to make. She was close
now. Closer than she'd ever been. Thanks to Jenna
McMillan.

"Amy, I think I've found him."

*Amy's fingers had tightened on her cell phone
when Jenna had called earlier today. "Where?"*

*"He's here. Back in Argentina. Can you meet me
in Buenos Aires?"*

*Yes, she could. She would. Just as soon as she
could get there.*

*"Let me give you an address . . . just in case we
lose cell contact," Jenna had added. "Got it? Okay.
If I'm not there when you arrive, ask for Alvaro.
He'll know where to find me."*

"Jenna . . ."

"Yeah?"

*"Thanks." It wasn't enough. After what Jenna had
done for her, Amy could never say or do enough.*

"Just get down here."

Yeah. She'd get there. "Be careful, okay?"

*"Careful's my middle name," Jenna had said with
a smile in her voice and broken the connection.*

It had been hell working through the rest of the
day. Amy had wanted to leave for Buenos Aires right

then. But she had to be so careful. Not to draw attention. Not to give anyone who might be watching her reason to be suspect.

Tamping down the anxious anticipation she'd felt ever since Jenna had called, Amy steeled herself for the confrontation to come. Her need for retribution outdistanced her fear—and her fatigue.

For the past five months she'd worked as an aid at Winter Haven so she could be close to her mother. Often, like today, she'd pulled back-to-back shifts when one of the aides had called in sick. That was fine. It gave her more opportunity to be close to her mother.

Her mother. Who was broken. Because of her grandfather.

Amy was ready for Edward Walker this time. Knew what kind of a monster she was facing now. Wouldn't be caught off guard and vulnerable again. Not ever again.

"Soon, Mom," she promised aloud.

But first, she had to get this car started in the sub-zero cold.

"Please, please, please," she pleaded into the red muffler wrapped around her neck and cranked the key.

After a long surly groan and a screeching grind, the engine of her ten-year-old Taurus finally, grudgingly, chugged to life.

"Thank you," she whispered through a shiver. With a shaking hand she felt under the driver's seat for an ice scraper.

She finally had to remove her mitten, lean forward

and grope around on the floor. Her fingers slide over the stone-cold barrel of her Glock before she found what she was looking for.

"Gotcha," she said in triumph. With the scraper in hand, she sat back up.

And choked on a scream.

A face, distorted by frost and shadows, pressed against her driver's side window.

"Hey . . . Relax, Erin. Cripes. It's just me." Ben Chambers' grin wasn't nearly guilty enough to compensate for the beating Amy's ribs were taking from her heart.

"Just making sure you got started okay."

Heart still hammering, pulse still spiked, Amy bundled her coat around her. She shoved her bare hand back into the mitten that matched her red muffler, put her shoulder to the door and pushed it open.

"Well, *that* took at least five years off my life," she said, working hard to sound good-natured. "It did warm me up, though, so thanks for that." She forced a smile.

Ben worked third shift—usually came in just as Amy was leaving. He was a sweet guy. And he meant well. Just like everyone else, however, he had no idea that she was wrapped as tight as wire coiled on a spool.

No one knew because Amy went to great pains to hide it. Just like she hid her true identity behind the mouse-quiet persona of Erin James.

"Car seems to be running fine." Ben had the good sense to sound a little sheepish now that he realized how much he'd shaken her.

"Thanks for checking on me." "Erin" brushed a fall of black hair back out of her eyes, careful not to dislodge her wig beneath her red stocking cap. Then, because Amy knew Ben would hang around if she encouraged him—maybe finally work up the nerve to ask her out—she turned her back, dismissing him.

It was cruel. Amy knew that. But she didn't want to encourage Ben's infatuation. She didn't want to hurt him. She didn't want to get involved.

Not with any man.

Not after what she'd been through.

And yet one man came to mind as she started scraping ice from her windshield.

Dallas Garrett.

She hadn't counted on liberal doses of what she had started to think of as the "Garrett factor" to plague her nights and days. Hadn't figured that hardly a day would pass in the six months since she'd left him in West Palm Beach that she hadn't thought of him. Played the "if only" game. If only she'd met him earlier. If only she was the same person she'd been before . . . well . . . before Dallas and his brothers had rescued her from the Abu Sayyaf terrorist cell on Jolo Island.

"Can't change the past," she whispered, angry that she'd let herself digress. Again.

The rhythmic chug of her car's motor and the sound of Ben's dejected footsteps trudging across the snow toward the hospital brought her back to the moment. She turned back to the task of clearing a thick film of frost off her windows, pushing away thoughts of the horror she'd experienced during the months she'd been held captive on the remote Philippine island. A horror that her own grandfather had arranged.

She squelched memories of Jolo and of Dallas, blue eyes dancing, soft smile encouraging, into her past where they belonged.

Her crepe-soled boots crunched and squeaked on the packed snow in the parking lot as she worked her way around the car. It was starting to warm up when she crawled back inside, fastened her seat belt and backed slowly out of her parking spot.

A tremor that had nothing to do with the cold eddied down her spine. She cut her gaze to the rearview mirror as she shifted into drive.

The dimly lit lot was empty. Ben had disappeared into the building. No one stood outside in this frigid New York January night watching her. No one had a reason to watch Erin James, and that's how everyone knew her.

And yet . . .

"Stop it," she muttered. There was no one there. Just like no one had been watching her last night. Or the night before—even though a sixth sense warned her otherwise.

Just because she'd been asking questions again. Just because she was close to confronting the monster responsible for placing her mother in Winter Haven—the same monster who had ordered Amy's abduction in the Philippines—didn't mean he'd found her.

She'd covered her tracks this time. Only Jenna knew what Amy was up to, and Jenna was as careful and concerned about secrecy as Amy.

Drawing a bracing breath, Amy steadied herself. Icy air seared her lungs; her fingertips stung with cold. She was safe. She was fine.

Because of her grandfather, she was also paranoid.

"Welcome to my world."

Inside her mittens, she flexed her fingers on the steering wheel as she drove into a darkness cut only by her headlights that sliced twin beams along the glistening snow-packed highway.

By the time she'd driven three miles down a road slick with patchy ice, she'd settled herself down. Warm air blew from the vents on the dash. She'd stopped shivering.

And then she spotted them. Headlights in her rearview mirror.

Her heart revved up several beats.

Headlights. On this road. At this time of night.

Headlights closing in fast.

All of her warning flares fired off. As she'd been taught in her self-defense class, she shot from condition yellow, aware of her surroundings, to condition red, sensing an attack.

She was the last one to leave on her shift. She was *always* the last one to leave. She made sure of that for this very reason. So she wouldn't have to wonder if anyone was following her.

No roads intersected the one she traveled—not for the first four miles. Which meant she wasn't so paranoid after all. Whoever was behind her had been hiding from her. Waiting for her.

They weren't waiting any longer.

Less than a city block separated the headlights from her taillights now. Telling herself to keep calm, that she may have missed someone leaving Winter Haven after her, she tightened her two-handed grip on the steering wheel. But she didn't recognize the vehicle—and she'd made it a point to learn the make and model of the vehicles of each of the staff members. She'd never seen this one. And it was too late for even a stray visitor to be leaving the facility.

It was an SUV. A big one. A Humvee, she realized as it closed the distance. Riding high on over-sized tires, blocky and bulky, the hulking black menace tailed her in the dark, snow-laden night.

Gaze darting between the road ahead and her rearview mirror, Amy slowed down, inviting the driver to pass her when the distance closed to a few yards.

Instead of going around her, the Humvee closed the gap to a few feet, riding her bumper. Bright lights glared in her side mirrors, blinding her.

She blinked away the spots dancing behind her eyelids, tried to focus on even breathing. On the survival lessons she'd studied and learned. Managing the immediate fear by controlling her heartbeat was crucial if she was to avoid setting off a chain reaction of escalating stress. If her motor skills became impaired, if her peripheral vision became restricted, if she lost her depth of focus, she was as good as gone.

She breathed deep, felt her heartbeat slow and focused on how to survive the very real possibility that whoever was behind her wanted her dead.

In her mind's eye she pictured the road ahead. A

sharp curve. A major incline. Tricky to negotiate in daylight on dry paving. A disaster to travel in the dark on ice.

To the right, a deep ravine fell away into a forest of maple, oak, hickory and aspen. To her left, a wall of exposed shale where the road had been cut through the hillside cast a deep shadow across the highway.

It was a deserted stretch of narrow road. The closest house was miles away. So was the nearest town. She'd just passed a green sign with white lettering announcing that Cayuga Lake was still miles away. Only forests and pastures lay ahead for miles. And more curves, more hills. Steep hills. She'd often worried as she'd crested a hill that she might meet another vehicle head on. She wasn't worried about oncoming vehicles tonight.

She was worried about the one behind her.

She speeded up.

So did the Humvee with its four-wheel drive capability clawing a firm grip on the road.

Palms sweating inside her mittens, she gave the Taurus more gas. Her heart lurched again when she felt the rear tires spin, fight for traction and lose. The back end of the little car swung to the left then started to fishtail.

That's when the Humvee hit her. And that's when training lost out over sheer horsepower and force and she fell prey to the laws of inertia.

The Humvee banged her bumper again, a jarring whack that snapped her head forward. Her forehead hit hard on the steering wheel. Pain exploded behind her eyes, momentarily blurring her vision. When it cleared, a solid wall of rock rushed toward her.

Gripping the wheel so tightly her fingers ached, she jerked it hard to the right, stomped on the brake. Too late, she realized she'd overcorrected. She shot across the center line like a bullet, caromed off a low metal guard rail and felt herself spinning out of control on the ice.

Then it was all velocity and impact and freefall. The nose of the Taurus dove toward the side of the road. Her airbag deployed when she plowed through the guardrail and plunged into the ravine.

Tree trunks flew by in a blur of black shadows as the compact car arrowed straight down the steep embankment; limbs and ground brush grabbed at the windows; the underbelly of the car thudded and screeched against the uneven terrain, dragging and bumping and tunneling through snow drifts that rose higher than the windshield. The noise was deafening. The speed terrifying.

And then, suddenly, it was over.

The Taurus ground to a shuddering, skidding stop at the bottom of a deep ravine. But for the soft ping of the cooling motor and the sound of her labored breaths, everything was quiet. Everything was still. Deathly so.

Moments passed—Amy didn't know how many— before she forced herself to move. To assess for damages. Amazingly, except for the bump on her head and a sore spot on her knee, she seemed to be fine. Between the airbag that now slowly deflated, and the seat belt, she was okay.

Yeah, she was okay. If you didn't count the fact

that she was alone, on a sub-zero night, in a wrecked car a hundred yards down from the highway. If you didn't factor in that the driver of the Humvee might, at this moment, be sliding down the steep grade to find out if she was dead or alive.

She had no doubt now that whoever was behind the wheel was hoping for dead. Or that he'd been sent by her grandfather to finish the job this time. And she couldn't sit here any longer waiting to see if he was coming after her.

She understood that she was running on sheer adrenaline now. She also understood that when it gave out, a world of trouble would crash down on her. Shock and hypothermia could kill her just as dead as a car wreck. It would merely take longer.

That's when her training kicked in. Her hands shook with adrenal overload when she reached around the airbag for the key. She wrestled it out of the ignition then used it to puncture the bag. The remaining air whooshed out in a sickly sigh along with a powder that burned her eyes. Tears welled up. She wiped them away and bent forward, searched the floor for her Glock. Because her hands were shaking, it took both of them to grip it then shove the .45 ACP into her coat pocket. Took several bumps of her shoulder to force the driver's door open and into a drift of snow. Finally, she crawled out into the knee-deep powder.

A glance back up the ravine told her she'd been right. Headlights angled down from the road; the bold stroke of a heavy-duty flashlight beam descended slowly down the steep slope.

He was coming after her.

She controlled the terror that shot through her blood, making her sweat and shiver, shake and stiffen up. She fought back the panic. Forced deep breaths. Slowed her heart rate. Consider the options.

She couldn't stay with the car. The unmistakable smell of gas permeated the night; the gas tank must have ruptured on the bumping skid down the ravine. One well-placed shot—she had to figure he had a gun—and she and the Taurus would blow like a bomb.

That left one recourse when facing a threat she had no way to size up: defense.

She slogged through knee-deep snow to the trunk of the Taurus. "Come on, come on," she pleaded through clenched teeth as she worked the key in the lock.

Finally, the trunk popped open. She grabbed her escape bag—the one she'd been carrying since she'd realized she was still a target—slung the backpack over her shoulder and moved. Wading, crawling, and sometimes digging her way through the snow.

When she encountered solid rock—a big one that she could tuck in behind—she stopped.

Here was where she'd make her stand.

Her throat burned raw from dragging in the frigid air; her breath trailed above her in telltale puffs that crystallized into ice; inside her heavy coat perspiration drenched her skin, soaked her winter-weight sweater.

She tugged off her mittens with her teeth. Reached in her coat pocket for the Glock. Reminded herself that the reason she carried it was because it was the best made revolver known to man. It never jammed, never misfired, never malfunctioned.

With it, after months of practice, she could unload a ten-cartridge magazine into a paper target at fifty yards, placing ten holes in a ten and a half inch grouping. Not expert. Not even close. But given that the average head size was ten inches, it was close enough.

Knees planted in the snow, she racked the slide to chamber a round. The sound of metal against metal rang through the still forest.

The flashlight went out. She knew she'd just lost any small advantage of surprise.

Whoever he was, he was a hired killer. He'd recognized the slide action of the Glock. Knew now that she was armed.

Amy steadied the barrel on the rock. Controlling her breathing, she clutched the grip with both hands and placed her right index finger on the trigger. Then she sighted toward the spot she'd first seen the flashlight. He'd been within one hundred yards of her then.

With every second that passed, he'd grown closer.

Killing moon.

Graveyard sky.

When she'd made those observations earlier, she'd never thought they'd be metaphors for what the night might turn out to be.

She searched the woods. Held her breath.

Watched. Waited.

Waited . . .

White. The snow was so white.

Black. The shadows were thick and black.

And still.

So very, very still.

Until one moved. Less than twenty yards away.

She aimed, sighted, and on an exhalation of breath, squeezed the trigger.

The shot echoed like a whip crack in the dark.

Sharp.

Deafeningly loud.

Deadly final.

She watched him drop.

Heard him hit the ground.

Saw the body twitch then fall still.

And trusted nothing.

Not what she saw.

Not the total absence of movement.

Not the devastating silence.

Long moments passed. Still she didn't move.

Blood pounded through her ears. Her rapid breaths froze in cloudy puffs.

Finally, she felt a sickening lurch of reality.

She'd hit her target. Had done what she'd trained to do.

Defended herself.

Taken a life.

Very slowly, she rose to her feet. Was surprised that her legs held her.

Slower still, both hands wrapped around the grip, one finger still on the trigger, she waded toward the dark outline, supine and still on the ground. Snow filled her boot tops, caked the knees of her pants as she approached the bulk of a man bleeding out on his back.

A 1911-A1 lay within fingertip reach of his open palm.

No threat to her now.

She'd hit him clean. Hit him square. Dead center in the middle of his forehead. A lucky shot. A golden BB.

Dead.

Blood ran black in the snow beneath his head.

A chill ran deep as he stared up at her through eyes as void of life as he'd been void of conscience.

Dead.

Him or me. Him or me.

Him.

Dead.

Not me.

Her adrenaline let go like a flood tide, sweeping away her strength with it. Her knees gave out. She sank to all fours. Vomited with a violence that matched what she'd just done. Tears spilled to the ground, melted the snow as she knelt there, her bare hands freezing. Recovering. Reliving. Accepting.

When she thought she could stand, she pushed slowly to her feet. Like an automaton, she wandered back to the rock. Retrieved her escape bag with cold, stiff fingers. Then she slogged back to the dead assassin and avoiding looking at him, pocketed his gun.

Breath heaving, she climbed, crawled, clawed her way up the ravine and away from the body that, like her car, may not be found until spring.

The Humvee was still running when she reached the road.

Without hesitation, she climbed inside.

And drove.

There would be others. When the man lying dead in the snow failed to report in to her grandfather, there would be others.

And there was only one place she could go to escape them. One man she could trust to save her. The one man she'd sworn she would never place in jeopardy again.

A hundred miles passed before she could meet the eyes that looked back at her from the rearview mirror.

She dragged off her knit cap and with it the black wig. But for the brown contact lenses, Erin James was officially gone.

And so, she feared, was Amy Walker.

A stone-cold killer had taken her place.

She'd taken a life tonight to save her own. . . . In doing so, she may have lost something just as precious. Her soul.

CHAPTER TWO

Two days later, West Palm Beach, Florida

So, what brought this on?"

Dallas didn't so much as glance at his brother who stood in the open bedroom doorway, a root beer in hand, a dark scowl on his face. "What? I'm not entitled to a vacation?"

A man on a mission, Dallas continued rifling through his bureau drawer before he addressed Nolan's long-suffering breath.

"E.D.E.N. can get along without me for a few days. You three overachievers can handle things here," he pointed out, referring to his siblings who were all partners in the security firm their old man had turned over to them several years ago.

"Besides, with Jase and Manny on board now, you've got plenty of bodies to fill the holes," he added, reminding Nolan that E.D.E.N. was at full force with the addition of Jase Wilson and Manny Ortega, two ex–special ops brothers-in-arms who'd recently joined the company. "Perfect time for me to take a break from bullets and bad guys."

Bullets and bad guys.

Without warning, a vivid assault of memory slammed him like a gut punch.

Dead.

Ski. Gates. Rodriguez. Stover. All dead or dying.

He sucked in air. Stalked across the carpeted floor. But he couldn't move fast enough to outdistance the six-year-old memory.

The stench of burning flesh seared his nostrils. The sick, sweet scent of blood and gore suffocated him. And the sounds. Jesus. Terrified cries of pain from both men and horses.

The ground was grave cold and running with blood, rubble and snow when he came to. Dead ahead . . . aw, God. Pain throbbing through his entire body, he clawed his way to Stover's mangled corpse. The lance corporal's eyes were vacant, unfocused as he lay sprawled in the debris, half of his face shot off. Twenty-three years old. His mother would never see him whole again.

Dallas rubbed a hand over the scar on his ribs, swallowed hard. Blinked to clear his vision.

Six years. Six fucking years and the images he'd thought he'd buried with his men were once again rising up out of the mucky swamp of his memory, sucking at his soul like leeches.

Never was a good time to relive this shit. So why the hell was this happening again? Why was it happening *now*?

"Bro?"

Dallas straightened. Wiped a shaking hand over his face and snapped at Nolan. "What?"

Brows knit, Nolan pushed away from the door-frame where, until now, he'd been attempting to look nonchalant. "What in the hell is wrong with you? You're either sniping like a great white, or as silent and stoic as a monk."

Dallas grunted and tossed several pairs of socks into the duffel that lay open on his bed. His brother was spot-on right. And Dallas was sorry about that. Just not sorry enough to muster the will to do anything about it. Except give Nolan a break and get out of his face. "So I'd think you'd be glad to get rid of me for a while."

"Talk to me." Concern knocked the edge off the ex-Ranger's command.

Talk to him? Christ. Dallas had made that mistake once already. Two weeks ago. The night their eldest brother, Ethan, had remarried Darcy Prescott.

Dallas had been shit-faced drunk—not his usual MO—and, light-weight that he was, he'd spilled his candy-ass guts. Cried to Nolan about the recent recurrence of the flashbacks, the night sweats, the black holes that had become a part of his life again. Nolan had wanted to play touchy feely ever since.

"You know, the VA has head men who specialize in—"

Fuck.

"Don't. Even. Go. There." Dallas cut Nolan off with a dark look. He was a marine. Okay, ex-marine. For over four years now. Still, the marine doctrine was forever ingrained in his DNA. And it was pig simple: Solve your problems, live with them, or shut the fuck up.

He wasn't about to flop down on a cushy couch in some psycho-babbling little cucumber's office and puke out his inner demons. "Philosophy" battalion in the mosquito-infested swamps of Camp Lejeune in South Carolina had made certain of that. The head "philosopher's"—AKA, the sergeant instructor's—therapy of choice had been to apply a size-thirteen boot directly to the ass whenever the urge to whine came over a raw recruit. He'd never felt the boot, but he'd witnessed the results. Effective as hell.

"Have you thought about looking for her?" Nolan asked quietly.

Double fuck.

He'd forgotten that he'd spilled the beans about Amy Walker that same night. Boo-hooed about the fact that he hadn't been able to stop thinking about the woman he'd helped rescue from that clew of terrorist worms with Ethan, Nolan and Manny when they'd staged an unsanctioned, civilian op to save Darcy from Jolo Island six months ago.

Amy had endured more degradation and torture at the hands of those Abu Sayyaf slime than any human being should be expected to bear. She'd survived because of her strong spirit and guts. But she would carry the scars—both physical and emotional—for the rest of her life.

Dallas respected her. Admired her. Cared about her. Wanted her.

But he wasn't going after her.

Hell, if that was going to happen, he'd have done it six months ago. Even though he'd suspected that she was planning to disappear from his life shortly after they'd returned to the States, he'd let her go. Didn't even try to stop her. Hadn't tried to find her.

Because he'd known. Alone, they might have a chance. Together, their excess baggage would break an elephant's back.

"Or is that what this sudden trip is really about?" Nolan persisted, crossing the room, a speculative look on his face.

Dallas watched his brother set his root beer bottle on the bedside table then lay back on the bed and get comfy, crossing his arms behind his head.

"You finally going after her?"

"That's going to leave a ring." Dallas evaded the question by glaring toward the sweating bottle.

Just like he'd been evading the probability that the ground assault they'd launched getting Darcy and Amy out of the terrorist hellhole had been the catalyst for the resurgence of his PTSD. Post Traumatic Stress Disorder. Long convoluted term that shrinks preferred to "fucked-up in the head." Go figure.

"Anal to the bone," Nolan grumbled after a long, silent stare and grudgingly moved the bottle onto a coaster. "Did you ever think that might be part of your problem?"

"No, but I've been thinking that *you* are. Don't you have a wife and a baby to go home to and harass?"

"You know," Nolan said, purposely ignoring Dallas' hint to leave him the hell alone, "I remember a day, not so many moons ago when you and Ethan invaded my inner sanctum and dragged my sorry hide out of a perfectly good drunken stupor."

"Too drunk to remember that Ethan came alone. If I'd been along—"

"Oh, right," Nolan interrupted with a tight grin. "You weren't with him. Guess I *was* drunk."

"Well, *I'm* not, so back off."

According to Ethan's account, Nolan had been close to the edge that day. Beyond drunk, deep in denial and ready to piss his life down the toilet. His little brother had DX'd out of the Rangers three months earlier, was laying a lot of blame on his big bad self for a buddy's death, and Dallas and Ethan had decided Nolan needed something to live for.

Having Nolan join the team at E.D.E.N., Inc. as a securities specialist and protecting TV anchorwoman Jillian Kincaid from a crazed stalker had started out as a job. A means to bring Nolan back among the functional. Who knew he'd not only straighten up and fly right, he'd end up marrying his client, the daughter of one of the fattest cats in the publishing business.

"Okay. So drinking's not your problem—and it's obviously not your forté," Nolan's voice dragged Dallas back to the immovable object currently stretched out on his bed, "but you're about a pin pull away from going off like a frag grenade."

Dallas worked his jaw. One thing about brothers. They understood things. Nolan wasn't going to let up.

"I'll handle it," Dallas said, because he also understood something else. Nolan was worried about him. And he wasn't going to back away. "I'll handle it," he repeated with a grim nod when his brother's expression relayed only skepticism. "I just need a little space, okay?"

Nolan studied him long and hard through narrowed eyes. "Give me more than crumbs here, D. You know I have to report back to the troops."

The "troops," Dallas knew, consisted of their mom and dad plus Ethan and Darcy, their sister, Eve, her husband, Mac, and Nolan's wife, Jillian. And he'd already figured out that they'd sent Nolan here to get the goods on the only Garrett who had broken army tradition and opted to join the marines—a decision that had always made his sanity suspect in their eyes.

"Do *not* sic Eve on me," he warned, figuring that would be Nolan's next move.

Their sister—Nolan's twin—was five feet two inches of blond hair, blue eyes and TNT. Eve loved hard, cared hard and wouldn't think twice about pinning Dallas to the wall if she thought she could protect him by doing so. The best thing that had ever happened to that woman was marrying Tyler "Mac" McClain. Mac gave back as good as Eve dished out, didn't take any of her lip and, Dallas was relieved to know, was crazy in love with her.

"Give me a reason not to send her over. Tell me where you're going."

That was the hell of it. Dallas didn't know. He didn't know squat—except that he needed distance. The concerned looks were wearing on him. The worry that seemed to perpetually crease his mother's brow fueled his guilt.

"Fishing," he said, making it up on the fly. He had
no idea where he was going. Anywhere but here.
"I'm going fishing, okay? With some buddies from
my old unit."

He'd go to hell for lying, but since odds were he
was heading there anyway, one more sin against
mankind wouldn't make a difference.

"So when do you leave?" Nolan clearly wasn't
taking the bait and was doing a little angling of his
own trying to catch Dallas in a lie.

"In the morning. Early flight to the gulf. I'll see
you in a couple of weeks. Happy now? Good. Now
get the hell out so I can finish packing."

Dragging a hand over dark hair that was badly in
need of a cut, he strode out of the bedroom toward
his condo's front door, swung it open and waited for
his brother to follow. The sultry heat of the Florida
night slogged into the room in thick, heavy drifts.
A sky that had been threatening rain all day finally
let go; a burst of fat, silver drops fell as he stood
there. Needing to be alone.

After what seemed like a decade, Nolan finally
sauntered toward him. Hands tucked in his hip pockets, he stopped about a foot away. Though Nolan was
the youngest of the three brothers, he stood within an
inch of Dallas's 6'1" frame, carried his weight in the
same lean, rangy build, and stared at him through the
same intense blue eyes.

"If your ass isn't straightened out when you get
back—"

"Yeah, yeah, I know," Dallas interrupted with a

weary roll of his shoulders. "You're gonna introduce it to my shoulder blades."

"Damn straight."

And then Nolan did the damnedest thing. This ex–special ops soldier who was now a full partner with Ethan, Dallas and Eve at E.D.E.N. Securities, Inc., this hard-as-steel warrior who took no prisoners and cut no slack, grabbed him in a bear hug and squeezed until Dallas' ribs cracked.

"Take care, man," Nolan said and let him go. Without a backward glance, he walked out the door and into the rain.

Thank God.

Thank Jesus God.

Because if his little brother had taken time to look Dallas in the eyes, he would have seen they were wet. And that was one humiliation he could not deal with tonight.

Half an hour later, Dallas was dry-eyed and hard-faced. He was about to skip out for the airport earlier than planned and blow out of town when he heard the knock on his door.

"Eve," he grumbled, a sick knot twisting in his gut. He hadn't gotten out of here soon enough.

Swearing roundly, he dropped his duffel by the door. "Damn Nolan and his good intentions." The little bastard must have gone straight to Eve—and she'd tear into him like a pit bull after a T-bone until she got some answers that satisfied her.

Muttering under his breath, he swung open the door, determined to nip this little inquisition in the bud.

Only it wasn't his kid sister standing there, drenched to the bone as rain slammed down like buckshot.

His heart cracked him sledgehammer hard, dead center in the middle of his chest as he stared into the face of a woman he'd seen for the first time in the fetid jungles of Jolo Island.

Amy Walker.

Soaking wet.

Sodden blond hair hanging in her face.

Cornflower blue eyes speaking to him without her uttering a word.

Jesus. Sweet Jesus Christ.

Dallas had thought of her, dreamed of her, worried for her . . . even cursed her for messing with his head after she'd disappeared. But he'd never planned on seeing her again.

Too much baggage.

Too many problems.

Too much work, he'd told himself over and over again.

Told himself now.

All of that flew out the window when she took a halting step toward him and collapsed into his arms.

Dallas caught Amy up against him, lifted her into his arms and kicked the door closed behind him, shutting out the rain.

"Can't . . . let them . . . find me . . . here," she murmured, turning her face against his shoulder as he rushed over to the sofa and laid her down.

Heart jammed like a pulsing pike in his throat, Dallas knelt on the floor beside her, her words barely registering. He skimmed his hands over her body, searched frantically for injuries. No broken bones, no blood, no swelling. Good. Great. Okay.

So why was his heart still jack-hammering?

"Are you hurt? Amy? Are you hurt anywhere?"

She shook her head. "Tired . . . so . . . tired."

Her eyes drifted shut and her head fell to the side, her wet hair and t-shirt and jeans soaking the sofa. Just like they'd soaked him.

Barely aware of his own damp clothes and not yet ready to take her words at face value, he used gentle hands to examine her scalp for bumps or lacerations, wanted to feel relief when he found nothing but a fading bruise on her forehead. But it wasn't until he checked her pulse and found it strong and steady that he breathed his first deep breath since he'd seen her standing in the arch of his open door.

"Amy?" he prodded gently. "Jesus, Amy. What's going on?"

Her eyes were closed. Her breathing even and deep.

Asleep, he realized with a mixture of concern and frustration. He was revved up like a Blackhawk at full throttle and she was out like a light.

Tired . . . so . . . tired.

Yeah. He dragged a hand over his face. She was tired all right. Dead tired.

And what had she said? *Can't let them find me here.*

"Can't let *who* find you?" he whispered, a million questions ricocheting around in his mind. He stood, strode back to the front door and threw the bolt. He hesitated over the drawer that held his HK USP tactical pistol, then unlocked it.

He chambered a round then tucked the weapon in his waistband above his right kidney. Just in case. Then squatting down beside the sofa, he sat back on his heels and watched her.

Just watched her.

Of all the scenarios he'd imagined when he'd thought of Amy Walker, this wasn't one of them. He'd imagined her full lips smiling, her slim body healed and healthy. And against all attempts not to, he'd imagined her in his bed. Naked and needing him to mend the part of her that had been damaged by brutality and violence.

His hand trembled as he scrubbed it over his face again. Yeah, he'd imagined her a hundred different ways, all the time knowing all he'd ever do was imagine because no way in hell was he ever going to act on his feelings for her if he ever saw her again.

Now here she was. Soaked to the skin, shivering and exhausted, sound asleep on his sofa.

Shivering.

Get a grip, Garrett. She was chilled to the bone.

Of course she was freezing. Her wet clothes and tangled hair were plastered to her body like a cold compress and his AC was jacked up full blast.

His knees cracked when he stood. His heart felt . . .

heavy or something. Thick in his chest as he hustled over to the thermostat, hiked up the temp, then snagged a blanket from the linen closet. And a lot of good that would do, he realized as he stood over her again, blanket in hand. He needed to get her dry. Get her warm.

Which meant getting her out of those clothes.

The thought had his pulse spiking again.

"Okay, badass," he grumbled, "her physical needs outdistance your schoolboy hormone rush, so just strip her, wrap her up and get her dry."

It was a plan. He liked plans. Liked things all tied up neat and tidy. Like his life used to be. Like he needed his life to be again.

There was nothing neat and tidy about Amy Walker. She'd been abused and used by the rankest of men. She might wake up, realize he was touching her, not "get it" that he was only trying to help and tear into him like a wildcat.

He remembered the first time he'd touched her. They'd been dodging rounds from AK-47s, making tracks away from a terrorist camp and running through the jungle for their lives. She'd been sick and hurt and half starved and yet the minute he'd laid a hand on her, she'd exploded. Fought him like a crazed animal. He'd had to wrestle her to the ground, haul her over his shoulder and run like hell or they were going to die. It was just that simple.

Only just as nothing about Amy Walker was neat and tidy, nothing about her was simple either. Not then. Not now.

He hesitated a moment longer before gently tucking the blanket around her. Then, reacting to the fear he'd heard in her voice, he double-bolted his door and drew the drapes before he snagged his cell phone and called Darcy and Ethan.

CHAPTER THREE

Dallas plowed a hand through his hair. Paced back and forth in front of the doorway of his guest bedroom. On each pass, he cast a worried glance inside. Amy Walker lay on the bed; his sister-in-law, Darcy, watched over her.

"Far be it from me to point this out." Ethan walked out of the kitchen with a beer in each hand. "But isn't that new carpet you're wearing a hole in?"

Dallas shook his head when his oldest brother held out one of the bottles. "Christ. Did you get a look at her?"

Ethan glanced past Dallas to the softly lit bedroom and his wife, who held vigil by Amy's side. It was Darcy who had gently roused Amy then herded her into the bedroom, helped her out of her wet clothes and tucked her into bed a little over an hour ago.

"Yeah," Ethan said. "She's a helluva mess, but she's okay, right? Didn't the doctor say she was just exhausted?"

Dallas tugged on his ear, gave a grim nod.

"Drink it." Ethan shoved the beer at Dallas' chest, putting a little force behind it. "You might not think you need it, but I'm sick of watching you pace."

On a deep breath, Dallas gripped the bottle. Rolled his shoulders. And finally drank.

"Any particular reason you're carrying?" Ethan walked into the living area of Dallas' condo.

Shit. He'd forgotten that he'd belted the HK. "Been a lot of unexpected traffic through here tonight," he said evasively. For reasons he didn't completely understand, he didn't want to bring up Amy's cryptic statement. *Can't let them find me here.* "It has a tendency to make a man a little punchy."

Ethan frowned but didn't press as he eased down into a chair upholstered in deep sand and terra-cotta. "Where do you suppose she's been all this time?"

Dallas reluctantly joined his older brother and sank down in a matching chair. It was a question he'd asked himself a hundred times. A question he intended to ask her. Later.

He shrugged. "Who knows."

"It's been, what? Six months since she split?"

Dallas said nothing. Like he didn't know *exactly* how long it had been since he'd last seen Amy. He'd thought of her each and every one of the six months and five days since she'd disappeared. Ethan didn't need to know that Dallas had been counting. It was bad enough that Nolan knew.

"Truth?" Ethan said with an arch of his brow when Dallas didn't respond, "Never thought we'd see her again."

Yeah. Dallas had thought the same thing. And

he'd tried to convince himself he was fine with it. But the way his pulse had spiked when he'd seen Amy standing in his doorway looking like a storm-beaten little bird proved he hadn't been fine with it at all.

Can't let them find me here.

He took another deep pull on the cold beer. Maybe he'd misunderstood her. Maybe she'd been delirious.

And maybe he should trust his gut—which was usually spot-on right when it warned him about impending trouble.

"What's her story, do you think?" Ethan asked, as much to himself as to Dallas. "Other than being messed up by those bastards on Jolo."

"Like that's not enough?"

Ethan cocked his head, surprised by the bite in Dallas' tone. He held up a hand in supplication. "Hey. I'm not the bad guy here."

Dallas let his head fall back against the chair cushion. Closed his eyes. "Sorry. It's—she just . . . she just looked so messed up, you know?" And he felt helpless to make it better.

"One of these days I'm going to learn not to second-guess my wife," Ethan said after a long, thoughtful look.

Dallas opened an eye. "What are you talking about?"

"Darcy tried to tell me that you had a thing for Amy."

Christ. Dallas leaned forward, cupped the beer bottle between both hands and stared at it. Was he that transparent where Amy was concerned?

"I don't have a *thing* for her," he finally lied because, hell, even if he did he wouldn't—more to the point *couldn't*—do anything about it. "She's a friend. That's all. And she's been through enough, you know? I was hoping she'd found her footing again."

Ethan was still watching him with that "*you can lie to yourself but you can't lie to me*" expression. "We can take her home with us if you want. She and Darcy got pretty close on Jolo. Maybe she'll open up to Darcy."

Yeah. Dallas contemplated the label on the bottle. Amy and Darcy had gotten close. Both of them had been captives of Abu Sayyaf thugs who'd hidden behind the cloak of Islamic Jihad. Both had been starved and terrorized. But while Darcy's ordeal, as bad as it had been, had totaled a daunting five days, Amy had been held for over five months before they'd gotten her off that island to safety. During those months, she'd been starved, beaten and raped.

That was Amy Walker's story—at least as much as his family knew. Unfortunately, Dallas knew there was more. While the motive for Darcy's abduction was now clear—Darcy had been kidnapped at the orders of a corrupt U.S. ambassador to the Philippines while she was stationed at the embassy there—no one knew why Amy Walker had ended up in the hands of those bastards.

No one but Amy. And in the few days after the rescue while she'd recovered with Nolan and Jillian here in West Palm, Amy hadn't been talking.

And then she just plain hadn't been here.

She'd left. No note. No explanation. No "so long, it's been good to know you."

"Dallas—I said, do you want us to take her home with us?"

"No," he said quickly. Too quickly, he realized when Ethan slanted him a tight grin. He settled himself down. "She's fine here. Until she wakes up at least. Then yeah, if she needs a place to stay, she's all yours."

Or not, Dallas thought, ignoring his brother's considering look. Until he found out what had brought Amy back to West Palm, he wasn't letting her out of his sight. Friends did that for friends, and it didn't have to mean there was anything more to it.

He glanced toward the bedroom again, absently working his thumbnail over the label on the sweating beer bottle, remembering the hollowness he'd felt in his gut six months ago when he'd realized she'd left. Reliving the edgy expectancy he'd been feeling ever since, wondering if he'd ever see her again. Kicking himself for his inability to shake it off and just get on with his life.

Now she was back. And he was royally pissed with himself over the way he felt about it.

Too much relief.

Too much concern.

Too much emotion all the way around.

Restless, he pushed off the chair, set the bottle on an end table. Ignoring his brother's contemplative look, he walked quietly into the bedroom, glanced at his sister-in-law, then focused on Amy, sleeping the sleep of the dead.

There were changes in her. Good changes.

She was no longer emaciated. No longer beaten

down and bruised. Her skin was clear, healthy, dusted lightly with the freckles that lent a youthful innocence and all-American-girl glow to a classically beautiful face. A face he'd missed far too much.

Only the scars remained of her ordeal. Scars from the rope burns on her wrists and ankles where they'd festered and become infected. From the knife-sharp leaves and vines that had sliced her arms and legs on forced marches through the jungle. A small crescent-shaped scar hooked at the point of her brow where it met her temple. He didn't even want to think about how it had gotten there—and yet he figured he knew. A hard blow from a big man.

He backed away from the rage that knowledge still bred, concentrated on the here. The now. She'd healed. She'd survived. And except for the fatigue, she appeared healthy now. Her muscles were toned and she had meat on her bones. She was round and lush in all the right places—there'd been no mistaking that when he'd found his arms full of her. Her pale skin was soft and sweet smelling. No mistaking that either.

But her eyes. In that moment before she'd passed out, those beautiful eyes had revealed the secrets and the sorrow and the burden she would carry for the rest of her life.

Can't let them find me here.

The hair on the back of his neck tingled every time he replayed those words. *Who* couldn't find her? Who was she hiding from?

Something told him he didn't want to know. Something else told him that whatever had driven her to his door might be big. Real big.

And, he suspected, real bad.

He glanced at Darcy, asked in a quiet voice, "Has she said anything?"

A frown turned down one corner of the pretty redhead's mouth. "She mumbled something about her backpack." She glanced up at him. "Did she have one with her?"

Dallas shook his head. "Nope. Just her."

Darcy shrugged. "Well, other than that—oh, and apologizing for passing out on you—no. She hasn't said a word. She's been out cold. But she's fine, Dallas. Trust Doc Hammond. She's just sleep deprived."

Dallas made a note to thank Nolan for sending over Jillian's doctor when Dallas had called him. Hammond was the same doc who had provided expert and discreet medical care for Ethan when he'd returned to the States sporting a gunshot wound he'd taken on Jolo. No way could they have taken Ethan to a hospital. Bullet wounds had a tendency to draw law enforcement; there would have been questions they wouldn't have been able to answer. Since their operation in the Philippines hadn't been sanctioned by anyone—specifically the U.S. military—they'd had to avoid those questions at all costs. Hammond had helped make that happen. And just in case there were "issues" with Amy, the doc had agreed to help again.

Dallas averted his attention back to Amy. Odds were, she had more issues than the military had boots. He didn't know what had happened to land her in that terrorist camp, but he had a sick feeling that it hadn't been an accident of fate. Hadn't been a "wrong place, wrong time" event as she had claimed back then.

No, there'd been a reason she'd ended up in the hands of those jackals. A reason she'd gone to the Philippines in the first place. A reason that had compelled her to risk her life.

Long after Ethan and Darcy left, Dallas sat by the bed and watched Amy sleep. Studied the smudges of blue beneath her eyes where her thick lashes lay on her cheeks. And wondered why she was here. Wondered if it was because she had been foolish enough to risk her life again.

"You been poking around in something that just might get you killed this time?" he speculated aloud.

Unfortunately, he had more than a hunch that he might have a vague, "big picture" idea about what that *something* could be. He rubbed his index finger over his upper lip, a niggling suspicion building to an acid burn in his belly. He'd done some digging on the Web. Run a search on Amy Walker even before she'd turned up gone. And what he'd found had made more than his short hairs curl.

She stirred slightly in her sleep. A reaction to his presence in the dark? Or to a nightmare that was far too real?

Night shadows fell across the bed as he searched her sleeping face. Nausea rolled through his gut in thick, oily swells. If his suspicions were even close to right, the hell she'd left behind on Jolo would be nothing compared to the hell that lay ahead of her.

When she settled, he left her alone. Left her to sleep. And to try to get a little sleep himself.

• • •

She was dreaming. *Amy knew she was dreaming, but she couldn't wake up.*

Hard hands tied her down. Hurting hands. And yet . . . something was different. It wasn't sunlight burning into her eyes through a thick rain forest canopy. Instead, the light was ice white and blinding, like one of those huge round orbs that surgeons used to illuminate an operating room. And the hands, oh God, the hands that bruised her weren't bare and filthy but gloved in sterile latex.

But the faces were the same. Ugly, mean, a little wild, but all she could see were their eyes above snug surgical masks.

"Don't, don't, please, don't," she whimpered as the scent of antiseptic confused her even more.

It should be earth scents assaulting her senses. Jungle scents of rot and green and loam, of filthy men and rotted teeth. She should hear the sporadic tattoo of automatic rifle fire break the silence; instead the beep, beep, beep *of life-support monitors and the* whoosh *of a blood pressure cuff echoed in the background.*

"Please, please, please." Her voice sounded hoarse from screaming, weak from exhaustion, and riddled with stark, relentless terror.

Even more terrifying, as she suddenly left the body on the cold metal table and floated above the operating room, it wasn't her face she saw staring back at her from below. It was her mother's.

"Mom. Oh, God. Mom. What are they doing to you?"

Tears spilled, landed in soft, soundless pools on the pristine white sheet covering her mother's torso and legs. Lying stark and deathly still, her mother's eyes were fixed and wide open—polarized with fear as one of the hunched, masked physicians attached electrodes to her temples and meticulously shaved areas within her hairline.

"Leave her alone! Leave my mother alone!" Amy screamed as she hovered above it all, helpless to stop the monsters as they tended to their hideous task.

"Don't hurt her. Please! Don't hurt my mother!" She screamed so loud it hurt her own ears. But no one heard her.

No one but her mother.

Tears filled the beautiful gray eyes that had once glittered with love and soft smiles when she sang Amy to sleep at night. "Hush, little baby, don't say a word, Momma's gonna buy you a mockingbird—"

"Don't cry, Momma. I'll help you. I'll make them stop."

But it was too late to help. And nothing would make them stop.

A white-coated doctor affixed the final electrode and, with a nod to his colleague, told him to flip a switch. Her mother's body jerked, arched, then spasmed.

Pain, sharp as a blade, hard as a fist jolted through Amy's body and suddenly she was on her back again. Not on an operating room table. Not beneath a sterile white light.

She was in the jungle again. Back on Jolo Island

in the Philippines and the terrorists who had kidnapped her were having their evening fun.

Harsh hands dragged at her clothes, shoved her legs apart, hurt her.

Hurt her.

Hurt her so bad she went away. At least in her mind. And she stayed away until it was over.

Please God, make it be over. . . .

"Amy?"

Amy flinched instinctively when a gentle hand touched her shoulder.

She opened her eyes.

To a strange room.

Dim light.

The shadow of a big man looming over her.

Instant, reflexive, involuntary terror gripped her like a vice. She scuttled backward until she felt a solid wall at her back. Instinctively lifted her arms to protect her face.

No room. No room. She'd run out of room.

"Amy. Sweetheart. It's okay."

Sweetheart.

She knew that voice. Had ached to hear that voice a hundred times since the man it belonged to had found her in that terrorist camp and taken her away from the pain.

It was too much to hope for. And yet . . . she forced her eyes to focus in the semidarkness. Forced her mind to clear.

There he was.

"Dallas?"

"Yeah. It's me." His voice sounded raw, choked with concern. "It's okay. *You're* okay. You were having a nightmare."

She heard a high, keening sound. Wasn't aware it was coming from her until Dallas swore, then turned on a lamp by the bed and flooded the room with soft light. He tentatively touched a hand to the back of hers.

"Come on, Amy. You're okay now. You know you're okay now, don't you? That's why you're here, right? That's why you came looking for me?"

She huddled into herself. Made herself think. Focus.

Not Jolo. Not New York. Not twenty years ago.
Not a dream.
Dallas.
Real.
Safe.

Yes. That's why she'd come to him. She'd needed to rest. Needed a safe place.

Dallas was safe. And she was tired. She was so tired. Tired of running. Tired of being tired.

She let her eyes drift shut again.

"Amy? Stay with me now. Come on," his wonderful voice coaxed. "It's raining buckets outside. You were soaked to the skin. Darcy . . . Darcy took care of you, remember? You're warm and dry now."

Darcy. Right. Darcy had been here.

And now she was warm and dry.

And wearing a man's t-shirt, she realized with a quick check beneath the sheets.

She was in a bed. Clean. Fresh smelling. Like Dallas.

"Come on, sweetheart," he said in that wonderful sheltering voice. "You know you can trust me. You know that, don't you?"

She did know it. She did.

Forcing herself fully awake, she blinked up into a pair of ocean-blue eyes set in a beautiful male face drawn into a frown of concern.

"Yes," she said and, for the first time in forty-eight hours, let herself relax. "Yes. I know."

CHAPTER FOUR

Dallas found a pair of navy blue boxers along with one of his gray t-shirts for Amy to wear. Both hung on her. She sat on a tall chrome stool, her elbows propped on the black granite island countertop separating his kitchen from the living area. Her bare feet balanced on a rung of the stool.

It was closing in on three A.M. She'd slept for around five hours. He hadn't slept at all.

"If you hadn't caught us on the road," Darcy had said when she and Ethan sailed into his condo around nine last night after Dallas had called Ethan's cell, "I'd have brought her something of mine to wear."

Dallas had no doubt Darcy would be over sometime later this morning with the makings of a wardrobe for Amy. Just like he had no doubt that, unlike six months ago, Amy's soft, healthy curves could fill out Darcy's clothes now. Amy may be exhausted, but she was far from the emaciated woman they'd dragged out of the jungle and smuggled back to the States.

And, he realized, as he poured himself a cup of

strong coffee and watched her from the corner of his eye, now that she was awake and acclimated to his condo, it was apparent that she was a far cry from the physically and emotionally bruised woman she'd been then, as well.

Despite her fatigue, there was a . . . hell, he didn't know. Kind of a combative edge to the way she squared her shoulders as she sat there. A self-assurance to the way she held her head. An almost militant determination to show him she was strong, composed and in control. As strong and in control as a woman who had a tendency to keep glancing toward the door and tense at the slightest sound could be.

She'd always been tough—she'd had to be to survive the hell she'd gone through—but she'd been far from strong when he'd seen her last. Fragile. Crushable. Those words had applied to her then. Not strong.

Now that she was awake and lucid, he was seeing a different woman. Tough. Determined. Self-possessed. And though he had no ownership over the emotion, he felt a swell of pride in her for the strength of character it had taken to bring her back this far.

"More?" Wearing a white t-shirt and worn jeans, he shuffled barefoot across the kitchen's cool terra-cotta tile floor, a coffee carafe in hand.

She met his eyes—something she once wouldn't have been capable of doing—and extended her mug in a two-handed grip. "Thanks."

He poured in silence. As he'd cooked in silence after he'd heard her stirring in the bedroom and decided that if he was hungry—which he was—she was probably hungry too.

Besides, it had given him something to do other than think about her long, slim legs sliding between his sheets. Something to do other than wonder what was up with her or pressure her for answers or wish to hell he'd had the good sense to take Ethan and Darcy up on their offer to take her home with them.

Instead, he'd held solitary vigil beside her bed for an hour or so after Ethan and Darcy had left with orders to call if he needed anything.

He hadn't called. He'd just sat there. Elbows on his spread knees, chin propped on his clasped hands. Watching her sleep. Cataloging her delicate features in the pale bedroom light. Resisting the urge to run the back of his fingers across her cheekbone just to touch the freckles scattered there. Feeling the weight and the whoop of his heart kicking up every time she made a sound, whenever her eyelids flickered, when she jerked restlessly in her sleep.

He'd finally made himself leave the bedroom. Made himself shut the door behind him after he'd gathered her wet clothes to toss in his dryer.

What he'd discovered when he'd emptied her jeans pockets had his heart double pumping—and wondering, *What the hell?* On a hunch, he'd gone outside, searched around his shrubs and found a backpack soaked with rain. He hadn't thought twice about rummaging through its contents. What he'd found inside had set him on his ass.

And there he'd sat. In his dark living room.

Where he'd brooded and wondered and worried

about more than the possibility of Amy waking up alone and scared.

Well, he thought, watching her over the steam ring above the lip of his coffee mug, *this* woman wasn't scared. A little on edge, maybe, but not scared. Free of whatever demons had haunted her sleep, she gave every appearance of being strong, together and composed.

And yet . . .

Can't let them find me here.

She hadn't yet uttered a word of explanation about her sudden appearance at his door. He wasn't sure how he felt about that. Or maybe he was. He realized, as he watched her, that in the rare moments when he'd let himself entertain thoughts of seeing her again, he'd still seen himself in the "savior" role. Pictured her needing him. And against all things reasonable, he'd liked the picture.

Which was crazy because he didn't now and never had wanted anyone needing him. Relying on him. Depending on him. Not on a personal level. Professionally, yes. It was the nature of the job. Emotional dependence, however, he'd wanted no part of it. And yet inexplicably he wanted it from Amy.

Didn't matter. Now that she was rested, he wasn't so certain she needed anyone now, anyway. Him included. And that knowledge spurred one more reaction he didn't want to explore: disappointment.

"More eggs?" he offered, placing the glass coffee carafe back on the burner and tried to deal with the undiluted truth that she could stand on her own two feet this go-round.

Which still didn't clarify why she was here. Or explain the contents of her jeans and backpack.

"No. Thanks. Those were great. I really appreciate it."

Yeah, he thought, a different woman from the one he'd dragged out of hell.

Now that she'd had some shut-eye, some food in her belly, it seemed she didn't need to be handled with kid gloves.

Which was a good thing. Because the gloves were about to come off.

Call it relief. Call it worry. Call it shock at her appearance out of the blue. Call it anything you wanted, but after several hours of concern, he felt mean suddenly. After six months of uncertainty and unknowns, he felt mean and mad and torn between worry and frustration.

She was about to bear the brunt of it.

"So," he said, as an anger that had simmered below the surface for almost half a year peaked to a slow, rolling boil. He started with what had been eating at him the longest. He'd get to the rest of it later. "You just forgot to say good-bye, or what?"

He gave her credit. She didn't flinch at the acid in his voice. She didn't pretend she didn't know what he was talking about either. And he didn't regret the bite in his tone nearly enough.

"I am truly, truly sorry for leaving like that." She looked at him through blue eyes brimming with apology.

"Oh, well." He nodded sagely. "Then that makes it all better, doesn't it?"

She heaved a deep breath, looked away from his bitter smile to her coffee mug. Hugged it with both hands. "No. It doesn't make anything better."

His first raw burst of rage—and yeah, hurt—spent, he settled himself down. Regretted that he'd sniped at her. He softened his tone. "You didn't think I'd worry about you? That we wouldn't *all* worry about you?"

She closed her eyes, tipped her head back. "I had a choice to make," she said then met his eyes again. "I could stick around, become more and more dependent on you and your family for support—and believe me, you all made it so easy for me to stay . . . and I will always be grateful for that—" She paused, gathered herself. "Or, I could do the right thing and leave."

"The right thing?" he repeated, concern now running tandem with a stubborn and lingering anger. "The right thing for you? For me?"

Sometime before she'd wandered out of the bedroom and shown up in his kitchen and found him cooking, she'd finger combed the tangles out of her hair. Silky blond strands draped past her shoulders, fell across a face that was as beautiful as it was sober. She dragged them back with a steady hand.

"Look. I owe you . . . you and your brothers . . . Manny and Darcy . . . I owe you all more than I can ever repay."

He worked a muscle in his jaw. Hard. "When did any of us ever give you the impression we expected payback?"

"Never," she said with a slow shake of her head. "And that's why I had to leave."

He grunted. "Is that supposed to make sense to me?"

She looked miserable.

He didn't let it waylay him. He wanted answers. And he wanted them now.

"Okay, let's try something I can make sense of," he suggested when she held her silence. "You left because you thought if you stuck around, you might drag us into something more dangerous than the trouble you were in on Iolo—does that about sum it up?"

Ah. He'd jarred her. He saw uncertainty now. And shock. He'd surprised her. He was about to surprise her some more.

"So . . . if that was the case then, why isn't it the case now? Why are you here, Amy? Why did you come back?"

She drew in a bracing breath, looked him in the eye and seemed to make a decision on the spot. "You know what? Chalk it up to a really bad decision, okay?" She stood. "I'll just get out of your hair."

"Right." He grunted. "*That's* gonna happen."

Her gaze flashed to his; his anger had surprised her. So did his next question.

"Who can't find you here?" he asked point-blank.

She blinked slowly. "What?"

"Before you passed out. You said: 'Can't let them find me here.' *Who* can't find you?"

He could see her mind racing a hundred miles an hour behind her eyes. She was going try to lie to him.

Tell him she must have been delirious. That wasn't going to happen either. He was about to make certain of it.

"Your grandfather? Is this about him? Yeah." He nodded when panic flickered in her eyes. "I know about the family you said you didn't have."

In the depths of the rain forest, hiding out from the Abu Sayyaf terrorists who were hunting them like dogs, she'd lied when she'd told him she had no family waiting for her back in the States.

Dallas had known the truth shortly after they'd flown back to West Palm and he'd caved in to the call of the Web and done a background search on her.

"How?" He preempted the question forming on her lips. "Because I'm good at my job," he said flatly and reached for the coffee carafe again.

While she stood in stunned silence, he filled his mug and sat back down on a stool opposite hers so the countertop was between them. It felt better that way. It kept him a safe distance from all her blond hair and soft skin and . . . Jesus. This wasn't about his unwanted attraction to this woman. This was about something much darker . . . although the outline of her soft breasts pressing against his t-shirt made for thoughts of the darkest, most carnal kind.

"E.D.E.N. is a security firm," he reminded her when she reluctantly sat back down at the counter and gripped her coffee mug in both hands as if she needed it to hold on to. "Background searches are part of what we do."

And what he'd found out when he'd conducted a

search on Amy Walker was that she had a grandfather whose name repeatedly popped up in conjunction with some very serious, very scary shit. She also had a mother. A resident of a mental institution in upstate New York.

"I'm sorry about your mother," he added quietly, and still felt like an ass because he'd purposefully gone for the shock value by mentioning her mother.

Only her eyes betrayed her reaction to his words. And he saw it all there. Pain, panic, then a concentrated bid to mask her emotions. It wasn't working. She was too shaken. Good. He wanted her unsettled. He wanted her talking to him.

Her continued silence and the rhythmic tap, tap, tap of her thumbs on the rim of her coffee mug gave away of how hard he'd jolted her composure. He was going to rock it some more.

"Jesus, Amy. You disappeared six months ago. Now, here you are again. Out of the blue. Running on fumes. Call me crazy, but I've gotta figure there's a tie-in to your abduction in Manila, the fact that you lied to me about having a family and the reason you showed up at my door. I've gotta figure there's a *damn good* reason.

"Which means, sweetheart," he added, more gently but in a tone leaving no room for doubt, "I'm not even close to letting you go."

He could see her struggle. She wanted to leave. She wanted to stay. What she didn't want to do was talk.

So he broke the silence for her. "How about we start

with this? Your grandfather, Edward Walker, popped up on some pretty dicey sites—sites like PARC-VRAMC."

Again, her silence told him she knew all about the nonprofit organization set up to educate the public about sadistic abuse, ritualized torture and invasive nonconsensual mind control experimentation.

"He was referenced several times on the site," he continued ruthlessly, ignoring the guilt slicing through him when her face drained of color. "Along with a list of German scientists and physicians who found refuge after World War II in any number of countries—the U.S. included—and were granted funding to conduct 'medical' research."

Medical research, hell. They were talking *Manchurian Candidate* shit. And when he'd discovered it, it had made Dallas as edgy as hell.

Watching Amy's face now, he fully understood the reason. He'd struck a vein. And he intended to mine it until she gave him the goods or the vein played out.

"Amy. Talk to me."

She closed her eyes, lowered her forehead to her palm. "I shouldn't have come." The agony in her voice broke his heart. "I never intended to involve you in this."

He didn't back off. "Involve me in what?"

Silence.

He dragged in a breath, then went for the throat.

"Let's go back to something you said earlier. You feel the need to repay me for saving your life on Jolo? Okay. Fine. Here's what you owe me. An explanation. A good one. And I want to collect right now."

His anger built when she remained stubbornly silent. "Can't find a place to start? Okay. I'll break the ice. Let's talk about these."

He dug into his pocket for the IDs he'd found in her wet jeans. Gaze locked on her face, he tossed them on the counter in front of her. There were five in all. All fake, all with her picture. All with different names, different hair color.

She stared at the IDs; her face drained to pale when he lifted her backpack from the floor behind the cabinets. He set it up onto the counter and fished around inside. Along with a cell phone, he tossed a short black wig, a pair of brown-tinted contact lenses and a fistful of cash onto the granite beside the IDs. Oh, yeah. And a fucking gun.

He pulled out the Glock 30 and an ammo pouch stuffed with two fully loaded magazines. He checked the pistol, ejected a round and swore under his breath at the size of the hollow-point cartridge. It looked like a teacup loaded on a .45 ACP case.

He extracted the clip from the grip, counted nine cartridges where there should have been ten. Balancing the magazine on his open palm, he held it out toward her. "Yeah. Let's talk about these. And let's do it now."

CHAPTER FIVE

Amy had always remembered Dallas Garrett's eyes as warm, welcoming. Like a low blue flame, a sunny day ocean swell. No warmth penetrated those eyes now. They were blue ice. Glittering sapphire. Opal hard.

He was angry. And he had every right to be.

It was aparent from the set of his broad shoulders as a jolt of thunder rocked the room. He abruptly stalked across the room to the sliders that opened on to a small deck. He pushed aside the curtain, then stared at the rain pumeling the dark. Settling himself down, she suspected.

God, what had she been thinking when she'd come here? Maybe that was the problem. Maybe she hadn't been thinking at all. She'd been scared. She'd been hiding out for six months, relying on disguises and a low profile to keep her identity hidden. It had taken a toll. So had driving down the length of the East Coast for two solid days and the fact that she hadn't slept in three.

She recognized now that she'd been in shock after the incident in New York. She'd killed a man. Almost died herself. She'd needed a safe place to fall. Just until she caught her breath, got her batteries recharged.

Dallas Garrett was the only safe place she knew. And no matter how hard she tried to deny it, she'd made the decision to come to him the night she'd made her first kill. It had been a wrong decision. At least it was wrong for him.

After a long moment, he turned, walked back again and stopped right in front of her. "Amy? What in the hell are you doing carrying? And talk about overkill. Christ—Corbon 200-grain Flying Ashtrays?"

She glanced at the magazine in his hand, her eyes defiant, her mind's eye fixed on the large hole dead center in the middle of a hired assassin's forehead. "They leave a big hole going in and an even bigger one going out."

"And you need this much firepower, *why?*"

It was more than a question. It was a command that brought her head up and sent her heart pounding again.

He wanted the truth. He deserved it. But did he deserve to be dragged into the thick of this? Guilt hit her harder than his anger. Just coming here could place him in danger.

"I'm already knee deep in whatever is happening with you," he said, as if reading her mind. "Give me something. Tell me what the hell is going on with you. I can help. You know I can help."

Yeah, she thought, feeling equal measures of relief and defeat. He could help. And before this was over, she would probably need help. But she didn't . . . she really didn't want to mix him up in this.

So why are you here?

Because she hadn't been able to stay away.

It was that simple. And she'd been that weak when she'd headed for Florida.

Okay. So she'd made a mistake. Well she was rested now. Could think clearly. And she knew what she had to do.

She snapped the magazine from his hand, pushed off the stool and attempted to look nonchalant. "The gun is for my protection, okay? That's all. Just in case. After Jolo . . . well, after Jolo I felt the need to be able to defend myself. It's that simple."

He wasn't buying it. His next questions told her just how much he wasn't buying. "And the wig? The colored contacts? Those for your protection too?"

"Fashion statement," she lied with a shrug and started stuffing her things into her backpack. "And I really do have to go."

He crossed his arms over his chest, narrowed his eyes. "On the off chance I'm actually going to let that happen, where exactly would you go?"

She checked her stash of cash then picked up the Glock along with the IDs. "Look. I was just passing through. I thought . . . well, I thought I'd stop by. See how you were. Okay?"

"For the last time, no. It's not okay." He gripped her upper arm, spun her around toward him. "Cut the crap. How many ways can I say it? You're not leaving. Not until I know exactly what's going on with you. And if you think you're protecting me from some big bad evil, well, forget it. I can handle myself. What I can't handle is worrying about you."

And what Amy couldn't handle was something happening to him. He was so ready to come to her defense. To slay dragons for her again if she asked him.

And she just couldn't ask him. She also understood that if she told him what she was about to do, he'd be on a flight with her to Argentina.

His eyes were so blue. So troubled. So angry. So determined. And the longer she stood here, the harder it was to resist a compelling need to tell him everything. When that had changed, she didn't know. She'd left here six months ago with no intention of ever coming back. It had hurt. Hurt a lot to know she'd never see him again. Hurt to know he must think she was ungrateful when she owed him her life.

It hurt now to look at him. His expression hard as onyx, he waited for her to start talking.

Sweetheart.

That's what he'd called her when she'd awakened earlier in the throes of a nightmare. A nightmare that she now knew had once been all too real.

Sweetheart.

It was a throwaway term of endearment. And she shouldn't give it import. She shouldn't want to melt into the strength he offered.

But she wasn't the same person he'd dragged off that island. Soft, naive. Vulnerable. She could take care of herself now.

During the last six months, she'd made certain of it. She'd taken classes. On the firing range. In martial arts. And she would never be a victim again.

She had a purpose now. She had intent.

And she had a raging need for answers. A consuming drive for revenge.

She planned on getting both. Even if she had to kill to get them.

A greasy knot of nausea rolled through her stomach. She had already killed. It still seemed surreal. And she didn't feel near enough remorse.

More than her body had been violated on Jolo. More than her innocence had been lost. They'd stolen her humanity, as well. Once, she would have sidestepped an ant to avoid killing it. Once she would have turned the other cheek before engaging in a physical confrontation that could hurt another human being.

Once.

Now she had killed. Was prepared to kill again. As her body had healed, she'd trained to make herself physically and mentally strong; killing those responsible for what had happened to her mother, what had happened to her, had been her driving force.

And hers might not be the only life in danger now. Amy hadn't been able to reach Jenna during the past two days. She had to get to Argentina. Had to find Jenna. Couldn't live with herself if something happened to Jenna because of her.

She glanced at the man who so patiently waited. A man who had a right to know.

Which was why she had to leave. Now. Before she

weakened and told him. Once he knew, she had no doubt he'd insist on going with her. And now that she was rested and thinking rationally, the one thing she could do was prevent that from happening.

For a long moment, she stood there, searching his eyes, his amazing face . . . wishing . . . wishing so many things could have been different between them. Wishing she'd met him when she was the person she'd once been, not the person she'd become.

Silence ticked like a clock. Anger and concern skipped on every beat. And somewhere in the mix an excess of another emotion confused and excited and frightened her.

He wanted more from her than an explanation.

He wanted her. He didn't want to. He'd never wanted to, but his eyes were heavy and dark with wanting.

Tempered with a measure of remorse.

She felt it too. In her blood. In her bones. In everything that made her a woman. Both the wanting and the regret. Both surprised her. Both made her weary and sad.

She knew there was no future for her with Dallas Garrett. It was possible there was no future for her at all.

And yet . . . for the first time since Jolo, as she stood there, so close to something so good, she yearned for the sweet side of intimacy with a man. The side filled with both taking and giving without humiliation or fear or pain.

She yearned for it. For the trust required to give

herself over to need. For the lovely anticipation of this man's—and only this man's—touch. The thrilling glide of his mouth across her skin, caressing, pleasuring, taking care and taking time to give her a memory that wasn't steeped in horror and degradation and loss.

Through a haze of longing, she understood something with a clarity that made perfect sense. If ever she were to reclaim that part of herself—the sensual part, the trusting part—her one chance stood before her. This man . . . this incredible, amazing man who knew what she'd been through and didn't see her as damaged goods or less of a woman because of it.

And she couldn't, she simply couldn't walk away. Not yet. Not . . . just . . . yet . . .

Not . . . without . . .

She leaned in close, her mouth mere inches from his. His breath whispered against her face as she closed the distance. Tentative. Testing. Trusting.

She touched her lips to his. Apologetic for placing him in this position. For asking him to be the one to give her back what others had so ruthlessly taken. For knowing he wouldn't have it in him to turn her down and using that knowledge against him.

His breath felt warm on her face, his scent clean and safe and so arousing she felt herself tremble and burn, overwhelmed by sensation and desire.

Desire, where there had been only pain for so, so long.

The shiver that rippled along her skin thrilled her. Clearly surprised him even as he met her halfway, then hesitated. She could sense the war he waged with himself. She could feel his reluctance battle with the wanting. Tension surrounded him like a force field. Heat radiated from his big body in sensual waves.

Even as his full, mobile lips opened over hers, moved against hers, he whispered an apology. And gave up the fight.

With ultimate care, with carefully controlled need, he kissed her. His hunger growing and giving and promising to take care, to restore all that had been stolen from her. Gentle loving. Desire without cost. Healing without pity. Taking without pain. Giving from bottomless depths.

Oh, God, she needed this. Two days ago she had almost died. Today she realized how badly she wanted to live. *Needed* to live what life she had left. Even more, she needed him to show her the way back to being a woman. To feel complete again. To return to hope and health and her own humanity.

"Amy," he whispered against her lips, parted them with his breath, wrapped her in his arms. "I'm sorry. This isn't . . . we shouldn't . . . you need—"

"You. I need you. Dallas. Please." She dived into a kiss that pleaded and seduced and left her breathless. "What I need right now is you."

Jesus. Jesus. He should end this. It was the right thing to do. The best thing to do. Dallas knew that. Knew it times ten. But she'd wrapped her slim arms around his neck, pressed those sweet, sweet breasts against him and clung to him like cellophane. Lush curves, warm woman, wanting and willing and strong.

And Lord . . . Lord God, he wanted her.

It wasn't right. In fact it was so wrong it scared the hell out of him. But he had wanted her and wished for her and thought of her like this for months. Of touching her. Of her touching him. Her fingers buried in the hair at his nape, his hands surrounding the delicate framework of her ribs. Thought of the two of them lying naked and breathless and knotted together like ropes in a give and sway as old as time, yet as new as a sunrise.

And now, here they were. Naked.

Somewhere in the midst of endless kisses and silken touches, they had removed each other's clothes. Made it to his bed. He'd even managed to suit up with a condom. Otherwise, they were stripped to the skin. Him on his back with her kneeling above him. Gloriously wanton. Absorbed in the moment. Totally in control . . . a control he gladly gave over to her.

It was a necessary submission on his part to let her direct the speed, the force, the unrelenting need. And her need was apparent in spades. Not to be taken, but to take. Not to be vanquished but to conquer. She needed to call the shots. To feel safe. To feel strong.

So he let her. Holy saints did he let her. Let her bend and shift and take everything she wanted, any way she wanted it. And she wanted it in ways he could never have imagined.

"Amy." Her name soughed out on a tortured breath as he gripped her hips while she rode him, relentless, focused, all lightning-quick reactions and wild, gasping cries.

He came like a cannon. No finesse. No control.

All velocity, explosion and speed. Given completely over to her will.

She clenched around him with a moan, arched her back and whispered his name like a prayer. Sighed her pleasure like an epiphany.

If he lived to be a hundred, hell, if he lived through the night, he'd never forget that moment. Never forget the feel of her moist heat convulsing around him, the fire and mist in her eyes, the tumble of blond hair falling across her face, the full swaying weight of her breasts as she caught her breath then collapsed onto his chest. Sprawling and spent. Wasted and sated.

Amazing.

She felt amazing, her weight liquid and hot pressed all over him. Her ragged breath feathered across his still erect nipple. Her knees tucked up against his ribs; the silk of her hair brushed his lips.

He lifted his left hand, pressed her cheek closer against his chest, caressed her sweet bare ass with his other hand and thought: *What have I done? What in God's name have I done?*

It was his last thought as he drifted off to sleep, his arms full of woman, his heart full of something that should have been regret but instead felt full and rich and rare.

CHAPTER SIX

Amy dressed in careful silence in the pale, predawn light. And tried not to think about leaving the man sound asleep on the bed.

He was so beautiful. Dark, unruly hair, damp from exertion fell across his forehead. Thick lashes brushed his cheeks as he lay supine and still on the bed where he'd given her back her sense of wonder.

What he'd given her . . . my God, what he'd given her. Tears filled her eyes. She had thought she'd never feel this way again. Never trust, never need, never feel clean and fresh and steeped in the heady pleasure of a man's gentle touch. A man's giving and gracious desire. Her own passion, honest and true.

And how did she thank him for giving her back that part of herself? The only way she could. By leaving him. She was going to leave him with his hands tied to the bedposts. Hands that had caressed her and finessed her into orgasms that still vibrated deep and woman-low inside of her. Hands he'd let her tie, giving himself over completely to her bidding.

This strong, dominant male had relinquished all the power. His blue eyes glazed with passion, his muscles quivering with the need to take her, he'd let her do the taking. Understood she'd needed control with a desperation born on a tropical island where paradise had been lost in a nightmare of degradation, violence and shame.

She stuffed the last of her things in her backpack then indulged in one last lingering look. Everything about him was beautiful. Vital. Strong, ropey muscles. Long, athletic legs. His skin a temptation to touch and taste and explore. There were scars. Scars that made her afraid for him. In particular the jagged remains of what had to have been a near-death injury that ran from his right rib to low over his abdomen.

The scars shouldn't have surprised her. He was, after all, a warrior who'd been willing to bleed, even die for a cause.

Well, she wasn't about to let him die for her. If she stayed, if she explained, he'd want to go with her. And if he did, he'd surely bleed again. Maybe even die this time. After what he'd given her . . . she simply couldn't place him in that position.

Regret skirted around the edge of determination as she grabbed her backpack, slipped out of the room and let herself quietly out of his condo and into the dark.

If anything, the intensity of the rain had increased and along with it the wind. She struggled against the force of it, lowered her head as thunder rolled with a teeth-jarring concussion of sound and fury. A lightning strike flashed on its heels as she cleared the parking lot and headed across the street at a fast trot.

That's when she heard footsteps closing in fast behind her. Since she'd left Dallas tied to the bed, those footsteps meant only one thing: they'd followed her. And they'd found her.

Pulse spiking, she kicked up her pace to a flat-out run, splashed through the water running ankle deep at the curb and dug frantically into her backpack for her Glock.

She was thinking of Dallas and hoping against hope she was leading them away from him when she was hit from behind. The force of the blow knocked her flat on her face in the grass. Her backpack, with the pistol inside, went flying.

Pain exploded through her body. Her knees and elbows took the brunt of the fall. She fought past the searing shock of it, reminded herself she hadn't spent the last six months just looking for answers or cowering in a closet, licking her wounds. She'd learned that there were ways to insure she would never become a victim again. There was a dead man in a snow-shrouded ravine in New York that proved that she didn't have to be.

She made herself go completely limp, as if she'd been knocked out by the force of the blow that had taken her down. When a big hand gripped her shoulder and rolled her to her back, she was ready. She laid into him with a swift chop to the windpipe— realized too late to pull it that it was Dallas.

"God damn it!" he swore, when she chopped his neck hard with her forearm. Capturing her wrists in his hands, he pinned them to the grass above her head. Rain pelted down like bullets, hitting her in the face, pouring from his hair. "Stop fighting me!" he croaked.

Tension, shock, surprise . . . all three vied for dominance as she lay there, feeling cornered and confused and relieved at the same time. If any other man—*any other man*—had dominated her this way, she would have fought, scratched, gouged, bit, screamed bloody murder. And she'd have relived the horror of Jolo every nanosecond.

But this was Dallas. The man who had saved her life and her sanity. The man she had just made love with and whom she did not want to lead into danger.

She searched his eyes as he loomed above her, soaking wet, his chest bare, imprisoning her with legs covered in soaked denim. "Please, Dallas, just let me go."

For a long moment, only their labored breathes and the relentless downpour broke the silence of the predawn darkness.

"In a pig's eye. Wherever you're going, I'm going with you."

Light from a distant security lamp cast his profile in misty, golden shadows. Emotions too huge to accommodate swelled in her chest. "Dallas—"

"Shut up," he ordered.

Rising to his feet, he held out a hand to help her up.

His hand was big. Powerful. Heavily veined. Rough with calluses. Waiting.

She lifted her hand, gripped his tight and allowed him to pull her to her feet. Her knees burned beneath her soggy jeans. She worked her sore elbows. Over-riding the pain was guilt.

She dragged sodden hair from her eyes. Had she really thought when she'd come here that he would let her walk away? That he wouldn't feel compelled to help her? "Dallas, I—"

"Back inside." He gripped her upper arm, steered her across the lot. "Where I can nurse my wounds in private."

"Oh, God." She stopped abruptly. Panic made her heart trip. She'd practiced her moves hundreds of times in class but had never employed them for real. "Did I really hurt you?"

He rubbed the side of his neck where she'd connected, then scrubbed rain from his face. "Let's just say you bruised more than my ego. And so you know, the last person to sucker punch me didn't live long enough to brag about it."

Nothing about this situation was remotely funny, but she smiled at the bruised pride in his tone. It was pained, knee-jerk, and riddled with a relief she felt guilty for feeling. "I'll keep that in mind."

"Yeah." He grunted. "You do that." Then he hustled her through the water-logged street toward his condo.

When he'd shut and locked the door behind them, he turned and leaned back against it. His wet hair lay plastered to his head as he considered her through narrowed eyes.

"Let's get something straight here. Whatever bind you're in, I want to help you. I need to help you. And you need to let me.

"You need to let me," he repeated, his gaze locked on hers. "There's no fighting it any longer. Got it?"

Yeah. She finally got it. He was right. What happened on Jolo, what happened in his bed . . . it bound them.

She didn't know what it all meant. Hadn't figured out the whys or the hows or if there was even a remote possibility anything further could happen between them. But he was right. And it was a relief to finally accept it.

"Yeah," she said. "I've got it."

A combination of relief and satisfaction crossed his face. "So, what happens next? Where do we go from here?"

Where they went from here was somewhere that might make it impossible for them to ever return. "Argentina."

If he was shocked, he didn't show it. He just pushed away from the door. "I'll get my passport. You can fill me in on the flight."

Two showers and two hours later, they were on a Delta jet bound for Atlanta. From there they'd catch a connecting flight to Buenos Aires. Once there, Amy figured, they would enter the fight of their lives.

She just prayed to God that they got to Jenna before it was too late.

Same day, Leleque, in the Argentinean Patagonia

Iraq. Lebanon. Argentina. One of these things is not like the other." Jenna McMillan sang the *Sesame Street* song whisper-quiet as she sat on her butt on the damp, dirt floor, her arms draped over her upraised knees.

Yeah, she thought as a cockroach roughly the size of an Abrams tank scuttled across the thick black bars of her cell, Third-World nations and terrorist strongholds equated to random abductions and indiscriminate, unjust imprisonment. But Argentina? Argentina was known for its beef, gauchos, Evita, the tango, and yeah, for a little drug action, for God's sake. American citizens weren't just plucked off the streets and thrown in prison.

Yet here she was. Locked in a six-by-six jail cell, miles from the civilized world, no charges filed, no jurisprudence or right to a speedy trial in play.

In short, as her daddy used to say, she was up shit creek without the proverbial paddle. And she wasn't really sure she had the balls for it.

Weary to the bone, she closed her eyes and let her head fall back against the grimy adobe wall. A single light bulb on a frayed cord hung from the ceiling in the hallway. It was almost more frightening with the light on than in the dark.

She was hungry. She was scared— although she'd never let those bastards see it. And after two days in this bug-infested cell, she was wondering if she'd ever see the purple mountains' majesty again.

God she missed Wyoming. Home. Hell, even Iraq had a certain appeal.

And was a breath of fresh freaking air too much to ask for?

"It smells like a cesspool in here!" she complained loudly. As if anyone would give a rip.

On a weary breath, she pushed to her feet. Her multicolored gauzy skirt was ripped and caked with dust, her sweat-stained silk tank hardly recognizable as white. And her hair. Gawd. She forked her fingers through the long tangled mass of auburn curls, attempted to work through the snarls. What she wouldn't give for a brush. And a shower.

She sniffed under her armpit. Made a face.

"How 'bout a change of clothes?" she yelled to some unseen, uncaring jailer who mumbled an annoyed, "*Mujer americana loca.*"

"*Loca?* You think I'm crazy now? Just wait and see how crazy I get if I miss my pedicure, you macho gaucho jerk!"

"*Cállate!*" he shouted.

Quiet? He wanted her to be quiet? All she'd been was quiet—and it rubbed hard against every grain in her body. But she'd thought if she played the demure card, acted the innocent, she could appeal to his sense of gallantry.

These yahoos were about as gallant as a herd of warthogs. And she done being quiet.

"I demand to speak with someone at the American embassy!" she yelled, walking up to the bars. She gripped them in both hands—immediately thought better of it—and jerked her hands away from the filthy steel. "You can't keep me here like this. I have rights."

The response was the creak of an old desk chair followed by heavy footsteps, followed by a slammed wooden door. The one that had been open between the small bank of cells and the outer office. The door that had provided the only influx of marginally fresh air in a cell that boasted a skinny cot with a mattress made of burlap and straw and alive with who knew what kind of vermin. One window—one foot by two feet—six feet off the floor provided the only source of natural light. A chipped porcelain pot in the corner of the cell was her toilet. A pitcher of stagnant water was her bath.

"And the goat you rode in on," she muttered, flipping a one-finger salute in the general direction of the outer office. Then she forced herself to settle down.

It wasn't that she wasn't tough. It wasn't as if she hadn't been in tight spots before. At one time or another, on one assignment or another, she'd been to every hotspot on the globe—Mogadishu, Beirut, Gaza, Kabul, Tikrit—dozens of others. She'd been shot at, survived mortar rounds, RPGs, and irate mullahs. She'd covered dicey hostage situations stateside and the grim reality of genocide in Rwanda. She'd even been bartered for by a Saudi prince who had a fascination for her green eyes and red hair.

She sank back down to her butt on the floor. Yeah, she'd been in some tight spots. But she'd never been locked up and alone, void of communication, cut off and uninformed. It was the uninformed part that got to her the most. Information was her life. She wasn't kidding herself. She knew this had something to do with Amy Walker's grandfather. And she'd known coming in what the man was capable of doing. When she thought about what Amy had gone through because of him—a shiver ripped through her body—well, she'd known she was dipping her spoon into a potentially poisonous stew.

Only one thing kept her halfway calm. They hadn't killed her. Had to be a good sign, right?

"*Right*," she muttered on a heavy sigh. They hadn't killed her. Yet.

She dragged her hair back from her face. Wondered if she'd ever see home again.

That kind of thinking was going to get her nowhere. She needed answers. Who exactly were these people? Where was she being held? And the big question: What did they plan to do with her?

CHAPTER SEVEN

Same day, in flight to Atlanta

The cabin was quiet. The passengers settled in. Beside Amy, wearing tan cargo pants and a form-fitting black t-shirt, Dallas waited patiently, his face hard, his eyes hooded.

He smelled of clean and of man. Now that they were on their way to Buenos Aires and she had time to reflect, her thoughts kept wandering back to the not so very long ago, when the two of them had been naked and joined in his bed. It had been . . . incredible. Easy. Pure. Right.

When she'd never thought that part of her life would be right again.

He was such an amazing man. Such a *beautiful* man. All the requirements of a hero—which he'd already proven he was. The amazing body honed with the musculature of a seasoned warrior. The dark, thick hair, the bold, hard lines of his face, the full lips that softened when he smiled and knocked the severe edge right off all those rigid angles and shadowed planes. Gentle hands and amazing grace when he'd touched her, smiled at her and made her a believer again in miracles.

He wasn't smiling now. He sat beside her with the intensity of a warrior. With the strength of will to wait until she was ready to fill him in. With the determination of a man who would play this out to the end.

And she'd kept him waiting long enough. He wanted to hear it all. And she needed to tell him.

"This is going to be hard for you to buy." She swallowed around a lump of apprehension that complicated her decision to give him what he wanted.

"Just tell it like it is, okay?" He was a big man. They'd been lucky enough to get an exit row seat so he could stretch his long his legs out under the seat in front of him. He crossed his ankles, folded his arms over his chest and got as comfortable as he could.

His eyes were dark and intent on hers, his expression one of encouragement and patience, when patience was probably the exact opposite of what he felt.

"My mother," she began, keeping her voice low so she wouldn't be overheard, "was a victim of mind control experimentation. Drug therapy, electric shock therapy, ELF waves, sensory deprivation . . . God knows what all they did to her."

"Jesus," he said after a long, stunned silence. "You know this? For a fact?"

She looked away, breathed deep. "There are documents. Documents written by my grandfather. And I have . . . memories," she said finally, and chanced a glance at him again.

"Memories?"

She swallowed hard. "Memories. Dreams. Of them doing . . . things to her."

"Them?" he prompted after a long moment, his voice lethally calm.

"My grandfather and his *associates*." She watched his face, waited for her words to take root. She didn't know if it was skepticism or flat out disbelief prompting his long silence.

"Are you saying that your *grandfather* experimented on his own daughter?"

He stared, eyes narrowed, head cocked, like he couldn't believe what he'd just heard, let alone grasp what she was implying.

"That's exactly what I'm saying. My grandfather was SS during World War II. And after . . . after he was one of the monsters responsible for destroying my mother's mind. For damaging a sweet, gentle spirit and turning her into a catatonic shell of the warm, loving woman I remember as a child."

Tears welled up in her eyes as she waited for Dallas to absorb what she'd just told him. Angry for showing weakness, she blinked them away as he slouched back in the seat, his expression thoughtful before his eyes transitioned to that caring blue she'd so needed to see.

He wiped a hand over his lower jaw. "His own daughter?" he repeated, still in disbelief.

"That's why I was in Manila." Now that she'd finally taken the first step, it was a relief to tell him everything. "I'd tracked him there."

"Are you telling me that's why you were abducted?

Because you were asking questions about your grand-father?"

"I was abducted," she said, meeting the challenge in his eyes, "because I was asking questions about Aldrick Reimers, also known as Edward Walker, sus-pected Nazi war criminal. It was insignificant that he's my grandfather."

Again, he grew silent.

"You've heard of ODESSA?" She felt the need to backtrack a bit in order to fill in the whole picture.

It was a rhetorical question. Dallas was ex-military. Ex-marine. Force Recon. He'd told her that and many other things in one of his monologues on Jolo when he was doing his damnedest to keep her from freaking out and folding in on herself. She seri-ously doubted there was a military officer—even an NCO, as he'd been—who hadn't studied the history of World War II and the Nazi machine. But she clari-fied anyway.

"ODESSA is a German acronym for *Organisation der ehemaligen SS-Angehörigen*. It's an organization of former SS members—an international Nazi net-work set up toward the end of World War II by a group of SS officers and sympathizers."

"Martin Bormann and Heinrich Himmler suppos-edly among them," he added, comfirming her assump-tion that he was well apprised of the organization.

"Yes," she said and swallowed hard. "Bormann, Himmler . . . many others. Including my grandfather."

She stopped talking when the pilot's voice droned over the speakers telling them they were right on

schedule and to relax and enjoy the rest of the short
flight to Atlanta.

"Okay," Dallas said, turning slightly toward her in
his seat when the pilot signed off. "I'm with you on
the probability of your grandfather being a badass.
But ODESSA? Amy. It's never been proven that
ODESSA actually exists. Common speculation is
that a lot of dark dramatic stories have fueled the fire
and kept the rumors going."

She understood his skeptisim. Many experts in the
field believed ODESSA was a myth. A fictional organization fabricated by the post-war propaganda machine.

"Tell that to my mother," she said, unable to hide
her anger. "Tell that to the people who—" She
stopped abruptly, lowered her voice, not sure how to
handle the rest of it.

"Tell it to the people who *what?*" The edge crept
back in his hushed tone.

She looked up, found his eyes hard and intent on
hers. Black, cobalt, even flecks of gold melded with
the cerulean blue that seemed to look straight through
to her soul.

"The people who had me abducted by those animals." She stopped herself, breathed deep to control
the rapid escalation of her heart rate and dragged
herself away from the nightmare of Jolo.

"Tell it to the others who are victims, like my
mother. Tell it to the hired muscle who found me two
nights ago and ran my car off the road."

She unbuckled her seat belt, suddenly needing to

move. Needing to do something to escape the memory of what she'd done that night.

"Whoa, whoa, whoa. Someone ran you off the road?" Dallas snagged her arm, held her in the seat. His eyes were wild when she faced him. "*Ran you off the road?*"

Settling herself down, Amy nodded. "In New York. As I was leaving my mother's facility. They'd found me there . . . no matter how carefully I'd covered my tracks."

She told him about how she'd been working there under an assumed identity so she could be close to her mother. About the Humvee, the plunge into the ravine. She didn't tell him about killing the man who had come after her.

Couldn't tell anyone about it. Not yet. Maybe not ever.

"Anyway, I managed to get away. Started driving. And ended up at your door."

He covered her hand with his. Squeezed. "Which is exactly what you should have done."

"Yeah," she said bitterly. "You saved my life once. And this is how I repay you. By dragging you back into my mess. Now you're probably a target too."

Dallas scrubbed a hand across his jaw, wished he'd taken time to shave. It was just one of the regrets he had. One of the many mistakes he'd made in the past several hours.

Among his biggest was giving in to a need so huge it had knocked him flat on his back with her on top of him. A close second was not clearing the air after they'd made love. Not apologizing, not clarifying . . . clarifying what?

Hell. He didn't know. He still felt like he'd been hit by an artillery round. What had happened between them in his bed—how could he clarify that for her when he didn't have a firm handle on it himself?

Sex—hell, yeah, he liked sex. With the right partner, with no strings, boundaries clear up front, sex was great. But sex with Amy . . . Jesus. Sex with Amy went beyond any boundaries he'd ever set, went beyond anything he'd ever experienced. It was . . . amazing. Wild. Out. Of. Control.

And he'd damn well better get back in control if he was going to keep both of them alive.

Not good. This was so not good. He had to keep his head in the game. They were on their way to Argentina, for God's sake. She'd actually thought she could sneak off without him. He was still pissed about that. Pissed that she'd thought she could talk him out of coming along—after he'd given up trying to do the same thing with her.

He'd called Ethan on the way to the airport. Told him he was taking Amy to visit her family—it was partly true—and they'd caught the first flight to Buenos Aires.

Where it was quite possible there were bad guys laying in wait. Or, quite possible that she was leading him on a wild goose chase.

"So that's what those fake IDs are about," he said abruptly, getting back on track with a much more pressing issue. He'd sort out the physical stuff later.

And the other stuff. The stuff that had him reevaluating everything he'd ever thought he'd known about what he'd wanted long term in a woman. "The disguise. The Glock with the elephant loads. You've been hiding out."

The cornered look on Amy's face was all the answer he needed. Now it made sense. At least one piece of this puzzle anyway.

Can't let them find me here.

She'd been on the run. Always looking over her shoulder. No wonder she was exhausted. She was in danger.

At least she thought she was.

And another issue rose front and center to play hell with his equilibrium. He didn't like himself much for what he was thinking. But hell. Her story was all so out there. He glanced down at the scars on her wrists, thought about the ones on her ankles. And wondered at the scars he couldn't see—the ones on her psyche. Wondered if those bastards on Jolo had succeeded in pushing her into the deep end. Wondered if during the past six months she hadn't lost a little more of herself than had been taken from her in the jungle.

ODESSA. Mind-control experiments. It was all so wild. And yet—Edward Walker *was* linked up to sites pointing in that very direction.

Still . . . his own daughter? Maybe . . . hell. He didn't know. Maybe Walker had simply been trying to stabilize Amy's mother all those years, treat a long-term mental condition and experimenting with cures, not creating her illness.

Maybe the problems that had landed Amy's mother in a mental institution had nothing to do with something as diabolical as mind-control experimentation. What if she'd always been ill?

And what, he thought reluctantly, if Amy's mother's condition was hereditary?

"You think I've lost it, don't you?"

Her gaze was sharp on his as the "fasten seatbelt" sign blinked on.

He didn't want to think it. God, he didn't want to. But Amy had been through hell on Jolo. Her experience could drive the most anchored individual over the edge. Man—and afterwards . . . she'd just disappeared. No word. For six long months, not a word. And now this. Showing up in the dead of night soaking wet, flying off to Argentina.

"Amy—"

She shook her head, disgusted, disappointed.

And pissed. She was good and pissed. Her integrity had been questioned—by the one person she had trusted enough to approach. To share her story with. A story he had bullied out of her. A story that he had just implied, he found suspect.

A story he *did* find suspect—at least parts of it.

"Look. I'm sorry, okay?" he conceded, attempting to settle her down. "And I don't think you've lost it."

She shot him a challenging look.

Okay. So she read his mind.

"Give me a break here. I'm still dealing with the fact that you're back. Six months," he pointed out with a lift of his hand. "For six months you're a no-show. And then, *bam*. Here you are—dead on your feet, on the run and toting a pocket full of forged IDs, a shitload of cash, a disguise and a goddamn cannon. I haven't got a firm handle on that yet. Give me a minute to absorb the rest of this, okay?"

He dragged a hand through his hair, met her eyes again and saw the same kind of frustration he was feeling. Saw, also, the woman—the flesh-and-blood woman—he'd lost sleep over, lost a measure of control over, lost the better part of his peace of mind over. The woman who had played hell with his hero complex on Jolo. And damn if she hadn't cranked it into high gear again.

On Jolo, she'd been a victim. Filthy, starved, bruised and battered. She might now be physically healed and free, but she was still a victim. Whether she was victimized by her own mind playing tricks on her or by a real and present danger, he didn't yet know.

He knew only one thing. From the moment he'd seen her standing in his doorway, he'd felt the weight of a thousand regrets lift from his chest.

Another chance. He had another chance. To see what the hell it was about her that made her so compelling. To find out what it was about her that made him want to step out of his comfort zone in the form of a major change of plans.

And the fact was, she wasn't the only one on the edge or on the run. He'd been ready to run too—from his family, from his career, from his own demons. He hadn't known where he was going, hadn't cared.

Now he had something to care about. Bold truth: He cared about her. Stupid. Pointless. Without future.

But still, he wasn't running anywhere until he figured out what was going on with her.

"We'll be landing in Atlanta in less than thirty minutes," he said checking his Rolex Submariner. "Before we catch our connecting flight, I want you to start from the beginning. Tell me everything. Don't leave out one piece of information."

CHAPTER EIGHT

My grandfather's real name is Aldrick Reimers," Amy said after a deep breath. "He was a German-born physician who worked in mental institutions in and around Berlin before World War II. His primary duty was to evaluate and decide whether mentally deficient children should be sterilized or killed. If the child proved to be good subject matter, at his suggestion, they were sometimes allowed to live and then were subjected to any number of inhuman experiments under order of the state."

Dallas pinched the bridge of his nose, rubbed eyes made gritty from lack of sleep and swallowed back his disgust.

"Like I said, he was SS," she continued, understanding the revulsion he felt. She felt it too. "A premier physician at age twenty-two."

"Twenty-two?"

"Young, yeah," she said reacting to the surprise in his voice. "One of Hitler's favorites. A perfect prototype for the superior Aryan race. He was a genius—and, I suspect, a little mad with it. Doogie Howser on LSD. He carried out experiments in the death camps. Horrifying, monstrous experiments."

She stopped, swallowed back the nausea that always accompanied this terrible truth. "After the war, the U.S. turned a blind eye to the atrocities committed by many of these men, 'believed' them when they denied being members of Hitler's death squads. My grandfather was one of many doctors and scientists brought to the States. Their medical expertise and the data they'd collected on their human experiments were considered vital to the Cold War effort in the forties and fifties."

"Some of the greatest and yet most perverse minds in the world," Dallas muttered.

"You're aware of the experiments at Brooks Air Force Base in Texas, the secret I. G. Farben Labs in Maryland, of Willowbrook?"

He nodded, his face grim. "Your grandfather was a part of Willowbrook?"

Willowbrook had been a snake pit in the 1950s and 1960s. A mental institution where the administrator and staff had systematically infected children with strains of the hepatitis virus in the name of medical research.

"No. Not Willowbrook. He was in charge of the Blackbird project."

"Blackbird?"

"One of their top secret projects. Established to counter Soviet and Chinese advancements in brainwashing and interrogation techniques."

"Okay, yeah. I remember reading about similar

programs. Artichoke. MKULTRA. Others that escape me now. The CIA was all hot to learn the state of the art of behavioral modification."

"Right. The government was concerned about the inexplicable behavior of persons behind the Iron Curtain and American POWs who appeared to have been subjected to brainwashing."

"*Manchurian Candidate*," he muttered under his breath. "*Bourne Identity*. Great book plots."

"Only what happened to my mother wasn't fiction."

Amy felt a chill eddy through her blood at the mention of the *Manchurian Candidate*. It was John Marks' book, *The Search for the Manchurian Candidate*, that might have landed Amy and Jenna McMillan in the danger they were in today.

"Tell me."

"My mother wasn't any more than a means to an end for him," she continued, forcing herself not to think about what might be happening to Jenna right now. "He wasn't in the States for over a year when most of his funding was pulled because the powers that be were getting squeamish about the government sanctioning the type of experiments he was into. But that didn't stop him. He conducted his own research, off site—until the CIA was formed in '47."

"And then they recruited him?"

She nodded. "Changed his name to Edward Walker so he wouldn't be connected to the SS. They put him in charge of the Blackbird project."

His silence encouraged her to go on.

"From what I've pieced together, he had an affair

with one of the nurses on his new project. He was twenty-seven at the time."

"Twenty-seven. That makes him . . . ?"

"Eighty-nine now," she preempted as he did the math in his head. "My mother was the product of that affair. According to the records, her birth mother died in childbirth."

She could see the reaction in his eyes and in the white in his knuckles as he clutched his hands tightly together. "Handy coincidence," he said darkly.

She became quiet for a moment, contemplating the horror of her next disclosure. "According to his notes, he started his experimentation on my mother when she was seven years old. Drugs. Shock therapy. Psychological deprivation—all under the sanction of the CIA."

He swallowed back his revulsion. Shook his head.

Amy understood. What was there to say that hadn't already been said? It was horrifying. Her grandfather was a monster.

"You keep making reference to his documents or his notes," Dallas said quietly.

"Right. About a year ago Jenna McMillan found my grandfather's name among some documents recently released by the government."

"Jenna McMillan?"

She watched his face as he processed this information.

"The journalist? Writes for *Time*? That Jenna McMillan?"

"Yeah. *That* Jenna McMillan. She'd been fascinated with Marks' book for years. Wanted to revive the story on the CIA'S mind-control experimentation—a kind of 'where are they now' piece—and had done some extensive research. She accessed several of my grandfather's papers through the Freedom of Information Act. She found out he'd had a daughter, located my mother, then found me."

"Go on," Dallas encouraged her when she fell silent.

"Jenna thought she was merely tracing a family history. She never dreamed she'd find an actual victim when she found my mother."

Amy stared hard at the seat back in front of her. "Jenna made all of his documents available to me."

She'd never forget that day. The shock of it. The horror as she realized that what she was reading was a history of the terror her mother had been through.

"Because of Jenna, I finally pulled my head out of the sand regarding the cause of my mother's mental condition. I accepted what I'd suspected but hadn't wanted to face. That my memories had been real. That the dreams had been real. My grandfather had done this to her. That's when I went looking for him."

"In Manila?"

"I had a lead that he was there at the time." She looked at her hands. Looked at him. They both knew what happened to her in Manila.

"Just what *is* your mother's condition?" Dallas asked gently.

Amy closed her eyes, gave a weary shake of her head. "It's a long story."

"I've got nothing but time."

Time. Once Amy had marked time in terms of

weeks, months, years. Now she measured it in how much longer she could stay alive. How much time she had before she found her grandfather and confronted him.

Time had healed her physical wounds. And time bred hatred. Changed her life.

She dragged a hand through her hair, met Dallas' probing stare. And went back in time.

"I was ten or eleven, I guess, the first time I grasped that my mother was emotionally unbalanced," she confessed, because to relay the entire story, she had to go back to her childhood. "Most of the time, she'd just be this normal mom. Baking cookies, going to work, shopping.

"On the days when she wasn't herself, I just took it in stride. It was the norm for me to come home and find her sitting in a chair or lying in bed totally gone. She wouldn't hear me. Didn't seem to see me. She'd just lay there for hours on end. I'd eventually go to bed, and in the morning, she'd be back. Mom again."

"What about your father? Was he in the picture?"

She shook her head. "Mom always told me that he'd died in a car accident right after I was born. It wasn't until Jenna made my grandfather's papers available to me that I discovered the truth."

Her stomach still knotted when she thought back to that day. She wasn't even aware that Dallas had reached out and covered her hand with his until the warmth from his skin seeped into her fingers.

"Subject 29. That's how he referred to her in his papers. Not his daughter. Not a human being. Not Karen Walker. Just Subject 29. Female. D.O.B. 2-4-45."

"Amy . . . I hate to point out the obvious, but if your mother was never mentioned by name, only by number—"

"I know what you're thinking, but I remember things, okay?" She made herself settle down when she heard her own defiance and anger at his doubt. "I . . . remember things. And the more I read, the more I remembered . . . and I knew he was writing about my mother.

"It explained so much. Like the dreams I've had for as long as I've had memories."

The dreams about them doing horrible things to her mother that now got all tangled up with her captivity on Jolo.

"I was experiment number 42, by the way," she added, almost to herself. "They—my grandfather and his *gang of merry men*—had attempted artificial insemination eleven times and Mom had always spontaneously aborted. They'd actually given up, but on a whim, decided to try one more time.

"She was thirty-six by then. The CIA funding had long since been pulled, the mind-control projects all deep-sixed. But he just . . . he just couldn't leave her alone. All those years he abused her, conducted experiments on her . . . controlled her even as an adult."

She had to stop. Collect herself. Rein in her anger. Dallas' voice steadied her.

"Amy . . . I'm trying to go with this, so, for the sake of argument, let's say these papers are about your mother. How did he hide the effects of his handiwork when *she* was a child?"

Again, she understood his skepticism. "Private

schools. Discretion at all costs. And money, the common denominator, talked as well then as it does now."

"What happened," he asked softly, "what happened to make you finally realize that she wasn't well? That she was different from the other mothers?"

"The catatonic states became more frequent. Started getting longer. Sometimes they'd last for days and I couldn't rouse her. When I started showing up for school in the same clothes, dirty, hungry, tired, the school social worker finally made a home visit. Long story short, Mom ended up hospitalized until she was stable again and I'd ended up in and out of foster care."

She could see in his eyes how that news affected him.

"It wasn't as bad as it sounds—not for me. She was the one going through hell."

"You were a child. Without a father. Often without a mother. How can that not be bad?"

Okay. It was bad. But she wasn't going there. He must have realized it, because he released a resigned breath and nodded.

"So where was your grandfather during all of this?"

"The Freedom of Information Act had been loosened up considerably and for the first time the public was made aware of the mind-control experimentation program—again, thanks mostly to John Marks' book."

"*The Search for the Manchurian Candidate*," Dallas reflected.

"Yes. Anyway, my grandfather must have known

that once the information was made public someone would be coming after him and his kind. He must have known that society was no longer willing to turn a blind eye to his atrocities and he skipped out— I was around ten years old."

"Did he . . . did he ever . . ."

His eyes were bleak when she met them. She realized then what he wanted to know, but couldn't seem make himself ask. She understood that he wasn't even certain he believed her story. And still, he was worried about what might have happened to her.

"No. No, he never experimented on me. At least I have no recollection of it. I was supposed to have been a boy, you see, and since I wasn't, I didn't hold any interest for him as a subject. He . . . he was into boys by then."

His long breath was weighty with relief. A prayer answered. His face was washed in it. His eyes were tortured with lingering thoughts that she might have been subjected to her grandfather's special form of abuse.

An unexpected sense of comfort and warmth enveloped her. She turned her palm under his, linked their fingers and squeezed. "I'm sorry. It hadn't occurred to me that you thought he'd used me too."

Yeah. He was starting to believe her. Good, bad, somewhere in between, she could tell he was starting to believe her.

"Look. I know it's a hard sell, but it's real. What they might be doing to people even now is a real possibility, too. Jenna said she found something," she added, countering his doubt. "Something to corroborate the stories about a second and third generation of SS operational and active in South American. Specifically in Argentina."

He looked incredulous. "That's what this is about? Argentina and the ODESSA myth?"

"Jenna's convinced it's not a myth."

"And because she believes, you do, too? Christ, Amy. A journalist goes on a hundred wild goose chases to uncover one valid lead."

"And how many of them disappear when they're on the trail of a story?"

Dallas sobered. "Disappeared?"

She had his full attention now. "She called me two days ago. From Buenos Aires. Said she had a lead on my grandfather. That he'd left Manila recently and returned to Argentina. I told her I'd come. That night I was run off the road. I've been on the move ever since. I haven't heard another word from her. And she hasn't answered my calls."

His eyes were on her face, but his mind was racing to parts unknown.

"So . . . this is as much about her as it is about your grandfather."

"I'm afraid something's happened to her, Dallas. The same kind of something that almost happened to me. She's running out of time. And so am I."

Time. There it was again. The element that couldn't be quantified. Not for Jenna. Amy didn't know how much time Jenna had. Or how much time she herself had before they found her again.

"He's still out there. My grandfather is still out there. I've got to find him. I'm *going* to find him and expose what he's done. I'm going to make him pay for what he did to her. For what he did to me when he made me fair game for those animals on Jolo."

"Amy." Cajoling. Soliciting reason. "He's eighty-nine years old."

To urgency she added anger. "And he's still a monster."

"An old man."

"I have to find him, Dallas."

"You almost died once searching for him."

She looked out the portal. Yes. She'd almost died. And there was a reason she'd lived. She had a debt to pay.

CHAPTER NINE

MC6 compound, El Bolson, Argentina

Erich Adler hung up the phone with calculated care. He leaned back in his desk chair to the creak of springs in need of oil. He was a big man: over six feet and stocky—built more like a laborer than a visionary. More like a brawler than the head of MC6, an organization that was on track to, someday, control the free world.

His nose was bulbous and crooked from multiple breaks, from the many beatings that had left scars on his ruddy face. He was battle hardened, purpose driven, and human life held as much sanctity for him as the fly he caught midair and squashed between his fingers.

He wiped his hand with a tissue and, fastidious as always, applied a small amount of liquid cleaner on his fingers. Then he contemplated where to go from here.

He could not afford any setbacks. Not now. Final plans were already in the works and he would be damned if he'd let an inconsequential fool of a woman do anything to disrupt his timetable.

He stared into space as a rage he fought to keep under control bred and beat against the wall of composure he always maintained.

His office door opened after a timid rap. Annoyed, Erich shifted his gaze to the thin, stooped man in the white lab coat and wire rim glasses walking into the room. Henry Fleischer was a brilliant scientist. He was methodical, precise, without conscience, and leading a team on the verge of the breakthrough that had eluded the organization for close to six decades.

Henry had as much at stake in taking Amy Walker out of the picture as Erich. They were the new guard. The future of MC6. The future of the world.

Unfortunately, Amy Walker and her meddling journalist friend, Jenna McMillan, were proving to be more than mere pesky flies in their ointment. Both had been on their watch list for over a year now. And both needed to be dealt with immediately. The time for discretion was long past.

That's why Erich had dispatched Subject 451 to New York to dispose of the Walker woman once and for all. Subject 451 had been programmed to kill. Had twice proven capable of carrying out direct commands. Efficiently. Proficiently. Without memory or emotion.

And yet, Amy Walker had destroyed him. Years of work, gone.

"Did you locate him?"

Fleischer's question jarred Erich back to the moment. "Yes," he admitted after a lengthy silence. "I just received a call. He was found dead. In New York."

Henry's lab pallor faded to the color of bleached bones. Subject 451 had been one of Henry's masterpieces. A perfect human receptacle programmed with care, tried and tested and proven.

"How?"

"Shot, apparently, by his assignment. Somehow, she managed to place a bullet between his eyes."

To his credit, Henry held back tears. It wasn't the human loss that affected him. It was the work. The destruction of his perfectly programmed assassin. "And the Walker woman?"

Erich rubbed a forefinger over his upper lip. "Remains a problem."

Henry's expression didn't alter. He knew better than to reveal his anger in Erich's presence. "We never should have agreed to that old fool's plan."

Henry was referring to Aldrick Reimers, of course. The Walker woman's biological grandfather. He was also the only remaining founder of MC6. The old man may have once been brilliant, but that brilliance had dulled and diluted into mad incompetence during the past few years. Yet his position must be respected even though Erich agreed with Henry's assessment.

It had been Reimers' idea to have his granddaughter abducted when she'd gotten too close to him in Manila last year. It had been Reimers who had assured the organization that she would die at the hands of the Abu Sayyaf terrorists and therefore eliminate the need for further MC6 intervention, guaranteeing no implications to cast attention on them.

But she hadn't died. She'd lived. And now she'd survived yet another attempt to take her out of the equation. Not only survived, but destroyed decades of work. Subject 541 had been forty years old. Had been programmed since birth. The loss was huge to the program. And they could not afford any more losses.

Erich intended to remedy the situation immediately. Amy Walker had to be silenced. Just like the McMillan woman.

"She won't stop, you know. She won't stop until she gets the answers she wants."

"I'm dealing with her," Erich assured the man who knew better than to question him further.

Henry hesitated then left the room. He'd had plenty he'd wanted to say, but nothing Erich had wanted to hear. Erich had already forgotten about him as he pulled up the list of candidates on his screen and scrolled through them. When he found what he was looking for, he dialed the extension for the holding compound.

"We need to move some product," he said, deciding he needed to take every precaution. "All twenty. I want them relocated at once. Keep them on standby for assignment details. I'll notify you when and where they need to be deployed."

After typing specific instructions into an e-mail, he shot the document to processing.

Then he sat back, steepled his fingers under his chin and contemplated when the surprisingly resourceful Ms. Walker would make it to Buenos Aires.

He knew everything there was to know about Amy

Walker, including the fact that she'd been working as a health aid at Winter Haven under the name of Erin James. No doubt to be close to her mother without being detected. A fine idea that hadn't worked. It had taken several months, but his people had found her. He also knew everything there was to know about the man who had rescued her from the Abu Sayyaf cell six months ago.

That's why Erich had been certain she would run straight to Dallas Garrett. Straight to her *hero*. Women were so predictable. Although, he conceded, he hadn't seen the extermination of 451 coming. He had thought any spark the woman had in her would have been extinguished on Jolo.

It didn't matter. All he had to do was wait for her to surface again. And she would. His man on the ground had tracked her to Florida, then followed her and her "watchdog" to the airport. It had been too risky to take them out then. No time to plan for an extermination to appear accidental. So at this very moment they were en route to Buenos Aires.

Which was actually very compliant of them. In the long run, it would make things much easier. She'd come looking for her grandfather, of course. And for the McMillan woman. She had no idea that Edward Walker and Jenna McMillan were as inconsequential as grains of sand. Minor elements in an equation that dwarfed the significance of a few human lives. It had always been about the greater cause.

No, little Miss Walker would never be allowed to get close to her grandfather, let alone the MC6 compound. Decades of preparation and hundreds of lives had already been sacrificed for the cause. A few more would make no difference.

Erich hadn't risen to his level of power in MC6 by being careless. He wasn't about to let anyone circumvent the prize that years of work was about to bring to fruition.

Very soon, Amy Walker would cease to be a problem. She and Mr. Garrett would meet a terrible fate. Uninformed *turistas* sometimes found themselves in particularly bad parts of the city—where they often found themselves dead. Terrible tragedy.

Problem solved.

He hadn't yet decided what to do about the McMillan woman. For the time being, he'd hang on to her. Use her for bait for Amy Walker if necessary. In the meantime, it might prove interesting to indoctrinate the reporter into the program. Test their latest therapy on such a headstrong subject and analyze the results.

He'd see. For the time being Jenna McMillan was out of circulation and any threat from that end was destabilized. First he'd deal with Walker's granddaughter. Then he'd decide what to do about the fiery redheaded reporter.

And then, once again, it would be back to business as usual.

Buenos Aires

The alley was midnight dark and cave quiet. The heat as oppressive as a ruthless dictator. Out on the street, a mere ten or so yards away, the bar district teamed with the rants and ramblings of boisterous drunks. The stench of booze, humanity and the South American summer funneled into the darkness on air as thick as paste and every bit as cloying.

"He said he'd be here," Amy whispered. "How long has it been?"

From a distance, the grating scream of a faraway police siren rent through a night dripping with heat, tension and second guesses.

Dallas checked his watch then cut a watchful gaze around the alley. "Half an hour."

It was a blip in time since they'd flown out of West Palm close to twenty hours ago and landed in Buenos Aires. He wasn't yet sure how that had happened. Or how he'd ended up armed and on the hunt in a back alley behind a seedy bar where a scar-faced man with a Fu Manchu mustache and hair as greasy as the oil in the crankcase of Nolan's vintage Mustang had told them to wait.

Hell. He wasn't sure of anything anymore. It was like a fuse had blown or something when Amy had taken him to bed. Instead of Afghanistan flashbacks, images of Amy, naked and moving above him, flashed through his mind's eye like a strobe. Like they were burned into his DNA now—the same way she was.

He'd deal with that later. Right now, her safety was top priority. He had no clue if there was a threat tonight, but he wasn't taking any chances either way. He'd never met a back alley that didn't bring some kind of trouble.

He glanced at her. Read her tension only in the

pinched focus of her eyes. She was in control. Rock solid. Impressive as hell.

"The trouble with these back-alley types," he said in a low voice as a rat skittered across the damp, cracked concrete alley that smelled of vomit, piss and rotted garbage, "is that reliability's not usually one of their strong suits."

Neither was integrity, trust or honor—but Dallas wasn't going to point that out to her now. Now, he was too busy concentrating on getting them out of here without getting their throats slit. The longer they waited, the edgier he got, and the more he was leaning toward believing her story.

"Jenna gave me the name of her contact," Amy had told Dallas right after they'd settled aboard for their flight to Buenos Aires where they'd arrived fifteen plus hours after they'd left West Palm.

Amy had slept damn near the entire transcontinental flight. Something she'd obviously needed to do.

He'd watched her sleep. Something *he'd* needed to do. A need he had to keep a tight grip on if another sunrise was going to factor into their future plans.

The garbage littering the alley wasn't the only thing that stank. This whole "buying information about the whereabouts of my grandfather" had the stench of setup to it.

"And where did you say Jenna got the name of this so-called contact?" Dallas shifted his body until he was positioned in front of Amy like a shield.

"I know what you're doing." They'd dropped their packs—his modified ALICE pack and her backpack—

on the street next to the cantina wall. When he side-stepped their packs and moved in front of her, she knew it was an attempt to stand between her and any threat that might confront them. "And I don't need you to run interference for me, got it?"

He glared at her.

She ignored him. "Jenna didn't say where he came from. Just that his name was Alvaro. Said he'd been helping her. She gave me a number to call and told me that if she wasn't at our designated meeting place, to contact him and he'd know where to find her."

Dallas glanced at Amy's profile in the diluted light. Her eyes were searching, watchful, her silence catlike and calm as she worked to control her breath. And yes, her stance was defensive, spring loaded, like she was ready and capable of striking at an instant's notice. Striking hard. Striking with lethal intent.

And lethal was just the word he'd apply to the weapons she carried. They'd barely cleared customs and spilled into a taxi when she'd asked the driver to take them to a gun shop.

"Work for you?" she'd asked as she'd settled back in the seat.

He'd lifted his hands, amazed at her boldness and focus. "Lead on."

She'd done exactly as he would have done. There'd been no time to apply for permits to transport weapons on their commercial flight, so he'd planned to arm himself as soon as he had a chance. She'd taken care of the necessity for them.

After the visit to the gun shop, where it had been

amazingly easy to buy any handgun they wanted, she'd bought a gleaming new KA-BAR knife—another unquestioned purchase—then strapped an ankle sheath on the inside of her right leg, just below her knee where it stopped above her hiking boot. The knife was a standard U.S. military issue. A tough knife, not flashy or trendy as the newer "wanna be a soldier" designs. The KA-BAR was a *fugly* knife, but the 1095 steel was properly heat treated and it did the job. Sixty plus years of combat spoke for itself.

A KA-BAR, Dallas thought, guarding her back. Jesus.

And then there was the Glock tucked in a shoulder bag along with her right hand. He knew the pistol was loaded with heavy-load hollow points and equipped with a high-tech LED weapon light. He'd watched, intrigued, as she'd mounted the executive flashlight on the universal rail beneath the barrel like a pro.

The Glock—another model 30—was well used but in good condition. The flashlight that, smart girl, she'd insisted on picking up before they left the States, was shiny-penny new, state of the art and a weapon in itself. The tight, diamond-shaped central beam had a deer-in-the-headlights effect and could temporarily blind a bad guy unlucky enough to land in the arc of the corona.

"So," he said, hitching up his pants and feeling the comfortable weight of a Sig P220 on his hip, "when exactly did you turn into Lara Croft, tomb raider?"

She even looked a bit like Angelina Jolie's portrayal of the female Indiana Jones equivalent, lean and mean and ready to wreak havoc and hell to defend and protect.

He could almost buy the woman warrior picture as she stood there in snug cammo cargo pants and a torso-hugging black tank. Her long blond hair was drawn back into a neat ponytail and secured with a leather thong at her nape; her bare arms and chest gleamed with a sheen of tropical perspiration.

Yeah. He could almost buy it—if he'd been able to shake the image of the fragile and wounded woman he'd dragged out of the jungle six months ago. Of the woman who had come apart for him in his bed less than twenty-four hours ago.

As if reading his thoughts, she lifted her gaze to his. Cornflower-blue irises had transitioned to cobalt in the dark alley's shadowy light.

"Lara Croft is a fictional character." The deadly calm look in her eyes shook him. "Lara Croft was never a victim. I was. Never again."

He believed her times ten. "So you learned how to handle a gun."

"Yeah. I learned. Took classes," she confirmed evenly, and cast a level gaze to the mouth of the alley where hookers plied their services, drunks stumbled into each other and users scored with their dealers. Big cities were all the same, only the venue was different. "And I learned how to take care of myself."

He considered her for a moment while sweat, as heavy as the stench of the city, trickled down his temple and ran under his jawline. The way she'd lit into him in the street in the rain back in West Palm, he figured she must have taken a martial arts class or two. Aikido came to mind. Karate. But both took years to master. So, no, she'd gone for something she could sink her teeth into quickly.

"Muay Thai?" he speculated, thinking the Thai boxing techniques would suit her build and the time frame she'd had to become even marginally proficient.

Dallas had studied that particular martial art for over ten years and knew students adapted the simple techniques in short order. Women benefited from Muay Thai because the strikes put a lot of power behind them. He'd witnessed even very slight women students deliver some pretty mean elbow and knee strikes. Remembered one, in particular, who came to class one night excited because she'd thwarted a mugger. As she'd handed the mugger her wallet, she'd stepped in and slammed him on the side of the head with an elbow strike. Knocked him out cold then dialed 911 on her cell. She'd been studying Muay Thai for all of three weeks.

"Krav Maga."

He narrowed his eyes when she named her training choice. Cocked a brow. "No shit?"

She grinned. "No shit."

He wiped his damp face on the sleeve of his black t-shirt. And didn't feel like grinning. Not one bit.

Krav Maga. Jesus. "It's a wonder I made it off the street alive. In the very likely event that I piss you off in the next few days, consider this an apology in advance, okay? So don't hurt me." He was only halfway kidding. He outweighed her by a good eighty pounds, way out-muscled her and had the edge on experience and actual combat situations.

They both knew he was safe from her, but he got the reaction he'd been after.

Despite the gravity of their current situation, she pushed out a soft laugh. "Feel the need for a little credit on the books, do you?"

He smiled. "Feel the need to *not* be on your bad side."

Credit the Israeli military for Krav Maga. And, yeah, after what she'd been through on Jolo, he understood why she might have selected that particular form of martial art. The basic techniques were relatively quick to learn, very direct, very brutal, and the basic intent—to "put 'em down fast"—was going to lay a world of hurt on or kill anyone on the receiving end.

Because Krav Maga was a military-developed system, there was never any consideration to the "blow back" a practitioner would be exposing themselves to in a nonmilitary situation. He wondered if she'd thought about that. The look on her face answered his question. Yeah, she'd thought about it. And she'd picked Krav Maga for a reason all right.

Lara Croft was never a victim. I was. Never again.

He wondered just how far she'd go to insure her own safety. Wondered how much she'd really changed. If the softness coupled with strength that had drawn him from the beginning had been compromised by cold deadly intent in her quest for revenge.

He thought about the cartridge that had been missing from the magazine of her Glock. More than once he'd revisited that fact in his mind. More than once he'd wanted to ask her about it. Wondered if the creep who'd run her off the road was the reason it was missing.

His questions would have to hold a little longer. The back door of the bar creaked open. A sliver of light, heavy with drifts of prime Columbian weed and tobacco smoke, curled into the alley. The silhouette of a man appeared in the foggy halo of light.

Beside him, Amy braced her feet in a firing stance and prepared for battle.

"Showtime," Dallas said under his breath and, whether she liked it or not, stepped protectively in front of her again.

It was as another man stepped out of the light and closer toward them that Dallas realized they were being tag-teamed.

His hand was already on his Sig when he caught movement in his peripheral vision. Amy caught it too. She pivoted, stacked up back to back with him and drew her Glock out of the shoulder bag, spotlighting the newcomer with the beacon-bright beam of her weaponlight.

Like rats crawling out of their hidey-holes, four more men joined the others . . . and bumped the credibility of her story from a minus to a double plus on the plausibility scale.

"I don't know what they taught you in your shooting classes," Dallas said in a hushed tone only she could hear, "but here's what I want you to do.

Start at the groin and work your way up. There are any number of interesting and major blood vessels and bones in the pelvic region that you can break and tear. Got it?"

She gave him a clipped nod.

"Good girl. Just ride the recoil up starting at the groin and if they're still standing when you get to the head, reload and start at the groin again. Besides messing with their head to have a woman pointing a gun at the family jewels, it'll also allow you to see their hands, which you couldn't if you're pointing a gun at their chest or head."

"Groin, recoil, head," she repeated. "I've got it." Stone cold. Totally in control.

Damn, Dallas thought as the rat pack started closing in, these assholes don't stand a chance.

CHAPTER TEN

Another man stood in the shadows, watching the tableau unfold. His name was Gabriel. Other than the Cold Steel Arc-Angel Butterfly knife strapped to his hip, his name was the only thing he had in common with anything godly.

Gabe Jones stood six feet five inches tall, checked in at a honed 225 pounds, and knew how to deliver a fatal blow to virtually every vulnerable area on the human anatomy—both in theory and in practice.

For too many years, he'd been a player in a game where the rules were made up as he went along and the stakes pitted life against the grizzly and gruesome reality of death. At thirty-five, he'd already played so long he could hardly remember another way of living—if that's what his current existence could be called. A time when duty and honor had been his driving force instead of stone-cold anger and a thirst for revenge was a distant and murky memory.

He'd lost friends, lost faith and, for the most part,

lost the ability to see life through anything but glasses made foggy with the film of gunpowder and red mist.

These days, he had contacts, not friends; enemies, not adversaries. He had access to an arsenal, yet it was his Butterfly he relied on. It was the Butterfly that had earned him the dubious handle of Archangel with the locals. He did nothing to dispel the stories that had bred and grown and were whispered with reverence and fear in the dark circles of the night.

Men stepped aside when he walked within striking distance. At first glance, women regarded him with sexy cat eyes and wondered what it would take to tame this man with the sleek stealth of a panther and the darkly alluring aura of *el diablo*. One long piercing glare from his devil black gaze, however, and they understood: No woman tamed the Archangel. When the need arose, he found a willing bed partner, not a lover—a distinction he made clear up front.

He was a mystery—and he liked it that way. Found it vaguely amusing and to his benefit that he was somewhat of a legend on the Patagonia and the back streets of this city. More to the point, he was an enigma, a lone *Americano* whose idea of a good time was to indulge in a single shot of Wild Turkey while shooting flies off a cantina wall with a Les Baer 1911-A1 .45.

Overkill turned him on.

Uninvited interest turned him mean.

And interference just plain pissed him off.

The confrontation unfolding before him in the back of this low-rent cantina reeked of interference. Two

Americans—a man and a woman—had just stumbled into a snake pit, the head viper a reptile Gabe knew well.

Alejandro had his own proclivities with tempered steel. He'd already drawn his Skean Dhu "Black" knife. The four other men who crept like rats out of the cantina's back door carried semiautos. So now it was six to two. With bang-bangs.

Christ.

Gabe could give a rip about the foolish American's lives, but he'd be damned if he'd let some thrill-seeking tourists out to catch a rush on the wild and seedy side of the city get themselves wasted in his carefully staked-out territory. A tourist homicide would draw *la policía* and U.S. Embassy officials like flies—a complication he neither wanted nor welcomed. Not after the groundwork he'd laid to trap Alejandro here tonight.

He searched the shadows and realized the Americans came equipped with their own firepower. And they obviously knew how to use it and defend themselves.

So. Not *turistas* after all.

That pissed him off even more.

Because that meant there might be a helluva lot more to them than met the eye—and that they might actually be here looking for him.

He considered walking away. Letting the pit vipers have their fun with their six-to-two odds and catching up with Alejandro later. But then a car pulled into the alley; its headlights cast an eerie glow on the deadly montage, and for an instant, flashed bright on the woman's face before it backed up, reversed direction and shot away on a shrill squeal of tires.

It was only a moment, but it was long enough for Gabe to see the woman's face—and he recognized every emotion etched deep there.

Recognized them because the relentless force behind them drove him, too. Revenge.

Well, fuck.

Now he *had* to help. Her specifically. And wouldn't that just go a long way to blowing his carefully nurtured cover?

He slipped the Butterfly out of its sheath and stepped out of the shadows.

Eight sets of eyes snapped his way.

"Throwing a party, Alejandro?" His gaze locked laser tight on the blood merchant's face. "It's not like you to forget to invite me. Should I be hurt?"

Gabe held the Butterfly easily and prominently in view. The familiar grip of the skeletonized solid titanium billet handle warmed in his palm. Closed, the knife measured five and a half inches long. Open, close to ten. But it was the scant four inches of the razor-edge carbon steel blade glinting in the arc of light from the open cantina door that drew everyone's attention. All told, the Butterfly weighed 4.3 ounces, worth a hundred times its weight in the right hands.

It was in the right hands.

And at least six of the partygoers knew it. The

looks on their faces was priceless when they saw him and low mumbles of "*muerto*"—*dead*—fell flat in the dark. The four thugs who had just joined the head rat shifted slightly toward the cantina door. They didn't look nearly as tough as they had before Gabe had crashed their little party.

Alejandro's low growl stopped them.

"What are we celebrating?" Gabe flashed a smile that no one in the alley mistook for amiable.

To their credit, the Americans held their ground, although they appeared to have serious doubts about him. As well they should.

The woman held her flashlight steady, the muzzle of her semiautomatic aimed directly at asshole number one's holy grail. He stood frozen like a deer in a searchlight.

Gabe quickly sized up the American who aimed his Sig dead center on asshole number two's forehead. Ex-military, he decided. Probably spec ops. He had the look. The intensity. The situational awareness.

The woman . . . she was a puzzle.

"The gringos are not your business, Jones," Alejandro growled with the tenor of a man determined to finish his dirty work but also aware that his party favors were at risk of going up in flames.

"*Amigo*," Gabe said, his smile tight. With a quick glance and a notch of his chin, he signaled the American to get ready, knew he would read the sign. "I think we'll have to agree to disagree on that point."

Alejandro swiveled and drew back his Skean Dhu.

Gabe's Butterfly was airborne before the knife ever left Alejandro's hand. The strike was deadly and true. A slice straight through the throat.

Alejandro staggered, dropped to his knees, clutching his neck to the wheezing, bubbling gurgle of blood filling his lungs. He collapsed onto his back with a jerky spasm and gasped one final, tortured breath. And then there was no sound at all but the echo of the rat pack's footsteps beating a path to anywhere but here.

Gabe was aware of the woman's eyes on him. She watched, her face expressionless as he walked up to the dead man, braced his boot on his shoulder, then leaned over to extract his Butterfly. It made a grating, sucking sound as he pulled it out of Alejandro's throat. He wiped away the blood on Alejandro's shirt and sheathed the knife.

He glanced at the American who still held his Sig at the ready. Then he nodded and turned to leave.

"Wait!"

It was the woman. Her voice was tight in a bid to mask something that could have been panic, disbelief, revulsion or all three.

Gabe stopped, expelled a weary breath.

"That's it? You killed him. And you're just going to walk away?"

He turned, impatient to be gone. "The party appears to be over."

"Who are you?" she asked as the man tried to step protectively in front of her. She wasn't having any of it. She pushed her way out from behind him.

Tough. She was much tougher than she looked.

And everything about her suggested a brutal loss of innocence that had made her that way. "I'm someone who knows that piece of rat shit doesn't deserve one ounce of your concern."

She still held the Glock in a two-handed grip, but she'd slipped her finger off the trigger. "You knew him?"

SF guy notched his chin in Gabe's direction. "Something tells me he knows a lot of bottom feeders."

Gabe glanced at the man, very aware that the Sig was still leveled dead center at his chest, trigger finger in place. He nodded, acknowledging the accurate assessment. "Occupational hazard."

"And that occupation would be?"

Gabe met the man's level stare—decided he'd be a formidable opponent. A capable ally. Neither of which he needed.

"Look, I'd love to stay and swap business cards, but—"

"We're looking for Alvaro." The blonde took a step forward when Gabe turned to go. "Do you know him?"

Alvaro. The name stopped him cold. Gabe knew a lot of Alvaros, but the fact that they were looking for a man by that name suggested they'd found their way into this alley for much the same reason he had.

Alvaro Rodriguez. Gabe clenched his jaw. In another life, another time, he would have called Alvaro friend.

But Alvaro was dead. Alejandro was the lowlife

who had killed him. Alejandro was the reason Gabe was here.

He met the woman's eyes, working to hide the rage that even killing Alvaro's assassin had not assuaged. Apparently he failed to disguise it. She saw. She knew.

"You *do* know him," she concluded.

"And if I did . . ." He let the line trail off, glanced at SF guy and reconfirmed his original assessment. Formidable. Competent. Deadly if the need arose.

"I was supposed to meet him here."

Very slowly, Gabe returned his attention to the woman, never losing awareness of the position of the man's Sig.

"Alvaro won't be coming."

He waited for the meaning of his statement to settle.

"Because of him?" She notched her chin toward the dead man.

Gabe said nothing. A nothing that rang of confirmation.

"Who did he work for?" she asked after a moment.

"Alejandro?" He grunted in disgust. "Whoever had the most coin."

"And who do you work for?"

He considered the man who had asked the question. Opted for evasion. "It's not important."

"It is to me," the woman said. "You knew Alvaro. Alvaro was my only lead in finding my friend."

Friend? Gabe waited with a deepening sense of doom.

"Jenna McMillan." She pinned him with a hard look from soft blue eyes. "Ring any bells?"

It rang more than bells. It rang of coincidence— something he didn't believe in. And it rang of complications of epic proportions.

Jenna McMillan was the reason Alvaro was dead. And whatever options he'd entertained about walking away from these two had just narrowed to a field of zero.

"Follow me," he said grudgingly, then turned and walked away from the alley.

Behind him, he heard them pick up their packs and hurry to keep up with him.

Fuck.

Dallas swore under his breath, wishing to hell he'd figured out a way to keep Amy in Florida.

But no. Here they were. Another back alley. Another bar. Another goddamn stellar opportunity to get their throats slit.

Are we having fun yet?

Not yet.

He kept a tight grip on Amy's arm as they followed the big man with the bad knife. They entered the building through a thick and scarred wooden door into yet another smoke-filled cantina.

He assessed the dimly lit room with escape and evasion in mind. Dallas didn't trust the man Alejandro had called Jones any further than he could toss a Humvee. What he did trust—fully and completely now—was Amy's story. He was now firmly convinced

that whatever was going on with Amy, her grandfather
and Jenna McMillan was as big and as bad as it got.
Which meant that this search and rescue mission now
had a full-blown protection detail component.

Someone wanted Amy dead. They wanted her
dead real bad—and that just wasn't going to happen
on his watch.

"Remember the drill," Dallas whispered, leaning
in close to Amy's ear.

"Groin and ride the recoil," she whispered back.

He squeezed her arm. "Good girl. Watch for the
flash of metal. I have no idea what we're getting into
here."

"He saved our lives," she reminded him.

"For his own purposes," Dallas pointed out as they
moved deeper into the bar. "Just watch your six."

It was another typical, low-rent cantina. Thick and
smoke-stained adobe walls. The back door, which
they'd come through, was directly opposite the front
entrance. Two open windows faced the street side—
more options if they had to dodge and run.

A slow, sad Spanish guitar played from an ancient
juke box in the background. The air lay heavy with
an assortment of tobacco and weed. Behind the bar, a
pock-faced senior with oily gray hair and tired, blank
eyes set up shots for shadowy men of questionable
character and heritage. Men who dressed like the
locals . . . but the similarities ended there.

They all made Dallas wary as hell. Hard men with
brittle eyes and dark scowls. Except for a poster boy
blond—a cowboy type all grinning swagger and

interested eyes—who was sizing up Amy like she was a sizzling steak and he wanted to be her platter.

With the exception of the cowboy, Dallas recognized the types who sat with their black bags close beside them on the floor. The go bags were filled, most likely, with assault weapons and a grenade or two. Spooks. Paramilitary. Private contractors. The bar was crawling with them. Sitting in silence, tossing back shots of Wild Turkey and blowing smoke rings in the clogged air. Operatives so long and deep undercover the lines between good and evil had blurred, bled and washed away like blood in a rain-soaked street.

And suddenly Jones started to make sense.

The Butterfly. Dallas fumbled around in his memory banks for a piece of information that danced just out of reach, flitted around out there, spun and stalled, eluding him.

He let it go. It would come to him. Eventually.

"Friends of yours?" Dallas asked conversationally as Jones led them to a table at the back of the room.

"Acquaintances," Jones said with a nod to the bartender. Then he sat down with his back to the corner, facing the room. "Make no mistake," he said looking directly at Dallas, "You're only here because I recognize you as Spec Ops."

"Was. Past tense. Marines. Force Recon," Dallas confirmed and dropped his pack on the floor beside a chair.

And Jones, Dallas suspected, was with Uncle—or had been. Water sought its own level just as Jones had sought his own kind. He wasn't a stranger in this bar. Dallas had caught the subtle nods. The quick dismissive glances when they'd recognized one of their own.

Dallas didn't exactly breathe easier knowing Jones was either CIA or a close black ops cousin, but he figured it was better than a stick in the eye.

And that's when it came to him: Jones, Gabriel Jones.

Shit. It should have clicked when the Butterfly made its deadly appearance.

Jesus Christ. Gabriel Jones. AKA: Archangel. AKA: Slice and Dice.

No wonder the thugs in the alley looked like they were confronting a ghost. They were consorting with a goddamn dead man.

CHAPTER ELEVEN

Dallas had heard stories about the Archangel—some of them from Ethan and Manny. Special ops and CIA often worked joint task forces. And a spookier lot Dallas had never encountered. Until they loosened up after an op with their drink of choice—generally Wild Turkey—and the stories started flying.

The Archangel was a legend even among the legend makers. And until this moment Dallas had often wondered if the Archangel was a myth. A good yarn on a drunk night. A tall tale about a loose cannon, a rogue operative who played by his own rules and damn the consequences.

A man who had supposedly died in a drug raid gone sour in Cartagena, Colombia, a year or so ago.

"Apparently, reports of the Archangel's death have been highly exaggerated," Dallas said quietly.

Jones cut him a look, but silence was as much as he got by way of explanation. Didn't matter. Dallas figured he had a pretty good idea what was going on.

More than one black ops agent had "died" in the line of duty only to resurface months or years later.

What Dallas didn't know was what the hell it meant that Gabriel Jones just "happened" to intercept Alejandro at the same place, same time, that Dallas and Amy were in that alley.

Before he could think it through, the pretty boy blond swaggered over. They'd barely gotten settled at a heavy wooden table, the top riddled with scars dug by any number and type of deadly knives, when he spun a chair around backwards, straddled it, and sat his grinning self down facing Amy.

"You, sweet lady, are a sight for sore eyes." He propped his chin on the hands he'd crossed over the chair back and grinned at Amy like a love-struck puppy. "Begs the question, what's a nice girl like you doing in a dive like this?"

"Back off, buckaroo." Dallas glared at the cocky cowboy with the sappy come-on, Hollywood looks and the growing possibility of a relatively short life span. "The lady's with me."

"Chill, man. I'm not moving in. Just admiring the view. Can't blame a guy for that, right? No harm. No foul." He extended a hand. "Name's Reed. Johnny Duane Reed, and it's been a damn long time since I've seen the sweet face of an American woman, that's all. It's a pleasure. A pure pleasure."

Dallas ignored Reed's good ole boy drawl and his extended hand. He glanced at Jones, who recognized the warning and notched his chin toward a man sitting in shadows across the room.

"Call your pup to heel, Lang. As usual, he's trying to piss in someone else's territory."

"God damn it, Reed. Get your sorry ass over here and leave the nice people alone."

Dallas glanced at the man with the deep voice. He couldn't see Lang's face in the diluted light, but there was no mistaking the authority in his bearing. Like Jones, Lang's shoulders were broad, his posture misleadingly relaxed. Just like Johnny Duane Reed's aw shucks grins didn't camouflage the operative's true calling, Lang's quiet command would never be mistaken for a request.

None these men would ever be mistaken for *turistas*, either. They weren't here for the scenery. They were here skirting around the dark fringes of international law. They were shadow warriors, men that no politically correct American wanted to acknowledge were on Uncle's payroll, but whose dangerous and shady activities allowed everyone from fat cats to the middle class to sleep safe in their beds at night.

So, no. Reed's just fell off the back of a bronc act didn't fool Dallas.

He was an agent. An adrenaline junky. Licensed to kill. Trained to react.

"Duty calls." Reed's grin never faded as he stood, sliced both Jones and Dallas a quick glance then nodded at Amy. "Ma'am. It's truly been a pleasure. You take care of yourself now, you hear?"

"I'll do that."

Dallas didn't much appreciate the smile in Amy's voice as he watched Reed walk away. He joined Lang in a lazy sprawl at the other table, his good nature never fading.

"Interesting character," Amy said after a moment.

"Character being the operative word," Jones grumbled, and thanked the bartender when he delivered a bottle of Wild Turkey and three shot glasses.

Amy covered her glass with her hand. "I'm good. Thanks."

Jones glanced at Dallas. Dallas turned his glass upside down. Waited.

"Suit yourself."

Jones took his time pouring a shot before lifting it and tossing it back in one deep swallow.

Then he settled his attention on Amy. "How do you know Jenna McMillan?"

Amy glanced at Dallas. He nodded. "Go ahead. Tell him."

Dallas listened in silence as Amy nutshelled it for Jones. She told him in short and concise statements about her mother's mental condition, her certainty that it was a result of her former SS grandfather conducting mind-control experiments on her. She told him about her first meeting with Jenna last year that had led her to Manila in pursuit of her grandfather. Told him, Dallas was interested to note, only that she'd been unsuccessful finding Edward Walker there and it wasn't until recently that she'd been able to pick up on her search—thanks to Jenna locating him here, in Argentina.

She left out everything about Jolo and her capture. Dallas understood. And thought again about how far she'd come in the aftermath of that horror.

"Three days ago," she went on, "I got a call from Jenna. She was down here following up on a story she's researching on mind-control experimentation while also searching for my grandfather. She was certain she'd found him here in Argentina. She asked me to meet her in Buenos Aires. Gave me Alvaro's name in case she didn't show. When I contacted him, he set up a meet at the cantina."

She stopped and Jones nodded for her to continue.

"The same night she called, someone ran me off the road as I was leaving my mother's facility. I have no doubt his intent was to kill me."

Jones sat back, his face unreadable. His thumb stroked up and down along the neck of the whiskey bottle. "What did he look like?

"The man who ran you off the road," Jones prodded when she didn't respond. "What did he look like?"

Amy looked at her hands. "Like someone who wanted me dead."

Jones looked at Dallas. He'd caught Amy's hesitation too. It was just long enough that Dallas knew she holding something back.

"How'd you get away from him?" Jones persisted.

Again, she looked away.

And Dallas finally put it together. "The spent cartridge," he speculated aloud. "You killed him?"

She said nothing. She didn't have to.

Jones leaned forward, eyes narrowed. "He's dead?"

Her eyes gave her away when they cut sharply to his. Finally, she admitted it. "Yes. I killed him."

And it was killing *her*, Dallas realized, understanding exactly what she was dealing with. He'd been there too many times to count.

"No guilt," Dallas said, and covered her hand with his.

She bit her lower lip. Finally nodded. "Maybe I'll have that drink after all."

Jones poured without comment, looked on in grudging admiration when she tossed back the whiskey and suppressed a gasp.

"Do you remember anything about him?" Jones probed quietly. "Any physical details? Identifying marks."

She shook her head. Stopped abruptly. "Wait." She touched a hand to her temple. "There was something . . ."

"A tattoo, maybe?"

"Yes." She looked stunned. Jones' speculation obviously surprised her, as well as jarred her memory. "A tattoo. On the back of his hand. I'd forgotten about it. Let me think. Numbers. Just . . . numbers. Four . . . four fifty-one. Yeah. Four fifty-one. Black ink. Small bold font."

Jones registered nothing. A nonreaction that made Dallas anxious as hell.

"How did you know about the tattoo?" Dallas turned to Jones, his sense of foreboding blimping up to elephantine proportions.

Jones sat back in his chair. Poured another shot. And just sat there, a look fathoms dark, coal mine deep masking his thoughts.

"Jones?" Dallas prompted. No inquiry this time. A demand to know.

Jones looked at Amy. Then at Dallas. "You need to take her back to the States. Get her the hell out of here and let me handle this. Forget you ever saw me. Forget about Alejandro and Alvaro. Forget the tattooed man. Just . . . forget."

Amy steeled herself against the stone-cold determination radiating off Jones in alpha-dog waves. The man scared her. But life terrified her these days, so the sensation wasn't new. And it wasn't going to stop her.

"I came here to find my grandfather, Mr. Jones. And I need to find Jenna. I haven't heard from her and haven't been able to raise her on her cell since she called."

"I'll take care of the McMillan woman. And your grandfather is old news. For your own sake, let it go."

Beside her, Dallas shifted in his chair. She refused to look at him. Knew without seeing his face that he'd like nothing better than for her to back away from this too.

It wasn't going to happen.

"Look. I appreciate your concern. What you don't appreciate is my motivation. Or my determination. My mother is little more than a vegetable. I owe Edward Walker for what he did to her. And I owe him for something else. Something I intend to make him pay for. And I won't turn my back on my friend."

She chanced a glance at Dallas then. Saw him

watching her with something she'd like to think was admiration but leaned more toward "damn stubborn woman."

Whatever it was, it bolstered her resolve. And it made her realize for perhaps the hundredth time today, how glad she was to have him with her. Not just because she felt safe with him. But because she felt the need of him. The need *in* him that he managed to relay with just a touch, just a look. By just being here.

Jones appeared about as happy as a man about to get a root canal without novocaine. "You can either help or get out of my way because I'm not leaving here until I find both of them."

Jones cast Dallas a look of appeal: *Can't you do anything about this?*

Dallas merely shrugged, relinquishing the stage to her. She would thank him for that later. And for a hundred the other things, large and small—but most of all for being the kind of man he was.

"You have no idea what you're getting into," Jones warned.

"Probably not. But since you have no idea what I've been through, I guess that makes us even," she countered.

Jones considered her, evidently "got it" that she was in this to the end and gave up the fight. He breathed deep, gave a fatalistic shake of his head.

"Okay, look. Do not construe this as me helping you, all right? I'm going to let you in on this for one reason and one reason only. If I turn you loose to your own devices and you stumble onto your grandfather, you're going to find yourself swimming in water that'll make a lake full of piranhas seem like a kiddie pool. And that's going to fuck up an ongoing op I have a personal stake in. And *that's* going to royally piss me off."

Too late, Amy thought. He was already pissed. That came through loud and clear. She didn't care. All she cared about was that he'd conceded.

"You aren't going to help us. Got it. Put any spin on it you want. You're going to help yourself by keeping us in the loop and out of trouble—works for me."

He grunted. "Lady. You have no idea what trouble is."

"Yes," Amy said meeting his hard scowl without flinching. "I do."

Jones held her stare for a long moment, must have seen something in her eyes that made him believe her. Understood that somewhere, sometime in her life, she had been through hell. Enough hell that she was ready to walk into the fire again to extract some justice.

"Fine. Don't say I didn't warn you. And let's get something straight up front. From this point on, you do as I say. When I say. How I say. Clear?"

"As crystal."

He gave her one last hard glare, cut his gaze to Dallas, who gave him a noncommittal look.

"And so you know," Jones continued, understanding that was the best he was going to get out of Dallas, "push comes to shove, my operation becomes priority one. You're on your own."

Amy expelled a relieved breath and took advantage of his grudging concession before he changed his mind. She had questions. He was the only ones with answers. "Who was the man with the tattoo?"

Jones drilled her with one last, probing look, as if he might still change his mind before answering with a weary breath. "An assassin."

"Hired by my grandfather," she surmised.

Jones shook his head. "Not hired. Sent. By MC6."

Amy glanced at Dallas, then back at Jones. "MC6?"

Jones hesitated, then swore under his breath as if he realized he was just about to cross the point of no return. "You've heard of ODESSA."

"Oh, Jesus." Dallas groaned. "I don't think I want to hear this."

"Doesn't look like you're calling the shots." Jones turned back to Amy. "MC6 is an offshoot of ODESSA. An enclave of scientists, ex-SS, and ex-military special operators who splintered off the U.S. government payroll years ago so they could continue with their 'research.' The guts of their mind control section is headquartered here, in Argentina—has been since the Peron era when Evita offered refuge to thousands of Nazis after the war. Subsequent governments have willingly turned a blind eye to their handiwork. Collusion might be a better word. In exchange for generous kickbacks, of course," he added bitterly.

"For God's sake, they have to be old men by now," Dallas put in, sounding a little like he knew they'd just stepped aboard a runaway train.

"True. And many of them are dead. Some, like your grandfather, however, are still alive and still plotting the downfall of the free world."

"Wait." Amy shook her head, stunned by the

implication of his statement. Surely she'd misunderstood. "What are you saying?"

"He's saying," Dallas said with a look that was all too knowing, "that jihadists and suicide bombers in the Middle East aren't the only ones with their finger in the terrorism pie."

"MC6 has been on the radar for over two decades," Jones continued. "It took that long to convince the powers that be that it and ODESSA are fact, not fiction."

"Don't say it," Dallas warned Amy.

Despite the gravity of this news, Amy smiled and resisted the urge to say, I told you so.

"This goes much deeper than your grandfather," Jones explained. "MC6 is comprised of second-, even third-generation members, all groomed or programmed to carry on the work started by their fathers."

"So the man who came after me—you're saying he was a member of MC6?"

Jones shook his head. "Not a member. One of their projects."

Amy met his statement with stunned silence.

"Congratulations, Ms. Walker. Lil' bitty you managed to eliminate a programmed assassin."

Amy stared at Jones.

Programmed assassin.

Her head felt light.

Her fingers numb.

Jones poured another full shot of Wild Turkey and pushed it in front of her. She lifted it to her mouth, downed it in one swallow.

Programmed assassin. The two words bounced around in her brain like twin hammers while the whiskey burned a path to her stomach.

The man who had been sent to kill her had been a victim too. Most likely tortured, abused, ultimately broken and remade into a killer against his will.

"Alejandro?" she asked when she caught her breath. "Was he—"

Jones shook his head. "He was just a bad-ass piece of shit. On the MC6 payroll, but he killed because he liked to, not because he was programmed to."

"And Alvaro?" Amy heard Dallas ask.

"One of mine," Jones said.

"I'm sorry."

Jones' eyes were bleak. "He knew the risks."

They all knew the risks, Amy thought. Like Dallas and his brothers, all of the men in this cantina played the odds on a daily basis. Instead of betting on sports or horse races, they bet on their lives. And not for one minute did she believe that Jones didn't grieve for the loss of one of his own.

"If Alvaro worked with you, why was he helping Jenna?"

"Intercepting would be a better word." Jones slouched back in his chair. His relaxed pose was deceiving. Like Dallas, his eyes were always watchful, his big body ready to move at the first sign of trouble. "Your friend was stirring up a lot of dust—as I said, we've had an ongoing op in the works for MC6. She was a very resourceful woman—not to mention a royal pain in the ass."

"For MC6?"

He grunted. "Them, too. Look." He leaned forward, elbows on the table. "Suffice it to say, it was in everyone's best interests if Ms. McMillan backed off—or at the very least, veered off course."

"Enter Alvaro, to muck up her navigation in the guise of a helpful local." Dallas' smile was tight.

"And to keep her out of harm's way." Jones rubbed a hand over his thigh, a gesture Amy had noticed several times. Nervous habit? Old wound?

"But she found my grandfather anyway," Amy pointed out. "And now she's disappeared."

"Alejandro's doing. No doubt ordered by MC6."

"Oh, God." With those words, Jones shattered the small hope Amy had clung to of locating Jenna safe and sound. "She's . . . dead?"

"No. I don't think so. But she may wish she was by the time they get through with her."

"You know where she is?"

"Got a pretty good idea." Jones checked his watch—a complex contraption with a wide thick face, a compass and dials that looked very much like the one Dallas wore. "Look, I've got business I need to tend to. Let's finish this conversation on the fly. I've got transpo out back. I'll drop you at your hotel."

He stood to the scrape of heavy wooden chair legs on a cracked tile floor.

Amy stood too. "But Jenna—"

"Will wait until tomorrow."

Dallas' hand on her shoulder steadied her. "He's right. If she's still alive, they're keeping her that way for a reason. Possibly as bait, to draw you in."

"That's the way I see it," Jones agreed, digging

into his pocket for his wallet then throwing some bills on the table. "You destroyed one of their favorite toys, Ms. Walker. I'm guessing they're pissed."

"You think they found the assissin's body already?"

"MC6 has eyes everywhere. When he didn't check in with a report, you can bet they sent someone to find him. And yeah, they found him—most likely retrieved the body—and tracked you here, or they wouldn't have sent Alejandro to take you out. As soon as they find what's left of him, they'll redouble their efforts to eliminate you as a threat. Jenna McMillan will be their ace in the hole. If they don't find you first, they'll count on you coming to her."

"What they aren't going to count on," Dallas assured her, cutting the tension with a soft smile, "is Lara Croft. At the risk of repeating myself, those assholes don't stand a chance."

CHAPTER TWELVE

Dallas let himself back into the hotel room, a to-go box full of food in hand just as Amy came out of the small bathroom. Around an hour ago, Jones had dropped them off a couple blocks from the Alcazar Hotel—his suggestion since they weren't booked anywhere. After writing an address on a napkin, Jones told them to show up there at 8:00 the next morning. Then he'd taken off into the night in an open jeep that looked like it ought to be traversing the sand dunes in Iraq.

The Alcazar was small, amazingly clean, boasted cheap rates —twenty bucks a night—and a private bath. While Dallas went out to scare up some grub, Amy had taken advantage of the shower.

He locked the door behind him and turned to Amy.

Her hair was wet. Her eyes were tired. Thousands of air miles and multiple adrenaline rushes and brushes with death had drained her physical strength.

He wondered how great a toll the past few days—specifically tonight—had taken on her emotionally. Knew it had to be high.

Still, she smiled for him as he shut the door behind him.

"Chow," he said unnecessarily and headed for the table in the corner of the room. Tried not to think about how hard it was to not walk up to her, fold her into his arms and take her straight to bed. Told himself to compartmentalize. It was a skill he'd developed early on in his military career.

Any combat veteran knew you lived in the moment, or you died in the confusion. During a firefight, a recon mission—whatever—thoughts of home, of a soft bed, a hot meal and a hotter woman got someone killed. So you blocked them out.

Like he'd been blocking since he'd agreed to this suicide mission. He couldn't think about her naked. He couldn't think about her needy. He couldn't think about her as anything but a job. A body he needed to protect.

Compartmentalize.

That was the key to keeping both of them alive. Jones had spelled it out in big block letters. Amy was a target. Whether it was back home or here, didn't matter. She was marked and Dallas was the only thing standing between her and certain death.

So the why the fuck could he not think about anything but burying himself so deep inside her it would take an act of Congress to get him out?

Jesus. Sex shouldn't even be a blip on the radar.

For more reasons than one. And yet . . . he was a man on the verge.

She'd exchanged her black tank and cargos for the gray t-shirt and boxers Dallas had loaned her back in West Palm. She was lost in them and lost in thought.

There wasn't one thing about the way she looked— her soft curves camouflaged by worn cotton, her expression pushing the rough edges of exhaustion—that should have made him feel he needed her more than she needed rest.

Yet it was all he could do to keep his hands off of her.

With purposeful motions he opened up the box with their dinner. And tried not to think about what had happened in his bed a little over twenty-four hours ago. Something he'd half-assed managed to do all day.

Compartmentalize.

Shit. He'd been kidding himself. It was always there. In the back of his mind. In the thick of his blood.

They hadn't talked about it. Hadn't rehashed or replayed or even acknowledged that, for one brief moment in time, she'd reached out to him. Asked him for something he'd wanted to give her but would never have expected her to take.

No, they hadn't talked about it. Not. One. Word.

Like it had never happened.

Only it had.

And he had to get past it.

Compartmentalize!

He could do this. Told himself he could absolutely do this. Liked to think he would have . . . if she hadn't picked that exact moment to walk up beside him, to turn her amazing blue eyes to his, to search his face in a silence that spoke as loud as any plea she could have voiced.

Oh, Jesus help me.

"Steak and beer," he said inanely, lifted a hand toward the food in a vain attempt to do the right thing. She needed food not sex. And right now, he needed a brain, not a dick.

Com. part. men. tal. ize.

He moved a step away, feigned concentration on retrieving napkins. "Hope beer's okay. It's actually cheaper than water."

Silence. Blue eyes watching.

"I get the sense that the city is just winding up, not down. Place is alive with neon and people. Could be NYC if the signs weren't in Spanish."

Damn he wished she'd quit looking at him like that.

"I asked at the restaurant. Seems dinner is usually served around eleven or midnight. Then the drinking and dancing start."

Drinking. Good idea. Maybe that's what he needed. He snagged a bottle of beer. Tipped it back, drank deep.

Then chanced a look.

She was smiling. And looking damn smug with it.

What the *hell* was up with that? Why wasn't she taking the hint? Why wasn't she letting him be heroic here? Why wasn't she just letting him feed her then get her to bed? Her on one side. Him on the other. Neat. Tidy. Done deal. The way his life would never be with her in it.

You waiting for Miss Perfect or what? Well, guess what? One of these days, some not so perfect woman is gonna knock the pins out from under you, brother mine. And I, for one, can't wait for that day.

Why his sister, Eve's, all too recurrent taunt trundled through his mind at this particular moment, he didn't know.

And he didn't want to think about it. What he had to think about was keeping Amy safe.

One room had been unavoidable. No way was he letting her out of this sight. And she, it seemed, was determined to keep him in hers.

She reached for his beer, lifted it to her lips and sipped. Savored. A sexy sort of languor on her face as she swallowed.

Deeper and deeper.

She made a little "umm" sound. He'd heard that sound once. Hell, more than once. In his bed. Flat on his back. And every muscle in his gut clenched at the memory.

Then she licked her lips. *He'd* licked those lips. Wanted to do more than lick them again. And damn if she wasn't offering them to him.

Okay. Subtle wasn't doing the job. It was time to swing the hammer and nail this thing head on.

"Amy . . . you and I both know that as good ideas go, this would never make the list," he warned, yet even as he said it, he felt his blood hike south from his big head to his little one. "What happened in

West Palm . . . it was . . . well, it was amazing . . .
but it was wrong. Two people reacting to acute stim-
ulation and too much adrenaline."

"Hm," she said. Just hm. What did that mean?

And then he found out.

"Are you afraid of me, Dallas?" She moved closer,
leaned into him, rubbed up against him. "Is that what
this is about?"

Cee-rist. She was actually baiting him.

"Amy—"

Two fingers touched his lips, demanding silence.
"Or are you afraid *for* me?"

He closed his eyes, tipped his head back and tried
to think about programmed assassins, paid killers,
slit throats. But all he could think of was her. Fra-
grant and warm. Soft and real. Willing and wanting.
And those damn sexy freckles.

"Hell yes, I'm afraid for you. You heard Jones.
You're a marked woman."

"That's not what I mean," she persisted. "Are you
afraid for me . . . in bed?"

Hell. Why couldn't she just let it go?

"Look." He swallowed around the desire clogging
his throat and thickening his cock. "Like I said . . .
what happened between us. Earlier. That was . . .
hell. It was—"

"Amazing. Yes, I know." She wrapped her arms
around his waist.

Melting. He was melting. "Yeah. Yeah. It was
amazing. It was *unbelievable.*"

She worked his t-shirt free of his pants. Warm fingers tunneled up and under, stroked his bare back. A

surge of desire ran down his spine, riding the sensual glide of her hands.

"You are killing me here."

"I'm not going to break, Dallas."

But he remembered her broken. God, he remembered her broken and battered and bruised. And he had no right. No right at all to forget about that.

"You're still on sensory overload," he pointed out again, trying to make her see their situation clearly. "Your adrenaline is ratcheting off the charts."

Talk about adrenaline. Her amazing hands worked around to his chest, slid downward, making his abs clench tight as sailor's knots. Then she started to work on his belt buckle.

He sucked in air through clenched teeth when she reached inside his shorts and touched him. Surrounded him. Stroked him. He almost came in her hands.

Rougher than he'd intended, he gripped her by the shoulders. Pushed her away. Held her at arm's length. Battled to get control of himself.

How did he do this? How did he tell her he didn't want her this way? That he'd already taken her when she'd been on the downside of disaster and that placed him off the charts on his own personal creep-o-meter? How did he do that when he wanted her more than he wanted his left nut?

"It's because of them, isn't it?" She asked in a quiet voice. Tentative now. Not nearly as certain. "Because of what they . . . did to me? Because of the way they . . . used me. Because of what they made me do."

Her eyes grew watery as she searched his.

"You can't be with me, can you? And not think about . . . about them . . . making me dirty."

His heart actually sank. He felt it drop. Dive straight to his gut and shatter on impact at the anguish in her voice. "God. Oh, God. No. Jesus, Amy. Not for a minute do I think that you are less because of those bastards."

Anguish transitioned to confusion. "Then *what* is this about? Is it medical? Are you afraid they gave me an STD? I'm fine. Medically, miraculously, I'm fine."

"Amy. Think. You are in the thick of a goddamn dangerous situation here, okay?"

He'd shouted. Damn it, he'd shouted at her. But somehow he had to make her understand. "A situation I should have talked you out of. You were stressed. Exhausted. Not capable of making wise decisions. And that made me a lesser man for taking advantage of you. I'm not going to do it again."

Her brows knit together. She gave a little shake of her head. "Is that what you think happened in West Palm? You think you took advantage of me?"

She just didn't get it. "Hell, yes, I took advantage!" It hadn't felt like it at the time. At the time, it had felt like heaven. Like a present on Christmas morning. One he'd dreamed about and wished for and never really expected to find.

So no, it hadn't seemed like he'd taken advantage. But in retrospect he couldn't spin it any other way.

He was miserable with guilt. And hell if she didn't look amused.

"So . . . you don't want to make love to me."

God save him. And damn her. She was baiting him again. "That's not what I said."

"Look. Dallas. Let's get something straight, okay? I may be tired. I may be stressed, but there's something you need to understand about me. That person you dragged off of Jolo? That wasn't me. That was a victim, in victim mode. Beaten down. Scared. Cowering.

"Wait—" She cut him off when he would have told her that she'd had damn good reason to be all of those things. "Let me finish."

Frustrated, he propped his hands on his hips. Buttoned it. Focused on the wall behind her. Anywhere but on her face, her mouth, the breasts that were clearly loose beneath his t-shirt.

"That woman," she continued, "never existed prior to Jolo. And that woman doesn't exist now. I went through hell. I had issues to deal with, I *am* dealing with them."

She paused, implored with her eyes. "I'll probably always be dealing with them on some level. But that's my cross to bear. Not yours. To the point, how I deal with them are my decisions to make. And so we are completely clear on this—you did *not* take advantage of me. If anything, it was the other way around."

Say what? She had his full attention now.

"I needed to know. I needed to know if . . . if that part of me, the part those bastards did their worst to destroy, had survived. I needed to know," she repeated, holding a balled fist between her breasts.

"And there was no one I trusted to show me the way back but you."

He closed his eyes, tipped his head toward the ceiling.

"You and Ethan. Nolan and Manny. You didn't just save me from certain death on Jolo. You saved me from torment and torture. I was a stone's throw away from letting the dark side take me. And I was certain that if I survived the rapes and beatings, the fevers and the starvation, I'd never be a whole person again. Never have hope again."

She touched her palm to his jaw. He couldn't help but lean into her caress.

"But you . . . you amazing heroic men gave me back more than my freedom and my life. You gave me respect. You gave me dignity. You didn't look at me as if I were damaged goods."

"You're not."

"No. Not to you. You . . . you even looked at me in a way I'd never thought I'd want a man to look at me again. Don't you see, that was the biggest gift of all . . . that and making love with you. Don't take that away from me. Not now. Not after you've brought me so far."

Man. Man, oh, man, she was getting to him. With those big blue eyes, with that firm, self-possessed posture that was doing as much to convince him as her words.

"I need to get on with my life, Dallas. And you've helped me. More than you will ever know."

He watched in wonder and awe as she moved into

him again, smoothed her hand around his jaw to his nape, pulled his face to hers.

"You don't have to take care of me, Dallas. You don't have to be my moral compass. You don't have to be my voice of reason, or decide what I can and can not handle.

"All you have to be," she whispered, rising up on her tiptoes and touching her lips to his, "is you. All you have to take care of," she said, nipping his lower lip while she slid a hand down and caressed him through his pants, "is this."

CHAPTER THIRTEEN

He was rock hard and wildfire hot in her hand. Amy felt power in that. In knowing that despite his misguided good intentions, despite his iron-willed determination to live up to some personal code of honor, she held the key to breaking him.

And when a strong man like Dallas Garrett broke, when he finally gave himself permission to give in to the need, the speed at which he fell was blinding. The fervor in which he embraced his downfall was electric.

And he'd lied. He'd lied when he'd said he wasn't going to let it happen again. The proof was in the pack of condoms she discovered in the pocket of his pants. Even when he was determined to stay away from her, he'd been thinking ahead to protecting her.

Oh, yeah. He'd wanted this to happen again. And when she kissed him, long and wet and deep, he gave up all pretense of denial.

Greedy hands slid down her back, paused at her

waist to squeeze and lift then lower to her hips, to part her thighs and guide her legs around his waist.

Heat, power, unrestrained desire. He surrounded her with it. Overwhelmed her with it. No silken surrender to her control this time. No tender kisses and tentative touches and letting her set the intensity and the pace.

This time . . . this time he devoured her. His mouth ravaged and bit and licked and sucked, demanding her tongue, then teasing with his. He walked them to the bed, lowered her to her back and covered her. The full, pulsing length of him. The wild, reckless joy of him. He rocked his pelvis against hers, his erection proud and thick and pulsing against her abdomen.

"Tell me." He strung wet, biting kisses along her throat, shoving his t-shirt off her shoulder and nipping bare skin. "Tell me if I scare you."

"I'm not scared," she whispered, breathless with need as his splayed fingers forked through her hair and he angled her mouth back to his.

"Well, I sure the hell am," he growled and sat up abruptly. Straddling her hips he tugged the t-shirt over her head. "Because you scare me to death. This . . . what you do to me . . . it scares the hell out of me."

She touched her hand to his face, smiled. "Don't worry . . . I won't let you get hurt."

The smile on her lips transitioned to wonder as he bent over her, his biceps bulging as he braced his hands on the mattress and caught her nipple in his mouth. Sucked. Feasted.

She loved it. Loved his dominance. His wildness.

His demands that she yield to him, as he had yielded to her.

His hands . . . his hands were everywhere. On her throat, on her breasts, between her legs, setting her on fire as he finessed and stroked and upped her level of sensation beyond the breaking point.

He claimed her in ways she had once thought would shoot her into a panic. Losing control, giving up this much power . . . she'd never dreamed it could be liberating. Never imagined it could be healing.

"Dallas." She breathed his name on a sigh when he sat back on his heels, watched her face as he touched her there, where he'd made her wet and swollen and pulsing with an aching longing for him to fill her.

She reached for him, her fingers stretched toward him. He clasped her hands in his, laced their fingers together then lowered their joined hands to her pubis.

"If we're going to do this, we're going to do it all. I want it all, Amy," he whispered sweeping his thumbs over her mound, separating the folds of her lips. Exposing her, opening her then sliding down the bed to take her with his mouth. "Need it all."

Liquid fire. Aching heat. Electric sensation. She lost herself in the lush, hungry strokes of his tongue, in the deep sounds of satisfaction rumbling in his throat as he selflessly gave her pleasure, selfishly indulged in the giving.

Lost. She was so, so lost, in the heat of his mouth, the depth of pure pleasure and mindless greed. She cried out at the joy of it, the unbridled wonder. Was desperate for him to go on and on and on . . . yet frantic for release. It came on a rush, hot, heady, insanely intense, profoundly physical.

Her entire body trembled as he kissed her there, one last time, then sheathed in a condom, entered her deep.

And the sensations began again. He pumped into her like a man possessed, like a man lost in a profound moment. A moment so profound, she was aware of every minute detail. The shadowy light spilling across the bed from the lamp on the table. The dampness of his hair beneath her fingertips. The blue, blue eyes that bore into hers as he filled her. The smooth skin at the small of his back where her ankles locked to hold him close. The tremor in muscles hard as steel and strained to the limit.

Yes, she absorbed it all along with his scent, musky now with the heat of their sexual energy. And when he took her mouth as he took her body, she tasted herself, and him, and the wonder that he had claimed a part of her that was most vulnerable.

She held him close when he came, thrusting into her hard on a deep masculine sound of supreme satisfaction. Smiled into the night, overjoyed, overcome with the delicious knowledge that in giving over her trust, in bending to his will, she felt more empowered than she'd ever felt in her life.

Dallas lay in the dark, wasted in the aftermath of hot, sweaty, amazing sex and marveled at the woman spread out on top of him like butter on bread. And fought another bout of guilt.

She was awake, he could tell by the cadence of her breathing.

Was she waiting? For him to say something? For a declaration of love?

No. Not going to happen. Even if that deck of cards were on the table, he wouldn't play them.

Couldn't play them. Not because they were too different from each other, but because they were so very much alike.

Both of them were damaged. Both of them fought to keep it together on a daily basis. She needed a man who could give her stability, pull her back to the light when she headed into the dark. How could he possibly help her?

Hell, he couldn't keep himself from plunging into the black hole. The big bad "hero" couldn't even win a battle with his own demons. Or the battle with his self-control.

So much for his grand gesture of not taking her to bed again.

Christ. He'd buckled, big time. Taken advantage—again—although she wouldn't want to hear it and would never let him cop to that in this lifetime.

Yeah. He should say something. And now that his heartbeat had settled and he could breathe without gasping, he ought to be able to manage . . . something.

"Our dinner is way past cold," is what came out.

The soft, sweet hand that had been sweeping up and down his arm stilled. She pushed up on her elbow, met his eyes. "Okay, good thing we got the good stuff done up front, 'cause I've got to tell you, Garrett, your pillow talk sucks."

She grinned at him. Actually grinned at him. "So, this is your idea of tender moments after?"

Lord. She was totally at ease with this and he was twisted up like a pretzel.

"Tender would be the operative word." Unable to stop himself, he lifted a hand and brushed that glorious fall of blond hair away from her face. "I was rough with you. I'm . . . hell. I'm sorry."

Her smile faded, became a frown. "You really have this hero thing bent out of whack, you know? Stand down, marine. I liked it. I liked the way you made love to me."

She pushed herself to her knees, sat back on her heels and folded her hands together on her thighs. Her skin was all rosy and pink, her lips and nipples swollen from the way he'd ravished her. Her hair—a sexy, sweet tumble—fell all the hell over the place. She should look used and abused. What she looked was lush and sated and pretty damn pleased with herself.

"Don't take this feeling away from me with apologies."

Strong, amazing woman. "You liked being manhandled?"

"I liked knowing that you wanted me. That you were wild and rough and intensely needing me. And I liked knowing that all I had to do was say one word, and the control would be mine again. Thank you for that. For all of that."

She leaned over, planted her palms on either side of his head and kissed him. Soft. Sweet. Lazy.

And took him under again. He dropped like a stone. Without a single punch.

With a helpless groan, he pulled her down on top of him, rolled her to her back and moved between her thighs.

Everything about her felt welcoming, riveting, lush. Her sighs. Her kisses. Her hands on his skin. Her body opening to take him home.

Home.

With every slow glide the word burrowed deeper and deeper into his head. Into his heart.

Making love with this woman felt like coming home. And this time, he made sure the homecoming was slow and lazy and sweet.

Amy forked a piece of cold steak into her mouth. "It's actually not that bad," she said, pleasantly surprised.

They'd finally made themselves get out of bed. Wearing only Dallas' t-shirt, Amy sat across from him at a tiny table in the corner of the hotel room.

He'd slipped into a pair of boxers. In the pale light of the dimly lit room he appeared to be naked. It was a look she could get used to.

"That's because you haven't eaten for hours. And for the record, it's your fault it's cold."

Amy sat back and grinned. "You just smiled." That was definitely something else she could get used to.

Of course, he frowned immediately. "I smile."

She shook her head, sliced off another bite of steak. "Not like that. Spontaneous. Unguarded."

He motioned with his fork, looking defensive. "Just eat your steak."

"Spoken like a man who's used to giving orders."

He glanced up at her, then resumed sawing on his steak. "Is this conversation going somewhere?"

Obviously, it wasn't, she thought with a twinge of disappointment. It had been so long since she'd felt this way. Happy. Safe. Flirty and a little reckless with it. And she knew it would probably be a long time, if ever, that she would feel this way again.

The past year had been a living hell. What lay ahead promised more of the same. But right here, right now, this moment, she felt cocooned in a protected pocket of time, where she was free to laugh, free to tease, free to love.

And she did love Dallas Garrett. It wasn't exactly a revelation, but it was the first time she'd admitted it to herself. The truth had been there for a long, long time. She even knew the exact moment she had fallen in love with him. It was the one moment on Jolo Island that she treasured and remembered with crystal clarity.

She could still picture the bower where he'd hidden them from the terrorists. Orchids dripped down in lush, summer colors, sunlight slanted through the canopy trees and birdsong rode on the tropical currents. He'd apologized. For touching her. For saving her.

And with those few, sincere words, he'd saved the part of her that needed saving most—her pride and her dignity. He hadn't realized it then. He didn't realize it now.

And he was right to keep his head in the deadly game they were playing. Here, in this room was the fantasy. Reality lurked only heartbeats away.

"I guess I was just wondering," she said, shifting gears, "how a man used to giving orders was going to handle taking them. Specifically from Jones."

He lifted a shoulder. "This is his territory. We're only as close to finding Jenna and your grandfather as we are because of him. I'll do things his way—as long as I agree with his plan of action."

She nodded, wondering about Gabriel Jones. "Do you think we can trust him?"

"About as far as I'd trust any Company man."

"Company?"

"CIA. Although I'm not certain exactly what role Jones plays for Uncle."

"Okay. Twenty questions time. Role? What does that mean?"

He sat back in the chair, lifted the warm bottle of beer and drank. "I don't know if he's on the payroll or if he's an operative for hire. Either way, he's our best shot. Just watch your back around him."

Thoughtful, Amy pushed a piece of meat around on her plate with a fork. "I got the sense he felt compelled to help me."

Dallas nodded. "Yeah. I think you're right. For some reason he seems to relate to you. Plus, he's pissed. Alejandro killed one of his men."

"What do you think his operation is regarding MC6?"

He shook his head. "Hard to say. Something's in the works, whether it's Company sanctioned or on Jones' own personal agenda, I don't know.

"What I do know," he said after finishing off the

beer, "with Jenna out of contact, Alvaro dead and MC6 on the hunt for you, Gabe Jones represents our best shot at finding your grandfather."

His face was grim as he studied her. "You're walking into a hornet's nest . . . you know that, don't you?"

Before she could form a response, he leaned forward, covered her hand with his. "You can still back out, you know. Hightail it the hell out of here, lie low until Jones gives the all clear. I can make you disappear, Amy. For as long as you need to."

"What I need," she said, understanding his concern but unwilling to appease him, "is to see this through. Too much depends on it. And I couldn't live with myself if I turned my back on Jenna."

He held her gaze for a long moment, finally nodded. A grudging consent. A measured understanding.

"You look exhausted," he said, his tone colored with a guarded intimacy that Amy suspected he really hadn't wanted her to hear.

You don't know how to handle what's happening between us, do you Dallas?

That's okay, she thought. That's okay. She didn't quite know how to deal with it either. She only hoped that when this was over, when they got to Jenna—please God, let her be alive—when she found and confronted her grandfather, that they would both be ready to talk about the future.

A future that, because of Dallas, she found herself desperately wanting. Yeah. For the first time in months, the quest for revenge and retribution wasn't the only thing driving her.

"Amy?"

She startled, realized that she'd tuned out on him. "Sorry. What?"

"I said you look exhausted. Why don't you get some sleep?"

"What about you?"

"I'm going to shower then I'll hit the rack."

Unspoken was the tag: Where I will sleep on my side of the bed and I expect you to sleep on yours.

Okay. She got it. In spades.

He disappeared into the small bathroom and she crawled between the sheets. She hadn't any more than hit the pillow and she was out.

And it seemed she hadn't any more than fallen asleep when she awoke with a start.

Beside her in the bed, Dallas slept. But not peacefully. His legs kicked with a restless urgency. His eyes were pinched tightly shut, his face contorted into a grimace that could only be pain as he thrashed his head back and forth on the pillow. Sweat drenched his body as he gripped the sheets at his hips with tight fists.

"Dallas," she whispered in the dark and touched a hand to his chest.

He groaned and jerked, flinching away from her touch.

"Dallas," she said, more forcefully, sitting up beside him.

He came awake the same way he'd been sleeping. Violently.

He bolted straight up in bed, hyper-alert, one hundred and fifty percent defensive.

"You were dreaming," she whispered, and only then did he turn his head and look at her.

Pain. My God, through the night shadows that separated them, she saw such pain in his eyes. And wretched, hopeless despair.

"It's okay," she whispered, winding her arms around him his neck and urged him to his back. "It's okay," she said again, a soft, soothing caress as she nestled up against him.

He stiffened at the contact, his heart still beating like an endless volley of artillery fire. Finally his muscles uncoiled. Almost reluctantly, he turned into her, wrapped himself around her and burrowed into her heat.

"It's okay," she murmured into his hair and held him. Held him close, held him to her breast as the tension in his rock-hard body slowly eased.

She lay awake long moments after he'd given in to the pull of sleep. Loving him. Afraid for him. Saddened by the knowledge that she wasn't the only one in this bed plagued by demons that prowled through the night.

CHAPTER FOURTEEN

What's the story here, do you know?" As they hurried along the Plaza Mayo, Dallas' gaze was riveted on the women marching in front of Casa Rosada, the presidential palace.

Amy hurried along beside him. Not disappointed, exactly that they hadn't talked more about last night. Not surprised that Dallas hadn't mentioned his nightmare that had awakened both of them.

There really hadn't been time. She was still dressing when he'd returned to their room with coffee and sweet rolls he'd picked up from the hotel restaurant. They drank the coffee and ate the rolls once they'd settled into a seat on the underground train. The noise from the rails had made it difficult to talk.

And now the urgency of finding Gabe outweighed any "heart to heart" she'd like to have with Dallas.

They'd ridden the underground to the crowded main square in search of the address Gabe had given Dallas last night.

A dog walker, a dozen panting, yapping, unruly

canines in tow, breezed by in a tangle of leashes and barks. Guards similar to those who guard Buckingham palace paraded stoically back in forth in front of the protesting women. High above the palace walls, the Argentina flag flew: two horizontal bands of light blue, separated by a white band, the center of which was filled with a radiant yellow sun with a human face known as the Sun of May.

"And what's with the white scarves?" he continued as they sidestepped the dogs, drawing her attention back to the women.

"In the 1970s and 1980s—during the Falkland war—" Amy explained, drawing from a passage in a guide book she'd read on their ride on the underground, "thousands of people were kidnapped by government decree and never seen again."

"The dirty war," Dallas said, and hiked his pack up higher on his back. "I remember now."

From the beginning, Amy had been taken with his intelligence. He knew something about everything. This was no exception.

"Since the war, a group called the Mothers of the Disappeared stage weekly demonstrations in front of the palace. The white scarves are symbolic. Even though over twenty years have passed, they continue to demand justice for their missing children."

All around them tourists and Portenios, as the people of Buenos Aires were called, moved with lazy grace under the heat of the Argentina summer morning.

The natives of the very busy seaport and city were known for their beauty and arrogance. Amy now knew why. The women were beautiful. The men, model perfect. She fully understood why the saying, Portenios know that God is everywhere but his office is in Buenos Aires, came to be.

"There's the corner," Dallas said, grabbed Amy by the arm and hustled her toward a busy intersection.

The traffic was heavy as they trotted across the street and were almost run down by an ancient and battered station wagon that screeched to a stop in front of them. It was a low-bellied boat with paneled doors, rusted fenders and a surfboard lashed to the roof, reminiscent of an old surfer movie she'd once seen.

The passenger door swung open and a voice rumbled out from the driver's seat.

"Get in."

Dallas bent down, glanced inside. Without a word, he opened the rear door, guided her inside then climbed into the front seat.

It took Amy a moment to recognize Gabe Jones behind the wheel.

Gone was the shadowy warrior who had killed Alejandro then led them through the back streets of the city last night. Today Jones' eyes were covered by dark glasses. On his head was a straw panama; a navy blue wife beater stretched tight over shoulders as broad as a building, baring biceps roughly the size of footballs.

The surfer dude disguise would have been convincing as hell if she hadn't already witnessed his deadly prowess with a knife. And if Amy didn't recognize the bearing of a man constantly riding the edge of intrigue and risk.

In the daylight, she could see how darkly attractive and dangerously intense he was as he maneuvered the lumbering station wagon in and out of traffic.

"Were you followed?" Jones asked Dallas as they waited for a light to change.

"Picked up a tail just outside the hotel."

This was news to Amy.

"But we lost him."

Jones nodded his approval and apparent trust that Dallas knew what he was doing.

Amy couldn't stand it anymore. "Where are we going?"

Jones glanced at her in the rearview mirror. "Surf's up. We're going to catch a few waves."

He was only half joking, Amy learned a little later. They drove east until the scent of the sun and the city melded with a saltwater breeze that rushed in through the wagon's open windows as they neared the busy seaport. Jones wove his way through back streets to a small, packed marina. He parked the car in front of a ramshackle building that appeared to be a charter fishing service.

"Wait here," he said, and disappeared inside. Five minutes later, he emerged with fishing poles and bait and motioned with a hitch of his head for them to follow him.

Amy scrambled out of the wagon. With Dallas' hand firmly gripping her elbow, they trailed Jones to one of hundreds of boat slips.

He'd already hopped down into a twenty-foot fishing boat and stood holding a hand up to help Amy on board. They were casting off and heading out to sea to the roar of a 200-horsepower outboard before Amy had a chance to shrug out of her backpack and sit down behind the windshield.

Then it was nothing but engine roar, sun, and the splash of salt water over the bow as Jones sped out of the harbor and headed south along the shore.

She glanced at Dallas, sitting behind her and to her right. The sun shone down as he stared into a wind that whipped his hair around his face—a face that never failed to make her heart rate alter. A face that reflected a dark passion and intense determination to protect her. A face she had loved from the first moment she had seen it, covered in cammo paint and sweat and resolved to save her even then. Even when he hadn't known her, he'd been ready to give up his life to save her from certain death.

Miles of ocean and shoreline passed. A little over an hour later, they slowed down to a crawl. Jones prowled the edge of a small secluded bay while a stout westerly wind rocked the relatively small craft around in the water like a cork.

Evidently satisfied with what he saw through a pair of binoculars he'd had pulled out from under the dash, Jones piloted the boat into the shallows and beached it on a wide expanse of sand in what appeared to be the edge of nowhere.

A man of few words, he cut the engine, hauled himself into the knee-deep surf and motioned for Amy to follow.

Dallas helped her over the side and followed her into the water, carrying both of their packs. As they waded toward shore, Jones shoved the boat back into the water and without a backward glance headed up the beach at a fast jog.

"Okay, is now the time to be nervous that our ride back to the city is drifting on the currents to Africa?" she whispered to Dallas, chancing a glance over her shoulder to see the boat bobbing and rocking on an undertow that was sucking it out to sea.

He didn't have a chance to answer. Jones had disappeared over a hill ahead of them and they had to move to catch up.

The sputter and grind of another kind of engine commanded all of their attention.

They trotted over a rise to see a sandy landing strip twenty yards away. Sitting on the strip, like a piece of tarnished metal deteriorating in the sun, sat a small twin-engine plane. Jones had already climbed aboard and sat behind the yoke in the pilot's seat.

Both propellers revved sluggishly to life, coughing and hacking like a tuberculosis victim.

"Oh, my God," Amy said, even as Jones shouldered open the cockpit door, stepped out onto the wing and motioned them to hurry the hell up.

As she stood there in shock, surveying the dinged-up fuselage, chipped red and white paint and—oh God, was that bailing wire hanging from the open door—Jones yelled, "Get the lead out!"

"Please, *please* tell me he's kidding," she implored.

"Doesn't strike me as a jokester." Dallas hustled her toward the battered plane.

"Is it . . . do you think it's safe?" she stammered, dragging her feet.

"Look at it this way. If he's willing to ride in her, he must not be too worried."

She didn't find Dallas' logic all that comforting. From what she'd seen of Gabriel Jones, whether he lived or died didn't make a whole lot of difference to him one way or the other.

But the bottom line was he was the only one who could take her to Jenna, to her grandfather. So she swallowed back the urge to upchuck her breakfast and climbed on board.

She fastened her seat belt as Jones fed the twin engines fuel and the plane bumped along down the makeshift runway.

"Where are the parachutes?" she asked in a small voice.

Jones angled her a look. And for the first time since she'd met him, he smiled.

Amy didn't exactly sleep, but Dallas was glad to see that after the first hour in flight and her initial white-knuckle reactions to the numerous air pockets peppering the lower currents, she was a least resting.

Dallas had enough broad-stroke knowledge of the older model Piper Seminole to know that although the cabin wasn't pressurized, they could still cruise at around 10,000 or 12,000 feet. Jones, however, kept the bird low to the ground, humming along between 600 and 1000 feet with the air speed steady at around

175 knots. He figured it meant one of two things.
Jones needed to stretch the fuel capacity of the
craft—which Dallas estimated to tap out at around
700 nautical miles—or he wanted to fly below radar.

After they'd been in flight close to four hours,
Dallas suspected both tactics were in play. But he
was tired of playing, weary of waiting for Jones to
fill them in.

Not that the flight hadn't been interesting. At this
altitude, north central Argentina, from the flat planes
of the Pampas, to cool grazing grounds peppered
with enormous flocks of sheep and fruit and vegetable farms, to the arid desert south of the Rio Col-
orado, had rolled by below them like a *National
Geographic* pictorial.

During the past hour, the planes and desert areas
had slowly given way to a rolling plateau of lush
green. The northern and western most edge of the
Patagonia, he suspected, as a network of lakes and
rivers unfolded ahead of them and eventually led to a
ridge of rugged mountains in the not so far distance.
Chile, he realized. They were almost to the western
border of Chile. Through the pitted windshield, he
could see what could only be the Andes grow closer
and loom larger with each nautical mile they traveled.

He glanced at the fuel gauge. Jones had switched
to the second tank close to two hours ago. The needle
flickered dangerously close to the empty mark.

Dallas figured they had to be running on fumes by
now. He was about to hit up the stoically silent Jones
for info when he banked the Piper sharp to the left
and cut speed and altitude.

Dallas glanced out the window. A small, narrow valley was carved out between the low-altitude foothills on the left and the snow-covered mountains on the right. With the ease of a pilot well experienced in flying bush country and improvised landing strips, Jones set the Piper down on a grassy stretch of ground.

"Welcome to the Patagonia," Jones said, and taxied off the landing strip toward a copse of trees where he carefully parked the plane then cut the engines.

In the rear seat, Amy worked at the buckle on her seat belt. "So where's the welcome committee?"

Dallas had to grin. She'd been scared shitless when she'd climbed on board, but she was back in control now.

That's my girl. Unsinkable.

He had no ownership over the feeling of pride swelling in his chest, but it was there anyway and he didn't have it in him to fight it. They'd have enough to fight before this was all over.

"If I did everything right," Jones said, unbuckling, "there won't be one."

Jones shoved open the door and stepped out onto the wing. "Grab your gear. We've still got a ways to go."

"Which is where?" Dallas asked, figuring Jones had kept them in the dark long enough.

"Soon," he said cryptically. "You'll know soon enough."

CHAPTER FIFTEEN

Gabe gave them credit. They kept their mouths shut and they moved when he said move. He figured it had to be a stretch for Garrett. He was clearly a man used to being in control. Relinquishing it couldn't be easy. Gabe respected him for that. And was counting on Garrett to be the tactical operator and experienced fighter he'd pegged him for.

The woman, hell, she'd been a surprise too. White-knuckled most of the flight, but she'd toughed it out. No bitching. No moaning. She was here on a mission, intended to complete it, and was tough enough and smart enough to accept that Gabe was the only game in town who could bring in a win for the home team.

He ducked back into the Piper, retrieved his go bag and a camoflague net.

When he jumped down and started unfolding it, Garrett pitched in and together, they covered the Piper, disguising it from any low-flying aircraft that might be on the lookout for them or the plane.

He was certain Garrett had questions—starting

with what the hell good the Piper was going to be to them now with two empty fuel tanks. Again, he kept them to himself and waited.

Gabe tugged a map out of his go bag and spread it out on the ground. Garrett and the woman squatted down on either side of him.

"We're here." Gabe pointed to an area far off any major roads and approximately seventy miles due east of El Bolson.

"El Bolson." Garrett squinted, thoughtful. "Why does that ring bells?"

"ODESSA," Amy supplied. "It was one of the stops on Evita Peron's rat line. A Nazi stronghold."

"For over sixty years," Gabe said. "It's also MC6's base of operations in Argentina."

"And Jenna—you believe that's where they're holding her? In El Bolson?"

Gabe shook his head, pointed to a dot on the map. "Close, but my men on the groud place her here. Leleque. It's a hole-in-the-wall hamlet—maybe two hundred population total if you count the dogs and chickens. It's close enough to the MC6 base that she's within reach, but remote enough that they can keep her under wraps should someone get suspicious of an American woman in the vicinity. A loud-mouth American to boot," he added with a grunt of disgust. "You sure you want to spring her?"

His suggestion earned him a glare from Amy. Gabe caught Garrett's grin.

Ah, so that's the way it is. Garrett's got a thing for her. Gabe had suspected as much last night. Was certain of it now. Fine. Whatever. As long as it didn't interfere with their op.

"What's the plan?" she asked.

"Barring a cake with a file in it, I guess we'll just have to bust her out."

"Wait, wait." Concern darkened her eyes. "That's our only option? She could get caught in the cross fire. Can't someone be bought? Like the local law?"

"MC6 is the local law. It's very hush-hush, but they own everything and everyone around here—and monetary payoffs seldom come into play. You cross them, you disappear. Or your daughter disappears. Or your son. No one ever sees them again."

He looked at her hard. "So the answer is no. No one can be bought. Whittles the options down to slim and one. We storm the castle."

He gave her credit. She got it. Nodded. "Then let's go do this."

Gabe stood, folded the map and shouldered his bag. Garrett gave him a hard look.

Nothing happens to her, it said. Loud. Clear. Absolute.

Gabe nodded. Nothing would happen to her.

Like nothing was supposed to have happened to Angelique.

He swallowed back the icy stab of pain her memory brought. He didn't think of her these days. Wouldn't let himself. He'd buried her memory along with her bullet-riddled body in a solitary grave one year ago. It was the best he could do for her then. At the time, he'd been half dead himself. Now, only his heart was dead.

And only his quest for revenge kept the rest of him alive.

He notched his chin toward the road ahead. "Our ground transpo should be around the bend."

"How does he arrange these things?" Gabe heard Amy ask Garrett as they hiked along behind him.

"I'm thinking friends in low places," Garrett said.

Ain't that the truth, Gabe thought.

Amy sat in the backseat of a seen-better-days Suburban, unenthusiastically munching on a sandwich made of baked ham and cheese—a *milanesa* Jones had called it.

His "friends in low places" had evidently thought of everything. They'd found the older model Suburban in a small, ramshackle building about a half mile from where they'd left the plane. In addition to the *milanesas,* a cooler in the back of the Suburban was well stocked with cheese, oranges, and avocados and the ever-popular Cerveza. The beer was cold and bitter but served its purpose. Even though it had been hours since the sweet roll and coffee this morning, Amy ate only because she knew she needed to refuel, not because she felt hunger.

She was too keyed up to register any physical needs. Too anxious about finding Jenna. About the confrontation to come. About the man behind the wheel. She still didn't know what to think of him.

Jones drove like he lived. Emotionless and with deadly intent. She supposed she should be grateful for his single-minded focus. Yet there were so many things about him that gave her pause.

She thought back to the night in the alley—was it just *last* night—and shivered, despite the heat. Jones had killed Alejandro without the blink of an eye—without an iota of remorse. Is that what happened? she wondered. After so many kills—and she suspected Jones had had many—did the act of taking a life become so rote, so mechanical, that guilt or repentance no longer factored in?

And what of Dallas? He was a warrior, too. She had no doubt he'd killed and killed often. In the name of good versus evil. In the name of freedom and protecting a way of life. He'd killed for her. In the jungle on Jolo, he'd taken more than one life to save her and Darcy. Were those kills the source of his nightmares—like the damage done to her and to her mother was the source of hers?

Someday, would she too, dream of the man she had killed? Would she agonize over taking a life? Of the life she intended to take?

Or would she become like Jones, stagnant of emotions or remorse or even grief?

She breathed deep, watched out the window as the terrain flew by. Grasses, dandelions and daisies tangled together on the long valley floor on either side of the dirt road. Orange-and-white butterflies and ping-pong-ball–sized bees flitted in the sun. Pink cone-shaped flowers topped long green stems and waved in the wind near a river bank that ran parallel to the road. Beyond, snowy mountains and dark bosque hills lorded over the valley while small birds flitted from tree to tree.

According to the map, the river flowed into a large lake, where glaciers glittered in the mountains above. This part of Argentina reminded her very much Montana. Beautiful. Peaceful. Serene. She'd spent a week hiking in Glacier Park—six, maybe seven years ago? Today it seemed like a lifetime ago.

Soon they would raid a village jail. With guns drawn. Someone could die. She could kill again.

If not tonight, then when she found him. She intended to make him pay. Her grandfather would pay with his life for what he had done to her mother and to her.

Braced by that goal to sustain her, Amy turned to the task at hand . . . and away from that long-ago life, understanding that circumstances other than distance had transported her as far away from home as she'd ever been.

Near dusk, same day, Leleque, in the Argentinean Patagonia

"**Why, thank you,**" Jenna murmured with no attempt to hide her sarcasm when the guard slid her "dinner" tray under the cell door. "This gruel looks absolutely divine—although I could have sworn I ordered the low-carb entree."

He grunted, not amused, then shuffled off without a word.

"Back atcha," she grumbled, then thought better of her surly routine and tried another tack. Scorn hadn't worked so far, maybe it was time to give sweetness and light a try. "Hey. Wait a minute."

He stopped. Turned with a dark scowl.

She flashed her *wanna be my bestest friend* smile. "What's your name?"

Another grunt.

Screw it. So much for charming him.

"Fine. Let's just call you Fido."

Her jailer had a flat face, dark pocked skin, rounded shoulders and the intelligence of a centipede.

And she was dependent on him for her existence.

Somehow that was even scarier than the unknowns.

Nothing, however, was as frightening as when the door crashed open half an hour later.

Three men with dark complexions and monster rifles stood before her cell door.

She did her damnedest not to cower, but clearly, it wasn't Avon calling.

The tall one had a jagged scar that ran from his jaw to the corner of his eye. He motioned with the business end of a gun that looked like every rifle every terrorist in every war-torn corner of the globe so cottoned to. "Up."

"Um, actually," she looked up at Scarface through wide eyes and tried to steady the kettledrum beat of her heart. "I'm fine. Really. I think I'll just sit this one out. Unless, of course, you're from the U.S. Embassy?"

Her little joke was met with stone silence.

"No. I didn't think so."

Gunman number two was built short and lean, like a hungry boxer. He yelled something toward the other room. Fido eventually appeared, rattling a set of keys and suddenly the filthy cell felt like home sweet home.

The cell door swung open. The end of Scarface's rifle swung toward her. And the look on his face said he wasn't going to take any lip or lagging on her part.

Jenna stood. "I can get money," she said, dropping any pretense of bravado. She was in seriously deep weeds here. And because of her habit—*stupid* habit—of infrequent check-ins with her editor, no one back in the States would have a moment of concern if a week or so went by and she didn't contact them.

Amy was the only one who would miss her. And Amy, she suspected, had her own problems. Jenna had had a lot of time to think about Amy while waiting in this cell. Had she made it to Buenos Aries? Was she, at this moment, searching for her? Or had Amy been snatched off the streets too, stuffed in the back of a van and thrown in a jail similar to this one?

What in the hell had they gotten themselves into? Jenna had gone looking for a story about a war criminal. And it seemed she'd landed in the middle of a cloak-and-dagger movie that would give *The Bourne Identity* a run for its money.

She couldn't think about that now. Couldn't think about Amy. She had to figure out a way to get herself out of this fix. And she had to do it now.

"I have connections," she informed Scarface, who seemed to be the leader of this little pack of miscreants. "I have big connections in the States. Whatever you want, I can get it."

Clearly, they could give a rip.

The third man joined her in the cell. He had a Rambo thing going on. He was short and heavily built; bare biceps bulged like softballs beneath the ripped armholes of a mud-brown t-shirt; the thighs beneath worn cargo pants were as thick as tree trunks. He'd caught his black hair at the nape letting the rest trail like a rope halfway down his back.

Scarface, Boxer, and Rambo. She couldn't have gotten Winkin', Blinkin', and Nod? she wondered with a desperate kind of hysteria. Moe, Larry, and Curly? The Three Amigos?

Rambo tugged a length of rope out of his hip pocket, handed his rifle to Boxer and grabbed her wrist.

Instinct had her jerking away. She stumbled, would have fallen if she hadn't run into the wall. Rambo was on her like a cobra after a mongoose. He backhanded her hard across her face. Her head snapped sideways. Pain, sharp, stinging, bell ringing, exploded in her head and she went down on all fours.

She lifted a hand to protect herself only to have him grab it, loop the rope around her wrist and jerk her to her knees.

She'd like to think it was clear thinking that kept her from fighting him. There were three of them plus the guard. Her chances of getting away were roughly the same as peace breaking out in the Middle East. But the truth was, she was so shocked—by the violence, by the pain, by the taste of her own blood—that she couldn't react with anything but submission.

She didn't fight him when Rambo caught her other arm and tied her wrists together in front of her.

Didn't resist when he grabbed her by her hair and jerked her to her feet.

Swallowing back a cry of pain, she recited every prayer she knew, then made up some she didn't when she saw the flash of a blade, then felt the sharp prick of its tip bite into her neck, just below her ear.

The moon had just slid above the taller peaks of the distant Andes when Jones pulled off the narrow road and tucked the Suburban behind a rock outcropping.

Dallas watched Amy as they all geared up, a sense of urgency cocooning them all in grim silence. Damn, she was something as she strapped a black nylon belt and holster with her loaded Glock around her waist. She double-checked her extra magazines, tucked them into her front pocket then strapped the KA-BAR onto her ankle like she could do it in her sleep. He wondered how many times she'd done just that in the past six months.

Someone had trained her well. Still, he had a hard time envisioning her using either weapon. A hard time seeing her pump lead into another human body—bad guy or not.

And yet he knew that she had.

She'd killed the MC6 assassin. And other than that one subdued admission, she hadn't said another word about it. He understood.

He wondered if the reality had even set in for her yet. If she'd blocked it. Or if she'd been second-guessing herself, replaying the scene in her mind, questioning if there had been another way.

Yeah. He'd played all those head games. Over and over again. And it always came down to one thing: life or death. And life won out every time.

Still, taking a life—even in self-defense—took its toll. Living with the aftermath was never easy. And living with the knowledge that he'd led good men to their death . . .

And there it was again. A vivid, violent flashback to the mountainside in Afghanistan. *The blood. The pain of snow and frozen ice on his face, the hole in his gut. The terrorized cries of his men.*

He shook his head. Fought to stow it away. Ignored the pounding of his heart, the sweat trickling down his back.

This was no time. This was no place to wander back into that abyss.

Amy. Depended. On. Him.

Aware of her quiet, methodical actions beside him, Dallas settled himself, then dry fired an M-4 Jones had dug out of the back of the Suburban to get a feel for the trigger action. The automatic rifle felt comfortable in his hands. Had always been a good fit for him. Grim faced, he loaded a thirty-round magazine with 5.56×45 mm cartridges, all the while wishing there was someway to keep Amy out of the mix on this one.

Fifteen minutes and a quarter of a mile later, the best he'd been able to accomplish was to make certain Jones delegated the driving duties to her. Her orders were to stay with the Suburban. Wait for them to contact her.

When Dallas and Jones set out on foot, Amy had

been sitting behind the wheel, a headset plugged into a no-frills two-way radio tuned to channel five. The plan was for her to play Bonnie to his Clyde and wait in the dark for Dallas' cue to pick them up.

Jones led the way through the dark back streets—obviously in his element. He pointed to a dingy gray cinder block building dead ahead. Their target. It sat amid weeds and dust with little else for landscaping, one block off the main street, which consisted of several cantinas, a gas station and a small provisions store. Jones had filled Dallas in as they'd geared up.

"Doubles as the city hall and the local jail. The kind of jail where the usual suspects are declared guilty without trial. Where the cell doors are locked and the keys are lost. Innocent until proven guilty is as foreign a concept down here as minimum wage."

The building dimensions were as unimpressive as the landscaping and paint job. Twenty by twenty, square. One story. Metal bars on all windows.

"Typically there's one night jailer, armed but old and slow," Jones told Dallas as they neared the target. "Three cells, northwest corner. Interior walls also cement block.

"How do you see this coming down?" Jones asked quietly, surprising Dallas as they plastered themselves against the night shadows of the wall of an adjacent building.

"Straight up snatch and grab," Dallas said without hesitation. "Crash in, guns drawn, catch him off guard, grab her and dash. No need to stay and play."

"Works for me." Jones peeled away from the building. "Provided there aren't other players on the court."

Dallas reconned the street as they crept along close to exterior walls still holding heat from the summer sun. It was dead quiet. Not even a stray dog wandered the narrow streets. One battered, older model brown sedan sat at the corner of the block. Empty.

Tire treads in the powdery dirt road suggested the car hadn't been parked there all that long.

Could be the jailor's ride. Could be "visitors." Which meant they could be walking into a nest of vermin. It was a chance they had to take. Jones knew it as well as Dallas.

With Jones on point and Dallas guarding his flank, Dallas spoke softly into his head mike. "We're about to go in." He'd previously radioed Amy directions to the jail. "Come in quiet and be ready to punch it."

"Be careful." Amy's voice was steady but concerned.

"Same goes," he said, and ended the transmission.

CHAPTER SIXTEEN

They reached the front door of the jail. Jones stacked up on the left, Dallas on the right. At Jones' signal, Dallas burst in the door, dropped to one knee, the butt of the M-4 pressed against his shoulder, his cheek against the stock, the jailer dead center in his sights.

Jones moved in behind him, his M-14 also in firing position and kicked the door shut.

"*¿Estàs solo?*" *Are you alone?* Jones demanded, pressing the business end of his rifle in the jailer's ear.

"*S . . . Sí*," he stammered, stunned and obviously scared shitless. "*Solo.*" *Alone.*

"*La mujer americana. ¿Dónde està?*" *The American woman. Where is she?*

The stricken jailor sat behind a banged-up metal desk, his hands raised on either side of his head. "*No sé de lo que vos hablàs.*" *I don't know what you're talking about.*

Jones cut him a hard look then walked past the

desk and through a door that Dallas assumed led to the cells.

He came back less than fifteen seconds later.

"She's not here."

"Shit. We've got the wrong place?"

"Right place. Wrong time. They've moved her."

With the M-14 suspended by a shoulder strap and riding his back, Jones grabbed the jailer's shirt front and hiked him out of his chair. "*Dígame. ¿A dónde la llevaron?*" *Tell me. Where did they take her?*

The jailor's eyes were wild with terror. "*No sé No sé nada.*" *I don't know. I don't know anything.*

He was lying. Dallas was certain of it. Evidently, so was Jones.

"Look, Paco." Jones shoved the man back down in the creaking chair, loomed over him. "I'm only going to ask you one more time."

"*¡No hablo inglés!*" *I don't speak English!*

"That a fact?" Jones picked up a dog-eared Louis L'Amour paperback that lay open, facedown on the desk. An English version. He fired it at the man's chest.

Then he got right in the guy's face. "Let's try this again, okay? You want to live to finish the book? Tell me where she is."

For added incentive, he slipped the Butterfly out of its sheath, flipped the blade open and held it to the man's throat. "This is the part where you get to tell me something I want to hear."

"The mountains," he croaked, his eyes as big as dinner plates at the prospect of possibly getting his throat slit.

Jones jerked him to his feet again and walked him over to a wall where a map of the area was tacked on a bulletin board. "Show me."

"Here." The jailor pointed with a trembling finger. "Maybe here," he added indicating a spot a few miles away.

"How many men?"

"*Tres* . . . th . . . three," he stammered. "Only three."

"And how many more when we find them?"

He shook his head. "This I do not know."

"How long has it been since they took her?" Dallas asked, hearing the low rumble of a vehicle pull up out front.

With the M-4 still trained on the jailer, he walked backward toward a low window, peeked outside. The Suburban rolled into view, stopped in front of the jail.

"*Una hora.* One hour," the terrified man said. "Maybe less."

Jones walked the jailor back to the desk. Shoved him down into the chair. "You know what they will do to you if they find out you ratted on them, yes?"

The jailer gave a tight, nervous nod, knowing he was as good as dead if he confessed to his "*compadres*" that he'd given up their location.

Jones pressed the Butterfly into the loose skin under the man's soft jaw until he drew blood. "Triple it if I ever find out you told them we were here. *¿Entiende?*"

"*Sí.* Yes! Yes! I understand. You were never here."

Jones backed away, closed and sheathed the Butterfly.

"The banditos, they're hung in the end," he said,

notching his chin toward the book that had landed on the floor by the desk. "Opps. Sorry. Guess I spoiled *that* ending."

And then he walked out the door. Dallas covered him, then followed him outside and jumped into the Suburban.

"Punch it, Martha," Jones said slumping down in the backseat.

Amy punched it.

Fifteen minutes later, Jones had her cut the headlights. Five minutes after that, they parked and headed for the hills on foot, packing an arsenal of ordinance and tech toys that would have made a recon team jump for joy.

Erich picked up his phone on the second ring. Dispensed with formalities. He was expecting to hear from only one person this time of night. "It's done?"

"*Sí. La mujer*—"

"How many times," Erich cut the man off crossly, "have I told you? English. Speak English."

A surly silence followed before Perez got control of himself. "Apologies—sir. The woman, she has been moved."

"Base Two?"

"Yes. As you requested."

"Eyes open, Manuel. Keep your eyes open. Do not get caught with your pants down. I'll be in touch with further instructions."

Erich disconnected. Sat back in his desk chair. And resisted the urge to throw something.

Alejandro was dead. He'd received this news only two hours ago.

"Dead? When? How?" he'd asked when Ramone' had called on the secure line from Buenos Aires.

He'd been knifed in the same alley where Alejandro was to have intercepted the Walker woman last night and eliminate her and the problem she created.

"And the woman?"

The terror in Ramone's voice had been palpable when he'd confessed that one of his men on the ground had found her then lost her early this morning.

Yes. She was proving to be very resourceful, Erich thought, and withdrew one of his special blends of Cuban cigars from a tightly sealed box. Maybe too resourceful for a woman and a man in a strange country. Too resourceful, perhaps, for them to be managing to evade his men on their own?

More even than the fact that Walker and Garrett had managed to escape Alejandro's special brand of elimination, it was the method that had been used to kill him that disturbed him.

Knifed.

For many men in this part of the world, the knife was the instrument of choice. Alejandro was one of those men. He was also one of the best with a blade. Erich highly doubted that the American, Garrett—and surely not the woman—would be any match against him. In fact, Erich knew of only one man who could beat Alejandro at his own game.

He stood, walked to the liquor cabinet. Poured a civilized finger of brandy. Took his time lighting the Cuban. Indulging in both, he returned to his desk.

Sat. Contemplated. Checked the time. Almost midnight.

He picked up the phone.

"Find out who's helping them," he said without
preamble. "Start with the Archangel."

"Jones? But all of our reports say he died in Co-
lumbia."

Erich had always made it a point to keep apprised
of Gabriel Jones' whereabouts and activities. He
made it a point to keep apprised of all of his enemies. And while he'd applauded the reports of Jones'
death, he'd never fully believed them. Jones was like
a ghost. He could materialize out of thin air at will.
And Erich's trust in his "intelligence" network was
always in question.

"Look for Jones," he repeated and hung up.

Jenna huddled into herself, shivering on the dew
damp grass, and pretended to be unconsciousness. It
wasn't too much of a stretch. Her head pounded. Her
mind was tripping on terror overload. It was tempt-
ing as hell to just let the darkness take her. Again.

But she fought it. Fought the memory of Scarface,
Boxer and Rambo dragging her out of the jail by her
hair and dumping her into the bed of a pickup truck.

She'd had to scramble to keep up with them, bite
back a cry when she bumped her hip, hard, on the
doorframe as they led her outside.

She'd always thought she was one tough cookie.
Thought she could hold her own in the worst situation.

Thought that she had been *in* the worst situation when she'd been stuck in that stinking jail cell.

Only the worst situation scenario of worst situation scenarios had gotten even worse.

It had taken everything in her not to cry out in sheer terror when Boxer had come toward her with a hood.

In the end, she'd pleaded, shaking her head as a hot trail of tears leaked down her cheeks. "Please . . . don't."

"*Silencio.*" He'd growled. Then just for kicks, he'd hit her again.

Her ears were still ringing when he jerked the hood down over her head then dumped her into the back of a rusted-out pickup. Through her pain and fear, she'd recognized the sound of a tailgate slamming shut.

Felt the give and sway of the truck bounce, heard one door slam shut then the other and the engine grumble to a start. Whoever was driving had shifted into gear and shot out onto the road so fast, the forward motion had sent her rolling backwards.

The last thing she remembered was a sharp, booming pain as her head hit hard against the tailgate. Then there was nothing but darkness.

And now there was nothing but here.

Wherever here was.

Ignoring the pain in her head, the swelling inside her mouth, she opened her eyes a slit. Gave them time to focus and adjust to a darkness cut only by a quarter moon hanging high overhead and a low flickering flame of a fire.

A campfire, she realized at the same time she realized there were several men either sitting or lounging around the fire, passing around a bottle.

Rambo was grumbling. Her Spanish wasn't the best, but she picked up a few things. Like the fact that he was pissed. Something about the damn German. Thought he was so superior. Tried to tell him how to do his job. And for the money he paid, he should be happy he even showed up when he called.

Then she heard the word *woman*. And the talk turned really ugly then.

Oh, God. She shrank tighter into herself as she listened to the things they wanted to do to her. Despite the German's orders to keep their hands off of her.

Low, mean laughter punctuated a lewd gesture and the bottle made another round.

Fido suddenly seemed like a prince among men, the filthy jail like the Ritz.

And the life she'd known became infinitely sweeter.

She wouldn't make it easy for them. She decided that right then. She knew she didn't stand a chance, but she'd fight them with everything in her.

She'd fight them, and somehow, she would survive.

The friendly speculation turned predatory as a growling discussion of who was going to have the first go at her broke out.

That's right, you bastards. Get greedy about it. Knock each other around. Hell, yeah. Whip out those knives. Use them on each other and leave me the hell alone.

But the most the bickering was going to give her was a reprieve. Jenna knew that. Just like she knew that if she survived what was surely going to be the longest night of her life, she would not be the same woman who had come to Argentina in search of a story.

"Paid thugs."

Amy heard Jones talk in a low, quiet voice beside her as they lay on their bellies, twenty yards away from a campfire surrounded by a dozen men, swilling from a bottle and arguing over the spoils of war.

Amy could see Jenna through the night-vision goggles Jones had passed to her. Jenna was huddled into herself, lying on the ground a few yards away from the men who were drinking around a campfire.

Fear for Jenna outdistanced the relief at finding her alive. Amy's heart broke for her. She felt Jenna's terror in every pore of her body. Experienced her revulsion with every heartbeat. And against all efforts not to, she relived those first few times on Jolo. The beatings. The rapes. The degradation of being reduced to something less than human.

Dallas' hand on her arm was meant to steady her. It startled her instead. She flinched involuntarily, scrabbled to the side only to bump run into the bulk of Jones' big body where he flanked her on the other side.

"Easy." Dallas' eyes were pinched with concern as he watched her.

"Sorry. I'm okay," she whispered. Collected herself. Nodded. "I'm okay."

She eased away from Jones, aware of his gaze on her—curious, thoughtful, before it shifted to Dallas. Beside her, Dallas nodded, reassuring Jones that all was well.

"What the hell are they doing out here?" Dallas asked picking up the thread of the conversation. "Looks like a permanent camp."

Amy lifted the NVGs again, realized he was right. A large canvas tarp had been fashioned into a roof for a lean-to, bolstered by a rock wall to the back and supported by wooden posts in the front. Looked like everything from ammo to food to communications equipment, bedrolls and dry firewood were stored there.

The fire pit, five or six feet in diameter, had been built of rocks. Layers of ashes drifted around its base, the sign of many fires. A separate pit, several yards away, was equally well used and equipped with cast-iron cooking pots. Amy could even smell the remains of what was most likely the evening meal. Lines had been strung between conifer trees. Clothing, blankets, even boots hung from the rope, the weight bowing the line almost to the ground.

"Just another band of local banditos," Jones said dryly. "Petty thieves, drug runner types. Scum like Alejandro, bought for little more than the price of the bottle they're passing around."

"Paid for by MC6?" Amy asked, handing the NVGs back to Dallas.

Jones slanted her a look. "Give the lady a Kewpie doll. They're pretty much the only game in town."

"Why'd they move her from the jail? I don't get it."

"They must have found Alejandro's body," Dallas speculated aloud.

"That's the way I figure it," Jones said. "And now they're doubly pissed. First you kill their programmed assassin, then you take out their go-to gun in Buenos Aires—at least, they're figuring it was you."

"My bet," Dallas speculated aloud, "is they aren't only pissed, their starting to sweat a little about now. Have to figure we'll show up here sooner or later. Moving Jenna deeper into their territory moves us deeper into their kill zone."

Jones grunted his agreement. "Where they have to figure sheer numbers are going to play in their favor."

"Can't fault that logic," Amy said fatalistically, and took one last look at the twelve men who were growing increasingly vocal and restless by the fire.

They all looked tough and lean. Hungry lean, mean lean. AKs lay by their sides; some wore vests, their pockets bulging with grenades. Many wore ankle sheaths.

"What we *can* fault is their stupidity." Jones started belly crawling backwards down the slope and away from the campsite. "We've got surprise on our side."

Amy followed Jones with Dallas protecting their flank. They regrouped in a hollow carved out by a cliff face.

"They have no way of knowing that you're aware of the location of the MC6 compound." Jones fished in his pocket for a piece of paper.

"Pardon me for pointing out the obvious," Dallas

said, "but you haven't pinpointed that little piece of information for us yet."

Jones' teeth gleamed white in the moonlight. "All in due time. The point is, they might figure you're coming . . . but we're ahead of the curve. They have no clue that you're already here."

"And I'm betting they're still thinking it's just the two of us," Dallas said.

"They'll connect the dots eventually, but you're right. Two Americanos in uncharted territory wouldn't appear to stand much of a chance against the nice gentlemen with the big guns.

"Got your flashlight?" Jones asked abruptly.

Amy dug it out of her pocket, shined it on the paper Jones spread out on the ground.

He quickly drew a map of the site, marked the location of the twelve men around the fire and Jenna's location to the back and left. "We'll hit them from the knoll, here."

He Xed the spot where they'd just done their recon.

"Figure we can take half of them out before the others even know they've got company. From the outside in, these are my targets," Jones said, slicing an X over the three marks representing the men on the right. "Garrett, you take the three on the left."

"And the rest will fire wild and blind," Dallas said with a nod. "We'll pick them off as they scatter."

"What about Jenna?" Amy was worried. "She could get hit in the crossfire."

"She's smart; she'll find cover. She's also out of our line of fire and we're going to be creating enough havoc the bad guys are going to be too busy covering their asses to worry about her," Dallas assured her.

"Here's where you come in." Jones glanced at Amy. "Keep your head down, but after our initial hits, you hit 'em with your flashlight. Lift it high and start firing wild. With luck you might hit one of them. For certain you'll blind a few and become their prime target, one they won't be able to see. In the meantime, we'll roll left and right. Hit 'em again while they focus on you. Then we'll mop up with these."

Jones handed Dallas two frag grenades, kept two for himself.

"You keep your head down," Dallas said sternly as he fixed the grenades to his belt. "No heroics."

Amy wanted to argue. Tell him she could hold her own in a gunfight and they didn't need to protect her by hiding her behind a berm. But she saw the logic of Jones' plan. They needed a reserve after the initial volley. She could provide it.

"Got it?" Dallas drilled her with a look.

She nodded. "Got it."

"Then let's do this."

CHAPTER SEVENTEEN

Jenna swallowed back bile and contemplated her impending fate. Scarface stood, drew a knife and threatened his loudest contender, who happened to be Rambo and who instantly decided he would wait his turn.

She braced herself and was wondering how many groin kicks she could land before he overpowered her when the night exploded in gunfire.

Scarface spun like he'd been hit broadside with a two-by-four, then dropped like a stone. Two, then three, then five other men fell in rapid succession.

"Jesus. Holy Jesus," she whispered under her breath and scrambled toward the biggest damn rock she could find. She'd heard and seen enough weaponry fired in Iraq to recognize the sound and muzzle flash from small-arms fire. Had figured out enough about these yahoos to understand there was little honor among thieves and wondered who in the hell hated them more than she did.

She heard a man scream. Another roar, then felt the concussion of an explosion that set her teeth rattling.

A ball of fire lit up the sky and she chanced a peek over her rock to see debris fly out of a crater where the campfire used to be.

"Holy shit!" Whoever these guys were, they meant business. She didn't plan to stick around long enough for introductions.

Clumsily gathering the folds of her tattered skirt together with her bound wrists, she crab-crawled at warp speed toward the lean-to. Found a heavy iron frying pan—*they couldn't have left one lousy gun?*—and crept behind a big conifer.

She hadn't any more than reached the thick trunk of the tree when a silence as loud as the gunfire crashed down like a bomb.

She closed her eyes, held her breath and listened.

"Jenna?"

Her eyes flew open.

"Jenna?" Louder this time. And sounding a helluva lot like Amy Walker.

Very slowly, she peeked around the tree trunk. Saw a slim, petite figure, flanked by two very large, very dangerous-looking soldier of fortune types picking their way through the bodies and the rubble.

"Amy?"

Oh, God. It *was* Amy.

"Get away from her," Jenna ordered, stepping out from behind the conifer, wielding the iron pan like a club.

Both men stopped. Glanced at her. Glanced at each other over Amy's head.

"What?" The biggest one grunted out a surly laugh. "Or you'll soufflé us?"

Okay. She was definitely going after him first.

"Jenna." Amy stepped forward. "It's okay. They're with me."

"Oh, Jesus. Oh, thank you, Jesus." Battling tears of relief, she started toward Amy at a trot.

She hadn't gotten five yards when a hand snagged her ankle. She skidded to a stop. Looked down to see Rambo, his face covered in blood, struggle to a sitting position.

Ten yards away, the rattle of automatic weapons told her both of the men with Amy had the lowlife in their sights.

"No," she said, "this one's mine."

She drew back the iron skillet and swung it at Rambo's head with a megaton of adrenaline fueling the blow.

She connected with a bone-crunching thud. The recoil shimmied up her hands to her wrists and rode all the way up her arms as Rambo dropped like the bag of dirt he was.

"Paybacks are hell," she said, a dizzying mix of vindication, agitation and delayed terror ricocheting through her blood.

Still wobbling from the recoil, she lifted her head high and sneered at the big guy. "Soufflé that, badass."

Then she ruined her big moment by bursting into tears.

• • •

Where are we going?"

Gabe pressed hard on the accelerator of the Suburban as they tore down the dark road. He glanced in the rearview mirror. Scowled at the woman with the wild tangle of red hair, nonstop questions and smart mouth.

He didn't like her by reputation, didn't like her on sight, resented her for being a party to Alvaro's death. And her snide "badass" remark had royally pissed him off.

"For a woman who was about to be passed around like a bong at an orgy, I'm sensing certain lack of appreciation."

As they'd hotfooted it back to the Suburban in the dark, there had barely been time for introductions, so it wasn't like she'd had a chance to fall all over them with gratitude, but a thank you would have done nicely.

Green eyes glared back at him. "Pardon me for the oversight. I tend to forget my manners when I'm terrified out of my mind and surrounded by blood and gore."

"Yeah, well, that's what you get for poking your nose around where it doesn't belong."

"Anyone ever tell you you've got a nasty disposition?"

He grunted. "Many have tried."

"Yeah, well try this." She shot him the finger.

"Whoa. Whoa. Wait." Amy's voice rose above the spit of gravel hitting the undercarriage of the Suburban. Stunned confusion colored her words. "What is it with you two?"

"I don't like him," Jenna announced baldly.

"Yeah. We got that part. Just settle down. Both of you. Give the adrenaline a chance to let down. We're all a little rattled. All on the same side here."

"Which made me think I might be entitled to know where we're going," Jenna grumbled with another sour look that Gabe caught in the rearview mirror.

"Someplace safe," he said grudgingly. "That's all you need to know. Deal with it."

That finally shut her up. About damn time, too. So why he felt like a bully and a brute when she dragged her hair back from her bruised face with a breath as weary and weighty as a broken dream, he didn't know. Just like he didn't know why he felt an uncharacteristic tug of sympathy when she lifted a hand and gingerly wiped a trickle of blood from her swollen lip.

"There's a first aid kit in the back," he said to no one in particular and concentrated on driving.

He had more pressing things to do than bicker with Jenna McMillan. Better things to do than think about her or to wonder how bad she was hurting. Or to get pissed all over again by the look Garrett was giving him from the front passenger seat. A look full of speculation. Kind of like the look Gabe had given Garrett when he'd figured out the way it was between him and Amy.

Hell. Garrett was so far off center he hadn't even hit the corners of the paper target. Gabe could give a rip about the reporter.

And the sooner he got her out of the hot zone and out of his hair, the better he'd like it. Problem was, that wasn't going to happen any time soon.

He glanced in the rearview mirror again. She had a face on her. He'd give her that, he admitted grudgingly. Classic. Regal. Intelligent. Even bruised and swollen, her lips made a nice statement—until she opened them. Closed and silent, they spoke volumes about what they could do to a man on a hot night and cool sheets.

He dragged his attention back to the road. Cursed himself for a fool. He'd been black ops for too long, that was all. Too many months on his own with nothing but his guilt and thirst for revenge to fuel his thoughts. Rule his actions.

Angelina.

He was thinking about her way too much these days.

Jenna McMillan was nothing like Angelina, who was pure and sweet and heroic. And dead.

Even thinking Jenna McMillan's name in the same breath was an insult and an abomination to Angelina's memory.

A memory he fought every day to forget.

Dallas figured they'd traveled about fifty miles before Jones slowed and turned right onto a road that was little better than a cattle trail. Cloud cover had moved in heavy and low, obscuring the moon, threatening rain. It made it difficult to see anything. A quarter of a mile or so down into a valley, however, Dallas made out the black silhouette of a small building dead ahead.

A barn, he realized when Jones pulled up in front of it. Without a word, Dallas got out and opened the double doors. Jones drove the Suburban inside, cut the motor.

Dallas closed up behind them, then walked back to the Suburban. Jones was already out from behind the driver's seat and opening the rear cargo door. He dug around and came up with a camping lantern and struck a match.

The interior of the small building was washed in soft light—enough to see Amy and Jenna's faces as they emerged from the backseat.

Shock. Both of them were feeling the aftereffects of the assault. He recognized the look in their eyes. The thousand-mile stare. They were caught somewhere between now and then and fighting like hell to make a permanent swing to the now.

"Don't think about it," he said.

Two pair of soft eyes lifted to his.

"Don't think about it," he repeated. "It's done. It was necessary."

Amy nodded. Jenna stared.

Jones came around from the back of the Suburban with an open bottle of beer. He shoved it in Jenna's hand.

"Drink," he said.

Dallas waited for the blowback. But she surprised him. She didn't argue. She drank. And then she drank some more.

"How long since you've eaten?" Dallas asked Jenna.

That got a reaction. "Like I could eat after that bloodbath? I am so not hungry."

No, he didn't suppose she was. But that was beside the point. He glanced at Amy.

She understood. They all needed fuel. "I'll see what's left in the cooler."

He stopped her with a hand on her arm. Studied her face. The smudges of dirt on her cheek, the halo of blond hair, the resolute determination in her eyes to soldier on.

He would hurt for her, for her loss of innocence if it hadn't been taken from her long before now. But regret would do no one any good on this night.

"You were okay out there," he said with a nod. "You were really okay."

She nodded. Seemed like she was about to ask him something, then shook her head and turned away.

He caught her arm, turned her toward him. "No," he said, answering her unasked question. "You never get used to it. You just deal with it."

He squeezed her arm, touched his other hand to her hair. "You just deal with it."

She nodded again, gave him a tight smile and he let her go.

Yeah, you just deal with it, Dallas thought as another barrage of memories assaulted him like a blast of C4. He'd fought his own demons all the way here . . . as he suspected Jones fought his. He didn't care how hard a man was. There was nothing noble about killing. There was simply necessity.

• • •

Jenna glanced toward the men. They were standing in the shadows by the back of the Suburban, talking in low tones. Jones pulled out a radio phone of some sort and Garrett looked on as Jones waited for a connection.

Whoever he was calling was super-secret, of course, Jenna thought in disgust. Macho jerk. Well, not a total jerk. A little while ago the badass had handed her a packet of wet wipes so she could clean herself up a little. He'd even tossed her a clean brown t-shirt and a pair of pants. Both hung on her, but it was better than her torn skirt.

A little later, he'd pulled a blanket out of the back of the vehicle. Amy had used it to make a little nest in a corner of the small barn. She'd tugged Jenna down beside her and insisted they both eat while Amy filled her in.

"Oh, my God," Jenna said, her mind reeling over what Amy told her about being run off the road in New York right after they had talked. About killing the man who'd been sent to kill her. About Alvaro's no-show in Buenos Aires two nights ago. And how Jones had implied that Alvaro was dead.

"Oh, my God," she said again, her voice full of pain and regret. "He . . . Alvaro. He was a cool guy. Man. So, that's why he didn't show up to meet me that night. And why I ended up tossed into the back of a van instead."

Jenna thought back to those long terrifying hours while they'd driven her across country then parked her in that horrible jail. Fiery images of the bloody assault back at the bad guys' camp flashed before her eyes like a surreal dream.

She forced herself to eat another bite of the sandwich Amy had given her. She couldn't absorb, much less process, all of this.

"So," she said, needing a diversion, "are there more back home like him?"

Amy glanced at her, then followed Jenna's gaze to Dallas Garrett. His dark good looks were striking. His bearing and the way he handled himself, confident and capable.

So unlike Jones, who, Jenna had decided, was a very short step up from Neanderthal.

Amy turned back to peeling an orange. "Two more. But they're both taken. Sorry."

Jenna studied Amy's face. "And what about Dallas? He taken too?"

Amy didn't look up from her orange. After a long moment, she nodded. "Yeah. I think maybe he is."

Jenna had figured that was the way of it. She'd seen the way Garrett looked at Amy. The way he always seemed to know exactly where she was.

"And Jones?" Jenna asked, not because she was interested in the man, but she was curious. "Where does he come in?"

"Dallas says he's CIA . . . or was CIA . . . or could maybe be a contractor working, loosely, for the CIA. Whatever he is, whoever he works for, the man has connections. He's the one who found you, flew us here and led the assault on the jail, then got the information about where they'd taken you out of the jailer."

Jenna rubbed her head, gingerly explored the knot on her temple. "This is . . . it's all so crazy. And Jones . . . he doesn't strike me as the benevolent type. Why is he helping you?"

Amy chewed on a section of orange, thoughtful. "Two reasons. Alvaro was one of his men. I think they might have been close. As close as men in this line of work can be, anyway."

"That would explain why Jones is so pissed at me," Jenna said, understanding. "He feels I'm responsible for Alvaro's death. Can't say as I blame him."

"Hey. You're not the bad guy here," Amy reminded her.

No. She wasn't the bad guy. But a good man was dead because of her. She couldn't think about that now either. "You said two reasons."

Amy nodded. "Yeah. Jones isn't happy about me being here, either, searching for my grandfather. He tried to convince me to go back to the States. Told me he'd find you, get you to safety. When he realized I wasn't budging until I found both you and my grandfather, he didn't have much choice but to help me. Seems he had some ongoing operation regarding MC6, and if he let me loose I would mess up whatever plans he had in place."

"MC6? Oh, God. That explains so much. Remember, when I called you, I told you I'd found something to corroborate rumors of a new generation of SS operational here? MC6 was the name that kept popping up."

"It's also the reason you were abducted." Amy

smiled tightly. "And that's my fault for asking you to help me. You were getting too close. Even though Jones had sent Alvaro to intercept you."

"Okay—shoe on the other foot time. *You* are not the bad guy here either. With or without you, I'd have been here, Amy. Are you kidding me? A group of rogue SS scientists still carrying on their horrible mind-control testing and research? Amy, it's the story of the century."

"Not yet, it's not. Apparently the local government is aware of the organization. Per Jones, there's a lot of hush money exchanged to insure anonymity."

"Which is why I was kidnapped. To shut me up," Jenna concluded. "What I don't get is why they didn't just kill me."

"Dallas and Jones both think they were planning on using you for bait."

"Bait?"

"To get to me. If they didn't find me first, they counted on me coming after you."

"And the reason they want to kill you . . ."

"Because I know too much about my grandfather. And, they have to assume that since I came down here, I know too much about MC6."

"So if Jones is CIA or something, why isn't the U.S. government all over these guys?" Jenna asked. "If they're aware of what MC6 is doing, why not just bring them down?"

"For the same reason they didn't take out Bin Laden when they had the chance years ago," Jones said, stepping in front of the lantern and blocking the light.

His shadow loomed large over them, dark, dangerous, deadly. "It's a little matter of chain of command, of the repercussions and the fallout if it gets out who's behind any takedown."

"You and I both know that's bullshit," Jenna shot back, weary of the man's need to show dominance and superiority. "The CIA is behind any number of 'takedowns' . . . many that have led to the downfall of small dictatorships and have derailed hundreds of terrorists plots."

"And you can prove this?" he said, shooting her challenging look.

"Hell no. Isn't that the point? Isn't that the way the *Company* operates? They get in, get out, get the job done and, like a ship at sail, they leave no trail," she countered sarcastically. "Why is this different? Why aren't they taking out MC6?"

"Maybe because ultra left-wing liberals like you do everything you can to expose covert activities and undermine the safety of good men—not to mention the security of your own country."

She laughed. "More bullshit. I'm a journalist, Jones. I'm neither liberal nor conservative. I seek and find the truth. That's all I'm doing here."

"No. What you're doing here is fucking things up. Your little search for the truth has compromised five years of groundwork and jeopardized a mission to put these sick bastards out of business."

CHAPTER EIGHTEEN

Gabe was pissed. And he felt mean with it. He didn't care. Didn't care about the stricken look on Jenna McMillan's face, either. She deserved the dressing-down.

Hell. She couldn't have known what she'd stumbled into, he knew that. It didn't, however, make it any easier to deal with the fact that the moment he'd committed to springing her out of that jail, he'd had to make one of the most difficult decisions of his life.

"So," she said, facing him down with an impressive amount of guts, "you *were* planning on taking them down."

He clapped his hands in mock applause. "You're quick, I'll give you that."

She shot to her feet—wobbled a little, then righted her, shoving his hand away when he would have steadied her. "You know, I've had it up to here with your crap. You think that I'd knowingly put an operation in jeopardy?"

He grunted. Made quote marks with his fingers. "*Reporter.*"

"Okay, guys." Amy rose to her feet beside Jenna. The voice of reason, again. "This isn't doing anyone any good. The question is, where do we go from here? What happens now?"

Gabe stared at the wild redhead, got back as good as he gave, then finally broke eye contact. Butting heads with her was a waste of time and energy.

"What happens now is that I've been forced into making a decision I didn't want to make just yet."

"What decision?" Amy asked.

Jones glanced at Garrett, who was leaning a hip against the side panel of the Suburban, watching Amy.

"To either pull the mission or accelerate the timetable."

"And what are you going to do?"

Again, Gabe hesitated. Heaved a deep breath. "It's already done. Once they find the remains of their rape and pillage squad, they'll know we're here, and we lose the element of surprise. That means we have to move tonight, or they might close up shop and disappear."

He glared at Jenna. "And it's on your head if I lose any more men."

Jones stalked back to the Suburban and started digging around in the glove compartment.

"How can he pull this together tonight?" Amy asked Dallas.

Dallas searched her face, looking for signs that the strain was getting to her. She looked concerned but steady. "Because the assault was in the works, like he said. A plan in place. He's simply bumped up the timetable. Already called in some of his men. We roll at three A.M."

"It's going to take them that long to get here?" Jenna rubbed her arms as if she were cold in this warm Argentina summer night.

"Has to do with biorhythms. The bad guys will be at their lowest at that hour. Their reaction time will be slower."

"And this is different for the good guys, how?" Jenna asked, incredulous.

"It's different because we'll be in the driver's seat. We know the assault is coming down because we staged it. And again, hopefully we'll have the element of surprise."

"Assault?" Jenna again, her eyes growing wider by the minute.

"Unless you'd prefer to just walk up and knock on the door and ask them pretty please to surrender?" Jones said from the shadows.

Dallas let go of a weary breath. Jones had a real hard-on for Jenna. And maybe that was the problem. He *literally* had a hard-on for her, and the only way he knew how to combat it was to snipe like the guerilla fighter he was.

"For chrissake," Dallas grumbled. "You two think maybe you can bury the hatchet for the duration? We've got enough hostile action ahead to keep you both busy."

Jones looked stubborn. Jenna looked pissed. Status quo.

"Fine." Jones cut a dark look at Jenna as he walked back toward her. "But let's get something clear up front. Believe me when I say that if I could, I'd evac you out of here before you could say news-flash. But I don't have the time or the extra re-sources to arrange that before this comes down. And I can't leave you behind," he added grudg-ingly. "That means you do exactly what I say, no ar-gument, no hesitation, no smart-ass cracks. Are we straight on that?"

Jenna crossed her arms over her breasts. "As an arrow."

Dallas breathed a small sigh of relief.

The tension in the barn was as tight as miser's wallet. Jenna's acquiescence went a long way toward easing the strain.

But Jones wasn't finished yet. "And if you have a shred of decency in you, when this is over and *if* we're still alive, when you write your little news story, you will not know who was behind the mis-sion, you got that? If you even hint, 'wink wink' that there was any U.S. involvement taking MC6 down, you will have personally signed death warrants for me and my men. Not to mention you'll be the reason for a Capitol Hill investigation the likes of which will make Contragate look like a nursery rhyme and up the national debt by another billion or so."

The tension ratcheted back up about ten twists as Jenna stared him down.

"A group of heroic local citizens took the law into

their own hands and righted a very big wrong," she said finally.

Jones studied her face then gave her a nod. It was the closest thing she was going to get to a thank you.

She shrugged as if to say, *whatever.*

Dallas heaved another breath of relief. Another disaster averted. Now if they just managed to live until dawn.

Without another word on the matter, Jones laid it all out for them.

"MC6 has been operating under the cover of an *estancia*—a cattle ranch," he clarified when Amy frowned, "for over fifty years."

He crouched down, spread a map out on the floor of the barn and circled the area with a pen. "It's a huge spread. Over twelve thousand acres of mountains, lakes, rivers and pastureland."

"A perfect cover," Amy put in.

"Yeah," Jones agreed. "For all intents and purposes it walks like, talks like, and moos like a working ranch. But it's all cover for what goes on belowground."

To the map, he added a diagram and several overhead aerial photographs of the inner compound, proof that the place had been under surveillance for some time.

"Here." He pointed to what appeared to be a barn or shed of some sort. "Carved out below this building is a cement block bunker. An underground lab— read: torture chamber. Woodpecker grids—"

"I'm sorry, what?" Amy asked.

"Hot-wired metal cages," Jones clarified. "Just one

of their many methods to break down the mind and create alter personalities that can be programmed to do their bidding.

"You need to be prepared to see some pretty bad shit," he added. "They'll have them floating in water tanks, locked in 'death coffins' to simulate being buried alive, hanging upside down, or locked in boxes with spiders and snakes."

"Oh, God." Jenna looked sick. "I've read about this . . . always with skepticism."

"You'll be a believer by the time this night is over," Jones said. "What they do to people here is as real as it gets."

"Where, in God's name, do they find their victims?"

Jones rolled a shoulder. "In parts of the Patagonia, a 'subject' can be bought for little of nothing. A child just disappears."

"Like the children disappeared during the Dirty Wars," Dallas concluded, thinking back to the women in the white scarves protesting at the palace in Buenos Aires.

"Yeah, like that."

"How do you know all this with such certainty?" Jenna asked.

Jones was silent for a long moment. "MC6 has been on the radar for years. But it wasn't until we managed to slip one of our own inside in the guise of household help a little over a year ago that we were able to establish anything concrete."

Dallas nodded toward the diagrams. "He provided this intel?"

Again, Jones was silent. "She," he finally said in a rough voice. "She provided the intel."

"Is she still inside?" Amy was so absorbed in memorizing the layout of the compound that she missed the change in Jones. Jenna, Dallas noted, had caught it. She was looking at him, a curiously soft expression on her face.

"No," Jones said after a long moment. "She's not inside. She's not anywhere."

Dallas watched Jones carefully. Whoever she was, it was clear that she wasn't only an operative to Jones. Her loss had been personal. Very personal. And it explained a lot about the man.

"Separate from the experimentation section," Jones continued, getting himself back together, "there's a confinement facility for the victims. I suspect we'll find the majority of them locked in there for the night."

Dallas spent a few moments studying the layout. "What kind of resistance are we going to meet?"

"Some of the head honchos live on site at the compound—three at the most—but most commute from El Bolson and the surrounding area. Remember, they've dug in here, have become a part of the landscape. No different from any other citizens."

"Except that they're monsters."

Jones glanced up at Jenna. "Yeah. Except for that." He turned back to Dallas. "I don't expect much in the way of resistance from the head guys. They'll rely on their hired muscle to hold us off."

"A security team?" Dallas asked.

"Thirty men on sight. A collection of misfits," Jones said. "They may or may not have the skills to defend the place."

"Know the type," Dallas put in. "Hired more on their loyalty—in the form of paychecks—than for their fighting skills."

"Right. We managed to place another operative inside on the security team a few months ago. He reports that their training is irregular, and since they don't get much action, their skills are pretty dull."

"So it goes something like, hey, no one even knows MC6 exists. No one has ever attacked. So what's the danger?" Dallas speculated.

"Right again. Remember, this encampment has been running since the early 1950's when the former SS scientists and doctors regrouped and slowly began building their organization. So the *estancia* appears as harmless as a family or corporate-run business."

"Which," Dallas said, rubbing his chin, "makes any overt security risky for the bad guys."

Jones nodded. "Also, from a business perspective, the security people really don't contribute to the bottom line. They're a necessary evil and an unwanted expense. So they hire the local riffraff instead of professionals because why should they pay fifty people a thousand dollars a day when they could half the number and pay them a hundred dollars a day? That's still a decent wage for this area and there's a limitless supply of hotheads ready to fill the bill."

"What kind of firepower are we looking at?" Dallas asked.

"A rotating two-man guard unit patrols the perimeters of the inner compound. One carries a holstered pistol, the other a slinged submachine gun. Other than that it's pretty much small arms, a few AKs—not much more unless they've got something stowed away, but our man inside hasn't found anything.

"Here's the other thing," Jones continued. "In this hot, humid environment, firearms need constant maintenance. Without a strong command staff hovering over them—which there isn't—I'm figuring they've let their equipment go."

"Based on what we found at the camp, the bulk of them probably spend their off-hours drinking," Dallas speculated.

"Roger that. And our man reports that the leader of the pack keeps himself away from the 'hired help.' Sees himself as a middle-management type and doesn't really have much security operations training. He talks the talk, but the men are aware that he can't walk the walk, so there's not much respect for him or his orders."

"Which," Dallas said with a nod, "should translate to a major breakdown in perimeter and interior defense once we're inside."

Jones nodded again, then pointed to the diagram. "The interior compound is about three-by-five square acres. Helicopter pad complete with a jazzy little Bell 206B-3. Armory's here. Barracks here. In the center is the ranch house slash corporate office for the operation."

Dallas studied the aerial photograph. "Even given their low profile and knowing they can't be overtly obvious so as not to create suspicion to the general populace, it seems to me there should be some sort of guard stations, surveillance cameras, towers, fences, etc., around the nucleus of the compound."

"Guard station here," Jones pointed out, "and here. Cameras mounted here and here. Four in all. We take them out first."

"Looks like they've clear-cut around the main buildings."

"But they don't keep it up well. Fence lines here." Jones located it for Dallas on a photo. "The wires are sensored, but in this area, with rain and animals around, there're bound to be a lot of false alarms. I figure they've grown lax. Breaching the inner compound shouldn't be much of a challenge."

He stopped abruptly, checked his watch. Glanced at Amy, then Jenna. "You two should get a little rest. We're looking at staging in less than three hours."

"And what about you?" Amy asked.

"Garrett and I have a little strategizing to do."

"I'm in on this," Amy said in a voice that both challenged and warned.

Dallas looked away, worked his jaw. He didn't want to think about what could happen to her, realized that to keep his head in the game, *he* couldn't think about it.

"We'll fill you in on the assault plan when we get it nailed down," Jones assured her.

"Go ahead," Dallas told her with a nod. "Sleep. It's the best thing you can do for everyone right now."

Dallas knew she wanted to argue. But she didn't. Evidently she'd decided to save her fighting for the bad guys.

CHAPTER NINETEEN

An hour later, Amy was still awake. Beside her, Jenna slept. That was good, Amy thought. After all she'd been through, it was a wonder she hadn't passed out from fatigue and terror.

But Amy knew from the most brutal personal experience that the mind and body were capable of surviving more than she had ever imagined possible. Capable of tolerating unspeakable pain, unforgiving torment.

She was fighting to keep those memories at bay when she felt the blanket tighten on the other side of her.

Dallas.

He lay down on a sigh heavy with fatigue. She turned to him. Studied his profile. The weariness on his face. The small lines around his eyes. The hard set of his jaw, tense, even as he closed his eyes.

"Why are you awake?" he whispered, never looking at her.

"Keyed up," she said, and moved into him when

he lifted his arm, inviting her to snuggle up against him.

"Yeah. Lot of that going around."

He ran his hand up and down her back, a methodical, unconscious motion. A comfort. A source of composure.

He was quiet for a long while, and when he spoke, his question came out of the blue. "So, what is it that you do when you're not being chased by or are chasing bad guys?"

Dallas' question threw her, until she realized how little they really knew about each other. And until it dawned on her that he was trying to take her mind off what lay ahead of them.

Or maybe he wanted to escape it for a little while himself.

Whatever his reason, she went with it. "I was a counselor in a group home for developmentally disabled children."

"Really?" He sounded surprised. May even a little approving. "Why? I mean, what made you decide on that course?"

"I wanted to give back, I guess. I know everyone hears horror stories about foster homes and the social services system, but I was lucky. The homes I was placed in were, for the most part, wonderful. And the older I got I realized just how lucky I'd been. I still keep in touch with some of my foster parents. Well, I used to."

Before Jolo.

"Mom was permanently institutionalized by the time I graduated high school," she went on, not wanting to get bogged down in that memory again. "When I visited her at the facility, there was a children's wing. I used to spend a little time with them, too, you know? They were kids. They were lonely."

"Like you were lonely," he said, his hand keeping up a comforting rhythm up and down her back.

"I suppose you could draw some parallels, but in truth, there were few. Anyway," she snuggled closer, loving the feel of him warm and strong beside her, "I realized I wanted to contribute . . . I don't know. Something. So I majored in social work in college and gradually settled on developmental disabilities. Specifically children."

"Think you'll go back to it?"

"Yeah," she said, realizing that's exactly what she wanted to do. "I will. Anyway, I'd like to. It's been a while. Over a year now, but there's always a need. I'm sure I can find a position."

He was quiet for a time. "Where did you go? Six months ago when you left. Where did you go?"

She lifted up on an elbow, searched his face. It gave away nothing as he lay on his back, eyes closed, resting. "I really am sorry about leaving the way I did," she said, knowing his carefully blank expression masked any number of emotions, anger and disappointment most surely among them.

He squeezed her arm and urged her back down beside him. "I know."

"I simply laid low for a month. Recovering. When I felt strong enough, I went to see my mother. Because I didn't know if I was still a target, I took a lot of precautions."

"The disguises."

"Yeah. The disguises. The fake IDs. One thing you
can always count on in a place like Winter Haven is
vacant staff positions. I checked and they needed a
nurse's aid. I applied for the job, started immediately,
and managed to keep close to Mom and hide at the
same time."

"Does she . . . does she know you?"

"Sometimes. Rarely," Amy confessed. "She has
brief, unexpected moments of lucidity. Those are the
special times."

Rain lightly peppered the roof of the barn as they
lay there, her thinking her thoughts, Dallas absorbed
in his.

"I'm so sorry I dragged you into this," she whispered, pressing her face against his chest and absorb-
ing the heat and the scent and the strength of him.

"I thought we'd gotten past that."

Maybe he had, but she hadn't. If anything happened to him—she shivered just thinking about it. She
touched her fingers to his chest, felt the beat, beat,
beat of his heart beneath her palm. He was strong. He
was capable. He was the reason she'd gotten this far.

"What if he's not there?" It was the question that
had been haunting her since the beginning. What if,
after all of this, her grandfather wasn't there?

"He's there."

She lifted her head. Met his eyes in the dim light
as her heart pumped several hard beats.

"Jones' man inside confirmed it a few minutes ago.
Your grandfather, his second-in-command, Erich

Alder, and a witch doctor by the name of Henry Fleischer. They're all inside the compound."

Amy eased her head back down on his shoulder as relief twisted into satisfaction, satisfaction into edgy anticipation. It was actually going to happen. She was going to confront her grandfather. Her heart pounded weighty and hard and irregular with the prospect of being this close.

"I've seen what hate can do to a person," Dallas said after a long moment. He turned his head, pressed his lips against her hair. "You've got reason for a huge hate. No denying that. But I've seen the need for revenge take over. Watched it change people."

She *was* changed. She'd been changed by so many events. "The need for revenge didn't change me," she said, hoping he would understand. "What he had done to me on Jolo—that changed me. What he did to my mother—the torture, the abuse—that changed me. He took everything from her. She never had a chance for a normal life. He's a monster, Dallas. A madman who has victimized God only knows how many others. Ruined their lives. And for what?

"What should happen to a monster like that?" she continued into a silence of night sounds and beating hearts. "He needs to pay. And who but me can make him? The U.S. government can't touch him. Not down here. He would never pay at all if we weren't here to make it happen."

More silence. More deep, heavy breaths in the dark. "It doesn't have to be you," he said, making it clear that he was offering to handle it for her. To take the blood off her hands and place it on his.

Love for him expanded to deeper, richer levels. "Thank you. Thank you for that. But it *does* have to be me. And he needs to know it's me. He needs to understand that he didn't win. That right wins out over wrong, that good trumps evil every time."

Dallas wrapped his other arm around her. Drew her close. Accepted.

"Sleep now," he whispered. "Just for an hour. You need to sleep."

Yeah. She needed to sleep. What lay ahead for her would take every ounce of strength she possessed.

2:15 a.m. Dallas shrugged into an assault vest, zipped it up and methodically filled the ammo pouches. He glanced at Amy, standing beside him. Awake and clear eyed. Silent, deep in thought, as she, too, geared up.

Jesus. He'd never get used to seeing her like this. Like a mini Amazon warrior, out to save the world. Or at least this little corner of it.

And he'd never get used to the crazy wild beat of his heart when he thought about anything happening to her. A hundred times in the past two days he'd wanted to reason with her, make her see the logic of staying out of the thick of things. A hundred times, he'd backed off. And it ended up that she was the one to make him see the light.

She was right. She was entitled. And unless her life hung in the balance and he had to intervene, she would be the one to see this through.

So there wasn't a damn thing he could do to keep her safe short of tying her up and locking her away somewhere. And he wouldn't do that to her. As she'd pointed out, this was her fight. Her call. He just wished to hell . . . well, there wasn't any room for wishes.

Rain plinked on the tin roof of the barn. Soft and steady. Almost calming. No fitting prelude to the chaos and battle to come.

He had to quit thinking about Amy and the way she made him want to reevaluate his feelings about commitment in general and relationships specifically. About why, exactly, he'd had tunnel vision most of his life about the need for a neat and tidy marriage to a neat and tidy woman—no baggage, no boogie men, no demons of her own to compete with the demons who rode roughshod over him.

"You actually expect me to shoot that thing?"

Jenna's voice jarred Dallas out of his thoughts. She and Jones were sniping at each other again. Huge surprise.

"What I expect," Jones said, his patience as thin as snakeskin, "is that you know how to fire it if you end up in a position where you need to protect yourself."

"I thought you were going to do that."

"Just pay attention, damn it!"

And so it went.

Dallas tuned them out. The rain had settled in, steady, but light. That was good. The moonless night would provide cover. The rain would already be creating havoc with the sensored wire surrounding the compound's inner perimeter.

"Do we have a plan?" Amy asked, breaking her silence.

Dallas nodded. "As soon as the rest of Jones' boys get here, we'll go over it."

No sooner had he mentioned Jones's men than they heard a vehicle pull up outside.

Silence dropped like a blanket. Jones walked to the door, his M-14 at his shoulder. Dallas backed him up on the other side of the door.

"Y'all havin' a barn dance in there?"

Dallas recognized the voice.

He lowered his rifle. Jones opened the door.

In came cowboy Johnny Duane Reed and his handler, Sam Lang, both of them loaded down with full ALICE packs.

"Howdy, ladies." Reed's grin was as obnoxious as his drawl when he spotted Amy and Jenna. "Nice seein' you again, ma'am," he said with a nod toward Amy.

"Ms. McKenna," he added with another nod as he shrugged out of his pack and settled it on the floor of the barn with a grunt.

"Do I know you?" Jenna asked, her brows pinched.

"No, ma'am, but your reputation proceeds you." Then he winked.

Jesus, Dallas thought, but couldn't quite suppress a grin. The cowboy never quit. He was annoying as hell—yet there was something about him that Dallas couldn't help but like. Maybe it was the way he flaunted all that cowboy swagger in Jones' face because he knew it pissed Jones off. Had to respect a man who was willing to give Jones grief. Took guts.

And a sense of humor, especially since Jones scored zero in the humor department.

The fact that Reed was here, however, told Dallas something else about the man. Jones trusted him to do the job. And that said more than anything else.

Same went for Lang. Dallas pegged him for about his own age—thirty-five. Maybe a few more. The lines on his face spoke of experience. The way he carried himself spoke of confidence, and the way he handled Reed, reining him in just before he hung himself, spoke of intellect.

Lang broke the tension by formally introducing himself and Reed to Dallas, Amy and Jenna.

"How'd they get here so fast?" Amy wanted to know.

"Call it the 'writing on the wall' factor," Jones said. "I sent them ahead last night just in case."

"So, what's the plan?" Lang off-loaded his own pack, ready to get down to business.

Dallas said nothing. He waited for Jones to brief the new arrivals on the assault plan they'd devised.

But Jones deferred to Dallas. "Go ahead."

"Okay," Dallas said, falling easily into the familiar role of team leader. "Basics first. Just to review. They're the bad guys, we're the good guys, and the end result is we're going to blow this hellhole to smithereens.

"Two issues. One: We've got innocent noncombatants on site," he explained. "We need to avoid collateral damage to the bunker that serves as cells and set those people free. Two: Many of these individuals are in various stages of programming. Some won't know up from down. Some may be hostile. So we'll need to keep them under tight supervision until we can evacuate them. I'll get to that later."

Dallas walked to the hood of the Suburban where he and Jones had spread the map, diagrams and photos.

"Here's our infiltration point." He pointed to the north side of the compound. "We'll drive there then proceed on foot and stage from here," he added, identifying an area where the sensored wire fence appeared to be overrun with brush.

"Once here, we'll make any on sight adjustments to the plan, double-check our gear, go over things one final time, and check radios." Most of this he explained for Amy and Jenna's benefit as Jones and his men were no doubt veterans of any type and number of land assaults.

"Our biggest threat will be the security team guarding the compound—which should, for the most part, be asleep."

Jones filled in Lang and Reed—who, as Dallas had suspected, were all business now—regarding the numbers and the weaponry they'd encounter once they breached the compound.

"So," Dallas continued with a nod, "We'll catch 'em with their pants down and take out their barracks first."

"Got just the ticket." Reed and walked to his pack. He unzipped and dug around, emptying the contents on the barn floor. Dallas saw extra batteries for NVGs, a GPS, radios, flares, rope, and wire cutters along with boxes of ammo and extra magazines.

Finally, Reed did some rattling around and came up with an assembled M-60 belt-fed machine gun—not so affectionately referred to as a "pig." The M-60 wasn't exactly what Dallas was hoping to see, but it would do. It had a reputation for jamming, but conversely, it could dump quite a few rounds downrange if they needed distance, and it was generally accurate as hell. In the right hands—and he strongly suspected Reed had the right hands—it would be the key to making this work.

"Your cue," Dallas said to Reed, "will be when you hear the pop of the M-14. That'll be Jones taking out the two guards who will be making rounds on the perimeter. Since we're talking about a total search and destroy, and the bad guys don't have reinforcements on site, don't worry about noise. The biggest challenge will be to not reveal we're there until after we have hit them very hard, taking out as many as we can in that first blow."

"Can do," Reed said.

"Lang—you're with Reed on the barracks assault. Toss in some satchel charges and grenades, then stand back while he cleans up on anything else that's still moving."

Lang nodded.

"Jones and I will back you up and keep an eye on the armory. Here." Dallas pointed to a building directly beside the barracks. "Once the barracks are secure, we take the armory, then for all practical purposes, we'll control the compound. We'll blow it on our way out. When the ordinance starts cooking off, I don't want to be within a mile of the place.

"In the meantime, Jones will peel off, take out the guard towers, and we'll all keep an eye out for any stragglers who escaped the initial bang.

"We good so far?" he asked, scanning the intent faces around him.

Dallas could tell that Amy wanted to say something, but to her credit, she kept her mouth shut. She merely nodded when she met his eyes.

"Okay, next we clear the barracks where the majority of the victims will be under guard."

"How many hostages?" Lang asked.

"Close as we can figure, fifteen to twenty."

"They'll be held in one of two underground bunkers." Dallas located them on the aerial photos. "The one to the east is the laboratory. We figure some of the victims will be held there in various stages of programming. The bunker to the west is the holding cell—most will be there, sleeping.

"Jones' man inside—" He stopped, glanced at Jones for help.

"Raul."

"Raul," Dallas repeated, "arranged to pulled barracks duty tonight. There are three other guards assigned to the prisoners. Raul will be guarding the door."

"He'll have a chemlight tucked in his bandana so you can ID him from the bad guys in the dark through your NVGs," Jones added. "It'd be nice if you didn't shoot him."

"Could I shoot you instead?"

All eyes turned to Jenna, whose gaze was locked on Jones.

"Joke, fellas," she said, then rolled her eyes. "Okay. Fine. A bad joke."

"Raul will make certain the barracks doors are unlocked," Dallas went on before Jones and Jenna could start in on each other again. "Reed and Lang will relieve us at the armory and watch for stragglers, so Jones and I will lead this stage. When Raul hears us outside, he'll toss some flashbangs to disorient the other guards and we'll go in and take them out.

"Here's where you come in." He glanced at Jenna. "Raul and Jones are going to need your help to keep the victims secured and again to help with transpo when the chopper arrives."

"Chopper?" Jenna stood at attention. "Where in the hell are you getting a chopper?"

Jones gave her a look.

"Okay. Fine," Jenna grumbled, reacting to his glare. "That's strictly need to know. Got it."

"It's a decent plan," Lang said, nodding, mulling it over, looking for holes.

"It would be better if we had more forces. But it'll fly if we hit them hard and fast," Dallas pointed out. "If it all goes down as projected, we're talking less than a five-minute time frame to secure."

"So, what are the big boomers for?" Reed asked.

Reed was referring to the blocks of C-4, blasting caps and detonators Jones had asked them to bring.

"This place is going to cease to exist once we get everyone out. Lang, I understand that's your specialty."

Sam Lang briefly studied the aerial photos. "I'll set charges here, here and here," he said pointing to the armory, the lab facilities and the main house slash office building. "Ought to do the trick."

"How much time are we going to have once you set them?" Jones asked.

"How much time do you want? I brought plenty of time fuses."

"Give us five minutes to clear once I give you the go."

Lang nodded.

"Does that do it then?" Reed was on his knees now, gathering hundred round lengths of ammo belts for the M-60.

"For your part," Dallas said. "As soon as the hostages are secured, Amy and I will move on to the main house. We'll deal with the brass in there."

The men exchanged looks but didn't say anything.

"Stay in close radio contact," Jones added. "We'll rally back at the staging point, count heads and get the hell out of Dodge."

"Questions?" Dallas assessed each face, liking what he saw. "Okay, then. Let's do this. Jenna—you're with Jones all the way." He shouldered his M-4. "Amy, you're with me."

"Some guys get all the luck," Reed said with that slow, sly grin and headed for the back of the Suburban.

CHAPTER TWENTY

They packed the ordinance, weapons and commo equipment into the back of the Suburban then passed out bottled water.

Dallas caught Amy's arm just as she was about to slip into the backseat with Jenna.

She looked up at him. True blue eyes. Wholesome face dusted with freckles. A crescent scar on her temple. Tragic. Strong. Beautiful.

He'd thought he'd known what he was going to say to her. *Stay safe. Stay strong. Stay with me.* But what came out instead was, "If anything happens to you—"

She cut him off with the press of her lips to his. "I'll be fine," she whispered against his mouth, then pulled away.

He dragged her back against him, kissed her with a desperation that scared the hell out of him. They were both breathless when he let her go.

"You damn well better be." He gave her one last hard look then got in the Suburban and let her go.

◆ ◆ ◆

Erich hung up the phone, lay back on his pillow. Contemplated the news he'd just received.

Jenna McMillan had been rescued. His men had apparently been ambushed. Worthless bastards couldn't even defend themselves.

He'd expected they'd try something like this. That's why he'd sent someone from security to check on the camp. Yes. He'd expected it. Just not this soon.

How had they gotten here so fast? Found her so fast?

And how the hell many men did it take to find Amy Walker, for God's sake? They should have located her long before she and her guard dog found the reporter.

So what did that mean?

It meant exactly what he had suspected.

He threw back the covers. Walked to the window.

It meant they had inside help. Someone who knew the region. Someone with the method and the means to pull off a rescue right under his nose.

Gabriel Jones. The Archangel lived. And he had his hand in this.

Erich felt his face flush red with rage, his skin crawl as sweat broke out over his body.

Jones was like a goddamn cat burning his way through his nine allotted lives. He was supposed to be dead. He *should* be dead. Right along with his lover, Angelina.

The satisfaction of knowing that he had played a part in destroying the one person the Archangel loved, however, was overshadowed with the certainty that Jones lived. And that he was the one who had led Amy Walker to El Bolson. Presumably he would lead her here. To the MC6 compound.

To expose their operation.

That would not happen. Could not happen. Not on his watch.

Without turning on the lights, he walked into the hall. Down to Reimers' private suite. Woke him. Then he walked down the hall and woke Henry.

"We have an issue," he said five minutes later when they gathered in the library, "And it would appear that we must take measures to deal with it tonight."

Amy wondered how many adrenaline rushes the human nervous system could deal with in a twenty-four-hour period and not shut down.

Many, evidently, because just driving out of the barn and hitting the road had revved hers right off the charts again. Her fingers trembled as she tucked her hair up under a black watch cap. Jones had given one to both her and Jenna. Dallas passed a tube of face paint toward the backseat. Amy smeared it on then handed it to Jenna.

Reed and Lang, in an older model Bronco, traveled along the road behind them. Lights off. Windshield wipers kicking back and forth in a slow, steady *swish, thump, swish, thump*.

Twenty minutes passed, punctuated by a silence that rang with the gravity and the danger of what they were about to do. By the time they crested a hill and turned off the main road to cut across an open stretch of pasture, the tension was as thick and weighty as a lead coffin.

And then they were there.

Jones cut the motor. One by one they peeled out of the vehicle. It took a while for Amy's eyes to adjust to the darkness. She'd have preferred a moon, but Dallas said the rain and cloud cover would work to their advantage as he went down on his knees by the fence they had to breach to get to the interior complex.

"If we set off a sensor," he whispered as he searched for a weakness in the wire, "the guards will most likely chalk it up to the rain. Fortunately for us, this system is old. It probably shorts out a lot."

Both Dallas and Jones wore NVGs—as did Reed and Lang. Amy and Jenna didn't have that advantage; neither did they have the advantage of the firepower the men carried.

In addition to pistols ranging from a Sig to a 1911-A1 and a couple of Glock 30s, all but Jones and Reed carried slick black M-4 automatic rifles with intricate scopes and sights. Jones stuck with his M-14. The belt-fed machine gun had to weigh a ton, but Reed handled it as if it were nothing. Jones, as always, carried his Butterfly. The other three had strapped on KA-BARs.

Jenna refused to carry a weapon, and while Amy understood that it was killing her to rely on Jones, she did as she was told and stuck to him like glue.

Amy watched as the men huddled, consulted quietly. Then broke apart. Apparently the plan stood. It was a go.

Breathing deep to control her heart rate, Amy racked the slide on her Glock to chamber a round. She double-checked her magazine pouch, then eased through the opening in the fence Dallas had made.

One by one they entered the compound as the rain slowly dampened their clothes. With Amy shadowing Dallas and Jenna sticking tight to Jones, they spread out. Crouching low, they scurried across approximately fifty yards of open area then ducked in behind a small building—a storage shed of some sort.

Dallas' eyes were spots of white in a face smeared with dark paint when he lowered the NVGs. He nodded to Jones, who promptly took of at a run, ducking behind a building that Amy was fairly certain was the armory. Jenna stayed close on his heels. At the same time, Reed and his M-60 headed for the building that had been IDed as the security staff barracks. Lang covered his exposed back.

Then they waited.

And waited for seemed like an eternity until finally . . .

Pop. Pop.

Jones' M-14. He'd taken out the guards.

Not five seconds later, the boom of a grenade rocked the silence. Then the rapid-fire staccato of Reed and his machine gun exploded into the night. Lang and Reed were taking the barracks.

Everything seemed to happen at once then. The security lights on the guard posts went out one by one—Jones, again, if Amy remembered right.

"Like white on rice," Dallas ordered with a meaningful look. Only when she nodded did he don his NVGs and move out at a crouching run.

Amy stuck right behind him as the barrage from the M-60 went on and on.

Ducking low, they raced across the wet grass toward the armory, meeting zero resistance. Jones came out of nowhere. Jenna had grabbed his ammo belt and hung on for dear life. He stacked up against the exterior wall of the armory building, pushed Jenna down and out of harm's way.

Then he kept guard while Dallas fired multiple rounds at the lock on the wooden door.

Like a well-oiled machine, they burst inside.

The armory was unmanned.

"Lax," Jones said, referring to security—and then they realized why.

The armory was empty.

Dallas ducked back outside. "What the fuck's going on?"

It was then that Amy noticed the utter quiet.

The M-60 was silent. Which meant that the bulk of the compound security team had been dealt with.

"This is way too easy." Dallas scanned the compound through his NVGs.

Jones nodded. "Roger that."

A whisper came out of the dark. "I thought we wanted it easy."

Jenna. She sounded shaken but in control.

Lang and Reed's sudden appearance at their side had all heads turning.

"I just shot the shit out of a bunch of sandbags," Reed said.

"The barracks were empty," Lang confirmed, then turned to Jones. "And yet you took out two guards, right?"

"Most likely sacrificed for the cause. So they'd suck us in deeper. Which means they knew we were coming," Jones concluded.

Dallas nodded. "They must have discovered the mess we made of their camp. Realized we got Jenna."

"Does this mean they're gone?" Amy felt her heart sink.

Dallas shook his head. "Only one way to find out."

"Keep sharp," Jones said, and with that cryptic advice, they headed for the west bunker that served as sleeping quarters for the victims.

"Jesus." Lang stopped cold when he saw the barracks door.

Jenna sucked in a gasp. Amy closed her eyes, swallowed back her horror.

A man—or what was left of him—was nailed, spread eagle, to the door. He'd been stripped, his throat slit. A swastika had been carved into his chest.

"Raul," Jones said darkly. "They must have made him."

The barracks door burst open.

"Take cover!" Dallas yelled.

He shoved Amy to the ground, lay across her and

started firing from his belly. A sea of men poured out of the west bunker, firing wildly from their hips. Another barrage charged out of the east bunker.

Reed bellied down with the M-60, mowing down the first wave that ran out.

"Go, go, go!" Dallas and Jones herded Amy and Jenna back toward the armory while the M-60 bought enough time for the rest of them to retreat.

"Bastards have pissed me off," Reed snarled, out of breath, as he backed into the open armory door. "They hit me in the face."

Lang grabbed Reed's jaw, turned his face toward him. "It's a just scratch."

"It's just my fucking *face*," Reed sputtered, then winked at Amy. "It needs to look good on a book jacket when I write my memoirs someday."

Amy did what Reed wanted her to. Hugging a wooden floor that smelled of gunpowder and must, ducking bullets, she grinned.

"Don't worry, pretty boy. It'll give you character." Lang sited down the barrel of his M-4 and tagged one of the guards.

"Like he needs to be more of a character," Jones grumbled, unholstered his Sig and beaded in on a bad guy hell-bent on meeting his maker. Jones made it happen with one shot.

"They're joking around," Jenna whispered, incredulous. "Men are dead. Bullets are flying, our takeover has turned sour, and they're making jokes."

"Welcome to the wacky world of black ops," Jones said. "Gallows humor. Get used to it."

"Why did they storm us?" Dallas speculated aloud,

no trace of humor—black or otherwise—in his tone. "I mean, we were going to walk in there. They could have picked us off one by one. Why expose themselves? They had to figure we wouldn't come in shooting because of the hostages."

"Figured they had the numbers?" Lang suggested.

"Stupid?" was Reed's contribution.

"Because someone made them do it," Jones concluded, seeing where Dallas was headed.

"Bingo. The big boys pulling the strings probably had guns at their backs threatening to kill them if they didn't."

"What about the hostages?" Amy asked.

"At this point? Most likely dead," Jones added on a grim note. "From scientific research material to liability in the blink of an eye."

"Jesus." Jenna closed her eyes. "Jesus. What kind of animals are they?"

"The worst kind. Now they're gonna be the dead kind," Jones promised. "What's your kill count, boys?"

Between them they figured they'd taken out close to twenty. "Add the two perimeter guards and that evens out the numbers."

Reed rubbed at the thin stream of blood trickling down his cheek, ducked as another round of gunfire peppered the armory wall. "Unless they brought in reinforcements."

Dallas shook his head. "No time."

"So that leaves half a dozen—give or take—still in the bunkers." Lang fired off another shot. "Make that five, give or take. And the head honchos."

"West or east?" Jones asked, referring to which bunker Reed and Lang wanted to attack.

"I think the son of a bitch that hit me was in the east."

"Guess that's settled. We'll take west." Dallas glanced at Amy then Jenna. "You two stay right where you are.

"Reed, leave the M-60 for them."

Reed did a double take but didn't argue.

"It's heavy," Reed said, giving Amy a quick lesson on how to fire it. "So keep it set up on the bipod and let her rip. Every fifth round is going to be a tracer so just lean on the trigger and point the flashes where you want the bullets to go.

"If it jams," he turned to Jenna, "you're going to need to help feed the rounds in straight." He showed her how.

"You're not a south-paw right?"

Amy shook her head.

"Good, 'cause I wouldn't want the belt feed cover latch digging into your pretty face."

"Are you finished yet?" Jones growled.

"We're good to go. Treat her right, ladies." Reed gave the gun an affectionate pat.

"Watch our backs," Dallas said with a direct look at Amy.

She nodded. "Be careful."

Weapons firing, they ran out into the open.

CHAPTER TWENTY-ONE

They've been gone a long time," Jenna said in a small voice. "And why did it get so quiet?"

Amy had been thinking exactly the same thing. It *was* quiet. And she didn't know if that was a good or a bad thing.

She kept her eyes on the open ground between the armory and the bunkers. Prayed to God she could tell the good guys from the bad guys if anyone charged toward them.

"I don't know. I don't know what's going on."

Just then a lone figure materialized out of the dark.

Amy sighted down the barrel of the M-60. She couldn't make out his face. It was too dark. She was too wired.

She held her breath, finger poised on the trigger.

"Hold fire."

Dallas.

She lowered her head to her shoulder, eased her finger off the trigger. Breathed. Uttered a prayer of thanks.

"What's happening?" Jenna levered herself to her knees beside Amy.

Dallas shook his head. "Nothing but bodies."

Amy felt heart sick. "The hostages?"

"Dead."

"Oh, God. All of them?"

"Every last one. They shot them in their cells."

"What about the lab?"

His face was as grim as grim got. "You don't want to know about the lab."

Reed, Lang and Jones joined them.

"I've been around some seriously bad shit in my life," Reed said. "Seen things, done things. None of it is the stuff of nursery rhymes. But this . . . what they did to those people. It's so fucking sick."

Stunned into silence, Amy was only vaguely aware of Jones talking on a radio, canceling the transport chopper that was on its way to evacuate the victims.

"My grandfather?" she said, lifting her eyes to Dallas.

Again, he shook his head. "No sign of him or anyone else."

"So who made the guards charge us?" Jones speculated aloud. "If the big brass got out before we came, who sent those guys on a suicide run?"

Dallas glanced back at the bunkers. "Double-check the bunkers. Look for a false wall, trap door—something. Blast your way through if you have to. They're here. They have to be here, hiding like rats in a tunnel."

He grabbed the M-60, tossed Reed his M-4. "I'll

cover the rear of both bunkers in case you flush them out."

"I'm coming with you." Amy scrambled to her feet—only to have Dallas drag her down to the floor again when another round of gunfire ripped into the exterior walls of the armory.

"What the hell!" Lang lunged for the floor.

Amy glanced from one man to the other as Reed dropped down beside Lang. "Where's it coming from?"

"The main house." Dallas risked a glance over a blasted out window ledge. "And the west bunker."

Which, Amy realized, meant they were pinned down.

Jones hunkered down in a corner by the door. He held up a hand. "Listen . . . you hear that?"

She couldn't hear anything above the steady barrage of AK-47 fire. At least she didn't think she could, until she picked up a faint whine.

"What is it?"

"A rotor blade revving up." Dallas made another quick check out the window. "Shit. They're firing up the chopper."

Amy had seen the helicopter when they'd passed it on the way to the armory. It was small . . . couldn't hold more than three or four people.

"It's got to be them," she said, desperate to find a way to stop them. "My grandfather . . . the other two. They're getting away."

"Cover me!" Dallas had to yell to be heard above the gunfire.

Rolling to his knees, he grabbed the M-60. Then he shot out the door, running into the crossfire of bullets before Amy realized what he intended to do.

The automatic weapon's fire doubled.

Lang, Jones and Reed all returned fire, aiming at the muzzle flashes, pinning back the shooters' ears to give Dallas a chance to get out of the line of fire.

"Fuck!" Jones yelled and never stopped firing. "He's down."

Fear coiled in Amy's chest like a snake. Dallas had been hit. And it was her fault.

She couldn't think past the fact that he was out there. Hurt. Possibly dead. And she couldn't sit here and not do anything about it.

She bolted to her feet, unholstering her Glock in one fluid motion, and ran out the door.

"Amy. . . . No!!" Jenna's cry trailed after her as she ran out and into the rain storm of bullets, searching for Dallas.

Rage rolled over fear when she spotted him. He was forty yards away, facedown in the damp grass.

Firing as she ran, she raced toward him as bullets whizzed by, one coming so close she felt it kiss her cheek.

When she reached him, she dropped to her knees. "Dallas!"

He lifted his head. "What the fuck?"

Thank you God. Thank you God. He was alive.

Fear for his life rolled over relief. "We've got to get you out of here. Where are you hit?"

"Take cover, damn it!"

"Not without you. Come on."

She crawled to his head, gripped him under his armpits and started pulling, thinking of stories she'd read about adrenaline rushes that allowed small women to pull big cars off of someone they loved.

"Don't let me down now," she prayed to the adrenaline gods.

They didn't. With Dallas digging in his feet and helping her, she managed to drag him the five yards to the cover of an out building and tuck them both out of the line of fire.

"Where are you hit?" she repeated.

"Calf. Forearm." He grimaced in pain. "It's okay. But those bastards are getting away."

She followed his gaze to the helipad where the bird was about to take off.

"No, they aren't." She ran back out in the open for the M-60.

"Jesus, woman!" Dallas roared, lunging for her and missing when she took off.

Divots exploded out of the grass, trailing each footstep as she ran. She ignored the fire. Reached the gun, hefted its cumbersome weight and hauled it back behind the building.

She hunkered down on her stomach, set the gun up on its bipod like Reed had showed her. She glanced at the helicopter. "Can this take it down?"

A grimace of pain tightened Dallas's mouth. "Guess we'll find out." He clutched his arm with one hand, hiked himself up on an elbow so he could help her set up.

"You hit it in the right place, it'll have the flying characteristics of a brick." He inched up beside her where she lay on her belly, fixing the chopper in her sights.

"Start from in front. Work your way back. And lead it when it takes off. It's going to need some forward momentum before it goes vertical."

Amy drew a breath, let it out slowly, remembered what Reed had told her.

Lean on the trigger. Point the tracer flashes where you want to bullets to go.

The chopper lifted, hovered, just as she fired.

The fire flash of rounds hitting metal sparked off the cockpit door.

"Keep firing!" Dallas yelled.

The stock recoiled against her shoulder like a jackhammer. It hurt like hell, but she kept firing.

The chopper rose . . . fifteen feet, twenty . . . and she kept firing. The gun jammed.

Dallas swore, reached around her and ejected the jammed cartridge, hand-fed the belt.

"Go!" he yelled as the chopper rose higher.

Amy leaned on the trigger, tracers flying, cartridges hammering the tail of the craft, which suddenly wobbled, then spun around. The nose dove and the bird started spinning out of control.

"Gawd damn! You hit the Jesus nut!" Dallas yelled, awe in his voice, as they watched the bird lurch and whirl and finally drop like an anvil.

Amy watched the helicopter fall, then crash hard at a thirty-degree angle. The main rotor chopped into the earth like a scythe.

Stunned, she caught her breath, stared at the wreckage. "What's a Jesus nut?" she asked absently.

Dallas laughed. "It's the bolt that holds the tail rotor, dead eye. You take it out and whoever's in that bird is going to see Jesus. Help me up."

With one eye on the downed chopper, Amy stood and helped Dallas to his feet.

"Is it going to explode?" she asked, supporting his weight with his arm slung over her shoulder, all the while searching for movement in the cockpit.

He grunted, shifted his weight to his good leg. "It's possible."

The cockpit door swung open, hung crookedly on one hinge. A man stumbled out.

Amy felt every cell in her body tense. Was it him? Was it her grandfather? There was only one way to find out

Heart kicking like the M-60, she forgot about Dallas. Forgot about anything but heading toward the crippled bird.

"Amy! Stop!" Dallas yelled, catching himself from falling with a hand on the building.

But she didn't stop. She couldn't. She kept going. As Dallas swore and roared and ordered her back.

Five yards were all that separated her from the craft before she slowed down, finally stopped. A man stood in profile, head down, leaning unsteadily against the tail section. An old man. A thin trail of blood ran down the side of his face, dripped off his nose to the ground.

Rain washed down in a steady stream. She brushed

damp hair from her eyes, absently wondered when she'd lost the watch cap. Her complete focus remained on the man by the chopper.

Heart hammering, she squared her shoulders. Called out.

"Edward Walker?"

He didn't respond.

"Aldrick Reimers," she said into the silence punctuated by the sporadic background fire of M-4s and the answer of Ak-47s.

Very slowly, his head came up. He looked at her.

And for the first time she saw his face. Pale. Sunken. Ravaged by time.

Yet she recognized him unmistakably her grandfather.

She'd seen enough photographs.

Stared at them enough times.

Had no doubt.

He squinted through rheumy old eyes. Then shook his head in disgust. "You look just like her."

Amy breathed deep as something cold and hollow slithered through her.

"You bastard." She held his watery gaze. "You cold-blooded, vile excuse for a human being."

Inside she felt a scream of rage build to a roar. So it surprised her that her voice sounded steady, calm.

"She was your daughter. How could you . . . how could you violate her? Destroy her mind. Take away her life?"

Her face was wet. From the rain. From her tears. She'd always thought . . . always thought when she finally found him, confronted him, she would feel nothing but loathing. Nothing but disgust and revulsion and an endless torrent of hatred so huge and strong that no other emotion could break through.

And yet as she stood there, the inescapable truth haunted her.

This is my grandfather.

This is my flesh and blood.

And through the hatred, she felt a loss so acute, so disabling, she could do nothing but stand there, frozen in pain as he shifted then leaned back against the disabled chopper. The hand that had been hidden behind him held a gun.

He lifted it.

Pointed it at her.

"From the first day you came bawling and squalling into the world, you have been nothing but an albatross around my neck."

She closed her eyes. And in that moment, she just wanted it to be over. The pain. The despair. The horrible truth of her life.

She braced herself.

A shot rang out.

She flinched. Waited.

For some sensation.

A jolt.

A burn.

A pain that eclipsed the ache caused by this man who should have loved her.

Then she felt him behind her.

Dallas.

She opened her eyes to see Edward Walker slump and fall to the ground.

Beside her now, Dallas lowered his Sig.

"It's over," he said. "It's over."

She leaned into him. The air hung heavy with the scent of gun powder, rain and a despair so huge it consumed her.

Numb with the weight of it, she watched as the old man breathed his last breath then lay still on the ground. Edward Walker—a monster who had destroyed without remorse, tortured without conscience—was finally dead. Dead. As final as it was, for as long as she lived, Amy knew that for herself, for her mother, for all the tormented souls he'd abused—that it was still way too little justice, carried out with too much mercy, delivered way too late.

Gabe left the clean up to Lang and Reed. It hadn't taken long to rout out the last of the poorly trained security forces and take them out.

He'd seen the chopper drop. Wanted to see for himself if Erich Adler had been on board. Wanted to see the bastard dead.

What he found was Dallas on the ground, Amy leaning over him.

"How bad?" he asked, standing over them.

"Just bad enough to piss me off," Dallas grumbled.

"He needs medical attention," Amy said using her Ka-Bar to slice off a piece of Dallas' shirt sleeve and tie around his upper arm.

Gabe eyed the wound, the blood on Garrett's pant leg. "And you still took it down?"

Dallas grunted. "Not me."

It took a lot to surprise Gabe these days. Amy Walker didn't weigh much more than the M-60. And she'd shot a bird out of the sky with it. He figured her shoulder had to hurt like hell.

"Walker is dead. Go check," Dallas said with a nod toward the wreckage. "See if there's anyone alive."

Jones gave Garrett a long look, decided he was okay and walked toward the downed bird. M-14 in hand, he approached the crash site.

One dead on the ground, Walker. Gabe used his foot to turn him onto his back, confirm that he wasn't breathing.

Silence, but for the ping of the cooling turbo engine and the hiss from a knot of leaking hoses. Smoke curled up from under the motor hood. The stench of fuel and oil, strong and thick, overpowered the scent of loam and rain.

The cockpit door hung open at a cockeyed angle. The interior lights hummed and flickered but still burned. There were two men inside. Both appeared to be dead.

Gabe reached over the man in the passenger seat and pulled back the pilot's head by his hair.

His face was covered in blood, but Gabe recognized him Erich Adler.

Gabe wanted to feel joy in his death. Adler was a monster. A murderer.

But all Gabe felt was hollow. He'd wanted Adler himself. Wanted to make him pay, slowly and painfully. For what he'd done to Angelina. For what the bastard had taken from him.

"You knew him?"

His shoulders tensed when he heard Jenna McMillan's voice close behind him. He collected himself, didn't turn around.

"Yeah. I knew him."

"Bad guy, huh?" Her voice sounded small and uncertain. Not at all like the mouthy reporter he'd grown to know and tolerate.

He nodded. "Very bad guy."

"What . . . what about the other one?"

Gabe pulled back his head. He didn't know him, but he recognized him from the dossier he had on MC6.

"Henry Fleischer. The witch doctor. He had a real penchant for electricity."

Gabe leaned further in to the cockpit, found twin briefcases on the floor. He grabbed them both, handed them back to Jenna.

"Don't lose those," he said. "I have a feeling we're going to want to read what's inside."

He turned then. Saw Amy still kneeling over Garrett. Jenna must have brought her Lang's first aid kit. She was playing doctor like crazy while Garrett grudgingly tolerated all the attention.

"We need to get out of here."

For once Jenna McMillan didn't have a response.

She nodded, looking lost and more than a little shocky as she stood in the rain, soaked to the skin.

Finally, she lifted her face to his. Her cheeks were streaked with rain and face paint. Her hair fell in sodden chunks out the watch cap. Her green eyes were misty. "So much death."

Yeah. So fucking much death.

"Come on," he said, feeling an uncharacteristic twinge of empathy. "Let's go."

CHAPTER TWENTY-TWO

It took both Jones and Amy to help Dallas back to the rally point, even though he insisted all the way that he could walk.

Amy knew different. The wounds weren't deep, but there was muscle damage in his leg. He was bleeding again by the time they reached the Suburban.

Jenna trailed behind, lugging the two briefcases. She was silent. Very silent.

She was strong. She'd be okay. They'd all be okay. Please, God, Amy prayed, working to staunch the blood flow in Dallas' leg, let them all be all right.

"Where are Lang and Reed?" she asked Gabe after they'd carefully settled Dallas sideways into the backseat of the Suburban and propped up his leg.

"Finishing up. We'll wait."

Amy wanted to argue. She wanted to get Dallas to a doctor. But she understood. You didn't leave men who had fought for you.

So they waited.

It wasn't long before they appeared over the hill. Reed carried the M-60 and Lang's rifle. Lang carried something big and bulky over his shoulder.

A body, Amy realized.

Raul. Their man inside.

She hadn't any more than digested the carnage they were leaving behind when a blast rocked the earth beneath her feet. A secondary explosion followed, then a rapid succession of booms split the air. Smoke and flames billowed up and boiled into the sky.

They'd destroyed the compound. The bunkers. The barracks. Even the helicopter. MC6 was gone. Along with it, the men who had made it what it was. A heinous torture chamber for dozens of lost souls. Amy only hoped that somewhere, somehow, the victims knew that someone had cared. Someone had sought and fought for justice.

Dawn burst over the valley in shades of pearl and lavender. The clouds began to break as they drove back to the road in silence. On another day, in another time, Jenna would have marveled at the beauty of the sun's first rays bouncing off the glittering white slopes of the Andes.

Another time, when she wasn't numbed by the carnage she'd seen. By the near-death experience of being pinned down by enemy fire.

She'd covered firefights in Iraq, but always with

full combat gear. And always they'd been minor skir-
mishes and always she'd been on the side with the
numbers and the firepower.

In the thick of the night, in the sights of bad, bad
men, they hadn't had the numbers. They'd had no
advantage at all.

And yet they had won.

She supposed she ought to feel a certain . . . she
didn't know. Concern, maybe. Guilt even that what
happened back there had been an unsanctioned, ille-
gal assault. Vigilante justice, some would call it. Taking the law into their own hands.

And maybe it should bother her that all she felt was
an overwhelming sense of accomplishment. Good had
triumphed over evil.

She glanced at Jones from the passenger seat.
Couldn't quite muster any contempt for him this
morning. He was a hard man doing hard jobs, jobs
few men had the backbone or the nerve to do. He did
his job well. Scary well. Like a machine. On auto pilot. Not once had she seen him falter or swerve from
doing what had to be done.

Yeah. Scary.

Because of him and the others, she was alive. To
tell the story. A story that needed to be told . . . if and
when she found the stomach to relive it.

He stopped the vehicle suddenly, then got out. Jenna
craned her neck to see Lang and Reed's Bronco brake
behind them, only then realizing they were at a fork in
the road.

It wasn't long before Reed poked his gorgeous

face in the window. He grinned at Jenna, then Amy, then at Dallas, who lay with his head on Amy's lap in the backseat. "You take care now, ya hear?"

"You too," Dallas said with a meaningful look. "Thanks."

"Anytime, man. You can watch my six any day." Then Reed was gone and Jones eased back behind the wheel.

Jenna shifted to her hip, looked out the rearview window as they took off, watched the Bronco swing onto the left fork and drive out of sight.

Brave men, she thought again.

"How are you doing?" she asked Dallas, another man who had been willing to lay down his life to right several wrongs.

"I've cut myself worse shaving," he said.

"Yeah, right," Jenna said. His face was pale beneath what was left of his cammo paint. A thin sheen of perspiration covered his brow.

He was hurting. Hurting bad, but it was clear he'd never admit it.

"It's going to be several hours before we can get him medical attention," Jones said with a glance at Amy. "Better start pushing antibiotics."

It proved to be among the longest several hours of Jenna's life. She'd known it was going to be when less than an hour later, Jones pulled the Suburban off the road, then stripped a camouflage netting off of a small, battered plane.

"No," she said, her heart dropping to her knees.

"Yes," Amy said. "Brace yourself."

"There's a little matter of fuel." Dallas lifted his head when he realized where they were.

"Don't worry," Jones said. "The fuel fairies have been here. Reclusive little critters—but they always come through."

Once they got past the takeoff, it was a quiet ride. At least the four of *them* were quiet. The little twin engines coughed and sputtered and the wings shuttered in the wind currents.

Amy couldn't help but grin when Jenna asked Jones about a parachute. Jones had given Jenna the same smile he'd given Amy when she'd asked.

With a sinking "ohmygod," Jenna had buckled her seat belt and closed her eyes. Then Jones had revved the engines to full throttle and plowed down the grass strip.

What seemed like seconds later, they'd been airborne.

"Um. Would you mind letting go of my thigh?" Jones grated out with a glance toward Jenna. "The circulation is starting to go."

Amy grinned when Jenna jerked her hand away like it had been burned. "Sorry."

"Relax," Jones said, and to Amy's surprise, he actually sounded a little sympathetic. Of course he had to ruin it. "I'd have figured a world-famous reporter like you would have flown in any number of risky transports in your time."

"Risky is the operative word," Jenna managed.

"This isn't a risk. It's a piece of shit. A damn death trap."

"There's that gratitude again. I guess I should have let you walk out."

Amy waited for Jenna to fire back another volley. Was surprised, again, when she didn't. She just sucked in a serrated breath and stared straight ahead.

Frankly, Amy could have used the distraction of a little bickering between the two of them. Dallas worried her. He was either sleeping or he'd passed out in the backseat of the Piper beside her. And that damn leg . . .

"He's bleeding again," she told Jones. "How long to Buenos Aires?"

"I have a friend. A doctor," Jones said. "She has a place in Bahia Blanca. Private landing strip. We'll go there. It's not much further."

Amy brushed the hair back from Dallas' face. His forehead felt clammy. His color wasn't good.

"He'll be fine." Jones' unsolicited reassurance surprised her. "He'll be fine," he repeated. "Get some rest. Both of you," he added, including Jenna in the suggestion.

He was right. Amy was exhausted. Jenna had to be too. Of course, Jones couldn't be in much better shape. But he looked confident and strong in the pilot seat.

Amy closed her eyes. Decided not to fight it.

Worry about the things you can do something about.

It was an axiom one of her foster mothers had lived by. *Worrying over something out of your control defeats you. Accept the things you can't change. Change the things you can.*

She couldn't change the fact that Dallas was hurt. Couldn't change the fact that they were airborne in this flying death trap. Couldn't change the outcome of the landing.

So she let go. Gave in to the pull of exhaustion— only to come wide awake what seemed like moments later when the wheels of the Piper touched the ground.

"Wow. That was fast."

"You slept," Jenna said. "For about an hour."

Another surprise.

An even bigger one awaited them when the plane taxied to a standstill.

They'd landed on a long carpet of green. To their right, a cliff face dropped a good fifty feet straight down to the pounding surf of the big blue water of the South Atlantic, sparkling like a jewel in the mid-morning sun.

To their left, a huge house— European in design with gothic arches, ornate gabled windows and expansive covered porticos—stood like a pearl on a nest of green growing plants and flowers. And walking toward them, a colorful skirt dancing in the breeze off the ocean, was one of the most stunningly beautiful women Amy had ever seen.

"Holy cow," Jenna whispered, her awe apparent.

Long, wavy hair, the color of roasted chestnuts, lifted with the wind. She walked tall and proud, her full breasts and round hips screaming sex appeal.

But it was her face that drew the eye and held it. Her complexion was the color of honey, her eyes wide and intelligent. There was drama in her face. Artful. Subtle. Breathtaking. Mature.

Gabe shut down the engines and shoved open the cockpit door.

When the woman saw him, she clapped her hands in delight and started running toward him.

When she reached him, she threw her arms around him, pressing all of her perfect pristine beauty against his grubby combat gear. And she didn't seem to mind at all.

His arms linked around her waist as she leaned back, bracketed his face with her hands and studied him. Like he was the world and she'd been lost without him.

"Hum," Jenna said and Amy couldn't help but notice that one syllable had an air of grumpiness to it.

Interesting.

But more interesting was the woman's reaction when Gave hooked a thumb over his shoulder toward the plane.

The woman released him immediately and hurried toward them.

"You have a wounded man," she said in perfect but beautifully accented English. "I'm Juliana Flores. I'm a doctor." She gave Amy a reassuring smile. "Come. We need to get him inside."

"Some digs." Carrying one of the briefcases, Jenna wandered out to a covered patio with a breathtaking view of the ocean.

Amy turned away from the intricately designed cement rail when she heard her. "And then some."

It had been at least three hours since they'd landed.

The late afternoon sun had dropped behind the huge monolith of a house, leaving the patio in the shade and the sea breeze to cool them.

"How's Dallas?"

"Sleeping," Amy said, and joined Jenna where she'd dropped down at a marble patio table in the shade. "But I think it's only because she gave him a sedative with his antibiotics."

"Slipped him a Mickey, huh?"

Amy grinned. "Seemed like the only way he was going to stay down. So . . . how are you doing?"

Jenna made a *humph* of a sound. "Fine and dandy."

Yeah. As fine and dandy as a person could be who had just survived a bloodbath.

Amy looked back toward the ocean. She didn't know what she was looking for. Solace, maybe. A little peace. A lot of perspective.

Edward Walker was dead.

She could no longer think of him as her grandfather. Or bemoan the fact that Dallas had been the one to end his reign of terror.

Much of the last year of her life had been searching for him. Her whole purpose in life had been to confront him and make him atone for the sins he'd committed. Yet somewhere deep inside, she understood that she had harbored some small kernel of hope that she'd been wrong. That he hadn't done what he'd done. That it was all a horrible, horrible mistake.

No mistake.

Edward Walker—Aldrick Reimers—was a monster.

A cruel and twisted man.

And now he was dead.

Yet instead of triumphant, she felt hollow. Instead of victorious, all she felt was empty.

"Do you think they're lovers?"

It took a moment for Jenna's question to register, then to detach from her own thoughts.

Amy breathed deep of the clean sea air. "Haven't decided. There's a lot of affection there. Almost seems maternal on her part, though."

Juliana Flores did indeed hold a great deal of affection for Gabriel Jones. And he for her. When he looked at her, more than fondness filled his eyes. There was sadness. And he seemed almost hesitant to accept the attention she lavished on him. Like he wasn't deserving.

Interesting.

But then, Juliana Flores, Amy had discovered, lavished attention on everyone. She and Jenna had been shown to private suites, each with their own sitting room and bathroom. Once Amy was certain Dallas had the medical attention he needed and he wasn't going to lose an arm or a leg or have permanent damage—and Juliana had proven to be an efficient and knowledgeable physician—Amy had succumbed to the lure of the huge marble bathtub. Shampoos, soaps, lotions . . . anything she needed had been provided in sumptuous and extravagant amounts.

And when she'd finally dragged her limp body out of the tub, fresh fruit, cheeses and sweet breads had been waiting for her. Along with new clothes: a soft butter-yellow peasant blouse, a colorful flowing skirt. Slip-on sandals.

"Do you think these are hers?" Jenna asked, lifting a fold of the skirt she wore. Her peasant blouse was green. Her skirt a brilliant floral print.

Amy lifted a shoulder. "Maybe she keeps things on hand for drop-in guests."

"Makes you wonder how often Jones 'drops' in unannounced."

Yeah, it made a person wonder. And wonder about Jones. Juliana Flores most definitely brought out a different side of the man.

He was softer around her. Almost gentle.

"She's older than I'd first thought," Jenna mused aloud as she opened up one of the briefcases they'd found in the downed chopper. "Older than she looks, I'll bet. Maybe very late forties. Early fifties. Jones might be one of those men who have a thing for older women."

"You know what's interesting?"

Jenna glanced her way as she dragged a sheath of papers from the leather case. "What?"

"That you seem to have developed an interest in Jones' love life."

Jenna grunted—a "get real" sound.

"You've got a thing for him, don't you?"

Jenna looked at her like she'd grown another head.

"Oh, come on. Admit it," Amy said. "You're attracted to him."

"You get hit on the head this morning? Have a mini-stroke on takeoff? Because you're not thinking straight," Jenna insisted. "He's a bully and a bore. He's crude and rude and suffers from the biggest lord-and-master complex I've ever seen."

Yeah, Amy thought, Jenna definitely had a thing for Jones.

She sat there several moments longer, needing a little time to simply decompress before she went to check on Dallas. Jenna was quiet too as she rifled through the contents of the briefcase.

Instead of decompressing, however, she found herself reliving the horror at the compound, alternately thinking about her mother. Wishing, always wishing things could have been different.

Wondering what would happen between her and Dallas when they returned to the States. He had feelings for her, she knew that. He couldn't have made love to her the way he had if he didn't. And he'd been so tender, so tuned in to her needs in those few hours before they'd staged the assault.

Since then, it had been all tension and danger and concern. They hadn't talked. There hadn't been any opportunity. Maybe now there would be.

"I think I'll go check on Dallas," she said abruptly, suddenly needing to see him.

Jenna mumbled an absent "okay," her nose buried in the papers.

Amy hadn't made it ten feet into the house when Jenna's voice stopped her.

"Shit! Holy, holy shit." Jenna flew out of the patio chair, gathered the papers and shoved them back into the case. Her eyes were wild with urgency as she hustled into the house. "Where's Jones? He's got to see this."

CHAPTER TWENTY-THREE

Jenna and Amy rushed into Dallas' room, damn near blowing the door of its hinges.

"Where's Jones?"

Startled, Juliana rose from the side of the bed, where she'd been taking Dallas' blood pressure. "He's in my study."

Dallas glanced at Amy, who shook her head, indicating she didn't know what was up.

"I need to talk to him," Jenna said, her voice filled with urgency. "He needs to see this right away."

"I'll go get him." Juliana hurried out of the room, reacting to Jenna's agitation.

"What's happening?" Dallas asked as Jenna scurried over to a Queen Anne table that sat near the window.

She dropped the briefcase on the table, selected some of the papers and held them out to him. "Read this."

The bed dipped slightly as Amy sat down beside him and started reading over his shoulder.

"Oh, my God," Amy said after several minutes. She looked up at Jenna, who paced back and forth at the foot of the bed.

Jones and Juliana walked in just then. Jones scanned the grim faces in the room and scowled. "What?"

"The compound. It was just the tip of the iceberg." Amy handed the pages to Jones. "Look at this. It's like MC6's mission statement or doctrine or something."

Jones read in silence while Jenna practically bounced off the walls.

"In a nutshell," Jenna preempted impatiently as Jones continued to scan the documents, "it says that MC6 cells have infiltrated every democratic nation in the world, that the network is wide and invincible—*their* words," she added when Jones scowled at her.

"We're aware of that," Jones said.

"Fine, fine. Look at the second page."

Again, Jenna paraphrased for everyone while Jones came up to speed. "Adler, Walker and the witch doctor—they were merely regional heads. They answered to bigger fish. Fish so big they aren't named, only alluded to."

"And?"

"Read the fourth page," Dallas said. "In addition to using their 'programmed' victims as assassins, this says they've programmed several others to use as mules to transport drugs."

Gabe nodded. "We've known for a long time that they've been running high-dollar heroin and cocaine traffic."

Jenna reached for the papers, searched until she found what she was looking for. "It points to facilities in the Philippines and Malaysia where they broker the bulk of the weaponry that finds its way into the hands of the jihadists."

Jones snagged the paper from her hand. Scanned it. "Can't believe they wrote this down. We've been trying to pinpoint these facilities for years. We've known for a long time that MC6 has been a major supplier."

"More radicals, more guns—more money for MC6." Dallas looked weary.

"And of course, an ultimate long-term goal of resurrecting a new Nazi regime from the ashes of the war between democracy and jihad," Jenna said, paraphrasing again. "God, these people are delusional."

"Dangerously so. This is what you need to see," Dallas said, handing Jones another sheet. "They have a plan in the works. Involves the deployment of twenty programmed assassins. Several respected Muslim religious leaders in the Middle East are targeted. Guess who's going to get the blame for their assassinations?"

Jones lifted his head. "The U.S. and its allies. That's a given."

"For what reason?" A worried frown creased Amy's brow.

"To circumvent and undermine and progress on ongoing peace efforts," Jones concluded. "If they pull this off, there will be an upsurge of radical terrorist acts that'll make anything they've done to date pale in comparison."

"An escalated 'holy' war." Dallas looked grave.

"And the motive?" Amy asked.

Gabe grunted. "What's always the motive? Money. Power."

Dallas stroked his chin. "So they figure that once we kill each other off or the superpowers have been so depleted by the devastation and economic costs of warfare—"

"They'll have easy pickings," Jones finished.

Amy shook her head. "This is insane."

"Of course it's insane," Jenna agreed. "But *they* don't think so. And the God's honest truth is, even if they fail, if they aren't brought under control, and soon, they're still going to create some major havoc."

"Twenty assassins." Dallas glanced at Jones. "And we found the bodies of how many victims at the compound? Fifteen?"

Jones nodded. "Many of them children."

"Which means," Dallas said, "they must have moved the assassins out before we got there. Presumably to set the plan in motion."

"I've got to make some calls." Gabe glanced at Juliana.

"There's a secure line in my office."

"Who's he going to call?" Jenna asked as both Jones and Juliana hurried out of the room.

"My guess? The State Department," Dallas said. "Someone he trusts, in any event."

"You mean someone who won't dismiss what he has to say as the ravings of a rogue agent?" Jenna speculated.

"Someone," Dallas said, "who can get some very big balls rolling. Someone who can make certain that within the next few hours an international manhunt for twenty programmed assassins will be on the ground and on the trail."

You could have had your dinner in bed, you know."

"That wasn't a dinner. That was a feast," Dallas said, hobbling into his room with Amy at his side.

Juliana had said they needed a celebration. Of life. Of the good they'd done. And in thanks for Gabe's contact in the State Department, who mobilized on the information Gabe had given him without hesitation.

The baton had been passed. Someone else would be dealing with the fallout. Who that someone was, Dallas didn't know. Most likely, no one ever would. The MC6 problem would be quietly handled. Like most terrorist threats were, quietly handled. He seriously doubted there would ever be so much as a newspaper headline about the foiled plot.

Dallas still wasn't certain where Jones fell in the chain for national security. But he was fairly certain Jones was no longer working in an "official" capacity for the CIA. The Company stretched the limits on their covert activities, but what they'd done at El Bolson was reaching, even for them.

Private contractor, he guessed. Part of an organization that was a law unto themselves, paid by the U.S. government, who would disavow their existence if their cover was ever blown.

These men did the dirtiest of the dirty jobs. Took the biggest risks. Like Gabe, many of them were ex-CIA, or ex–special ops. Seals, Delta, Force Recon, Rangers and Special Forces. Men used to violence, who lived for adrenaline, but deep down, were patriots.

Juliana Flores . . . Dallas didn't know where she fit in to the mix. A humanitarian, certainly. A covert operative? Or merely a sympathizer? Only one thing was certain. She and Jones had a bond that went beyond the normal working relationship.

He caught a crutch on the edge of a lush rug covering the cool marble floor, swore when he stumbled.

"This is what I'm talking about," Amy said, fussing. "You're not ready to be out of bed yet."

Dallas wrestled with the crutches and eased down on the side of the mattress. "The day I can't sit up at a table and eat is the day I pack it in."

God, he hated this. His arm was more of a pain the ass than a real pain. It burned and ached, but it wasn't really slowing him down. His leg was the problem. He still couldn't put any weight on it. And, according to Juliana, he needed to stay on the crutches for at least a month, or he'd tear the repairs she'd made and then he'd be looking at surgery.

He eased back onto the pillow, got pissed all over again when he saw the guilt on Amy's face.

"No." He held a hand out for her. "Don't even go there."

But it was too late. Had been too late the moment he'd gone down in the compound. She blamed herself. And he couldn't bear that weight of her guilt anymore.

"Come here." At his urging, she climbed up on the bed, folded herself against his shoulder. Stretched out beside him.

And said nothing.

She didn't have to. He knew exactly what she was thinking.

He cupped her head in his hand, loved the feel of her sleek, silky hair beneath his fingers. The slender warmth of her body against his. And knew he could get used to it.

Strike that. He could *not* get used to it. But he could set her straight.

"Amy, listen to me. What I do. The choices I make. They're mine. Only mine. The consequences of those decisions—mine.

"Mine," he repeated when she sighed heavily. "No one else's."

Silence. Only the warm wetness of her tears dampening his shirt.

It broke his heart. He hugged her hard. "I'm fine."

"You're *not* fine. You've been shot. You could have died. You can spin it any way you want, but if it weren't for me—"

"If it weren't for you," Dallas interrupted, "some very bad men with some very bad plans would still be doing very bad things to innocent people.

"If it weren't for you," he repeated, whispering into her hair, "no one would have known what was in the works at MC6. If it weren't for you," he said again for emphasis, "several Muslim clerics would be sitting ducks right now instead of alerted to the threat and there would be no one on the hunt for the assassins.

"Amy . . . do you think—do you actually think I could have lived with myself if I'd turned my back and let you come here by yourself? If I'd missed an opportunity to be a part of something that made a difference? We made a difference. How many people can say that?"

She was silent for a long moment. Sniffed. "I didn't come here with any great humanitarian mission in mind. I came here for retribution."

"You came here to right a wrong. You did that. And so much more."

She lifted her head, gazed at him through lashes heavy with tears. Her next words confirmed that her anguish went far beyond her misguided sense of responsibility for his injuries.

"He should . . . he should have protected her. Should have . . . loved her."

She broke down then, let the tears fall in earnest. Tears she needed to shed, tears she'd held for too long.

"He should have . . . loved . . . me."

"Yes," he whispered as he drew her close against him and held her while she finally gave herself permission to fall apart. "He should have."

In that moment Dallas wished he could kill the bastard, Walker, all over again. He'd make it take longer this time. He'd make him suffer for the hell he'd put Amy through.

Yeah. Walker should have loved her.

And Dallas couldn't.

If he'd learned nothing else, he'd learned that he couldn't love Amy Walker.

She deserved more.

She deserved someone who could bring light into her life. All he could offer her was more darkness. Action, exhaustion, adrenaline—they'd all acted as buffers against the flashbacks during the past forty-eight hours. But they'd be back. They'd be back with a vengeance, and with them the black holes that could suck him in for days on end.

The one good thing he could do for her was not weigh her down with his ghosts. She deserved a man who could lift her up, not drag her down. A man who could help her heal, not a man who needed healing himself.

His gut knotted at the thought of some other guy touching her, making love to her. The lucky sonof-abitch had better, by God, understand that she needed special attention, special handling.

He couldn't think about that. Not and keep his sanity. Not when she was liquid and warm and so very, very pliant in his arms.

He breathed deep. Breathed her in.

She'd settled. Seemed content now to lie beside him, her breathing even and deep.

Asleep, he realized.

And told himself he needed to sleep, too.

And he would have. He would have slept, would have left her be.

If she hadn't sighed just then.

If she hadn't lifted her hand, touched his face, covered his lips with her fingertips . . . like she was checking.

Just checking to make sure he was here.

That he still held her.

In the dark.

And in the dark, with his pulse jumping and his heart racing, he told himself, one last time. He needed one last time . . .

Just. One. Last. Time.

He kissed the ultra-soft pads of her fingertips, knotted his fingers loosely in the silk of her hair and drew her head back. Kissed her. Long. Sweet. Deep.

She responded with her tongue. All woman. All need and hunger and heat.

With a lazy grace, she pushed to her knees beside him. Watched his face as she lifted her blouse up over her head, tossed it to the floor.

Her breasts were bare. Pink and perfect and heavy. Her waist was small, her hips a gentle flair of soft flesh and smooth skin as she shimmied out of her skirt and panties.

A dream. A goddess. A reason to reduce his world to this bed, to this moment, and shut out everything else as she went to work on his shirt.

He lay submissive. Let her happen to him. Let this amazing woman, as soft as velvet, as fierce as fire, strip him to the skin. Skin that was sensitized and tuned to the glide of her hands, the heat of her touch, the . . . God . . . the silky wetness of her tongue as she bent over him, took him in her mouth and reduced him to begging.

He arched his hips and she took him deep. All suction and sensation and golden hair trailing over his belly.

"Amy . . ." Her name eased out on a groan as she loved him—imperfect, inexperienced, and all the more incredible for the knowledge that she wanted to gift him with something she'd never given any other man.

"Amy . . ." It was as much as he could manage as her glorious, untutored mouth drove him to the brink of insanity.

He reached for her, held the hair back from her face and watched her make love to him. It was beyond erotic. Beyond exotic.

It was a sweet and selfless giving. Rich and rare and ruthlessly thorough.

He didn't want it to end. Knew it had to.

He pulled her head up. She shook her head *no* and took him in again.

He couldn't help it. He laughed. In pure, prurient joy.

It was exactly the wrong thing to do.

She stopped abruptly. Lifted her head. Looked up at him, uncertain. She was on her hands and knees. Straddling him. Looking like a wild creature about to bolt.

"No. Oh, no." He cupped her face in his hands, reading the insecurity in her eyes. "You are wonderful. I laughed because . . . hell, I can't believe what a lucky sonofabitch I am."

Her doubt faded. Replaced by a shy smile. "I . . . I . . . ah . . . I've never . . . you know."

He drew her toward his mouth. "I know. You were wonderful." He kissed her gently. "Thank you. Thank you."

She snuggled on top of him. Her hair fell across his face, her lush breasts crushed against his chest.

"Turnabout's fair play," he whispered, brushing aside her hair and nipping her earlobe.

"No. You rest. You're hurt."

Again, he laughed. "Never too hurt for that."

He urged her to her knees, guided one on either side of his ribs. Then, caressing her thighs, he eased her slowly forward until she was straddling his shoulders.

"Dallas . . ."

"Shh," he whispered, then shattered her hesitation when he gripped her hips and lowered her to his mouth.

She tasted like everything woman. Honey and sex and sensuality. And the sounds she made. They called to something deep inside him. Something basic and carnal and more necessary than breathing.

He was wild for the need of her. Wet and slick and hot and vulnerable.

She came with a soft cry, a shudder that wracked her entire body. A whimper as she braced her palms on the wall above the bed and let the sensations take her.

Limp and languid, she slid down his body, shaken, trembling and spent.

It was enough. More than enough for him.

And that was something new for Dallas Garrett.

He gave, yes. But he took too . . . and he was still pulsing and rock hard.

Didn't matter. As he held her, as she drifted off to sleep, he felt more fulfilled than he ever had in his life.

Until he thought about the fact that very soon now, he had to let her go.

CHAPTER TWENTY-FOUR

How are you, Gabe? Really? Truth now. Don't whitewash things for me."

Gabe glanced up into Juliana's eyes and experienced the pain he always felt when he saw them.

They were Angelina's eyes. They could have been sisters instead of mother and daughter.

And Angelina could have been alive today if it weren't for him.

He rolled a shoulder, averted his gaze to the towering windows running the length of Juliana's study because he couldn't stand to bear to witness to a sorrow she tried to hide with soft, forgiving smiles.

The morning sun broke through the beveled windowpanes like lasers, glanced off the gleaming cypress flooring in dancing prisms of blue, yellow and green.

"You know me, Juliana. I'm fit and fine."

The silk brocade settee was feminine and old. Expensive as hell. He felt like a bear sitting in it. Hell, everything in her house made him feel like a bull in

the proverbial china shop. From the draperies to the
tapestries to the dead king's furniture, everything
was refined and regal—like Juliana. He was cob
rough and clumsy with the delicate china coffee cup
that he balanced on his knee.

He drank it dry, set the cup on a Louis XIV side
table.

"She chose her life, Gabe. They both did." Juliana
walked to the settee, sat down beside him, knowing
instinctively that he was thinking of Angelina. Blam-
ing himself. Hating himself for her death and for Ar-
mando's.

She took his hands in hers. "We can miss them.
We can mourn them. But we can't die with them."

He'd wanted to. God, he'd wanted to.

"I wanted to be the one to kill him," Gabe said,
staring down at their joined hands. Hers were silken
smooth and graceful, his were big and hard, cal-
loused and scarred. "I wanted to kill him myself."

"I know. But he's dead. And you were involved in
making it happen. The important thing is, he's gone.
Erich Adler will never harm another soul again."

He didn't dispute her, but Erich Adler's death had
come too late for him. The man who had ordered Angelina's assassination, had damaged Gabe forever.

Retribution was not sweet. It was only necessary.
And empty.

"We have to be going." He made himself meet her
earnest smile. Squeezed her hands. "I don't want to
be anywhere near here when the local authorities respond to the call I made to El Bolson this morning."

They would suspect. Whenever any unexplained

event involving multiple deaths of multiple bad guys happened in this part of the world, he and his men were always suspect.

Of course, for over a year, Gabe had been a "dead" man as far as anyone knew. So he was in the clear. Reed and Lang, however, needed to lie low for a while. And he needed to facilitate making that happen.

"I understand," Juliana said, sounding cheerless at the thought of him leaving. "What of your friends? They are welcome to stay for as long as they have need."

Gabe shook his head. Thought about correcting her on the issue of Garrett, Amy and Jenna being "friends." Wasn't sure what stopped him.

"Thank you, but no. I don't want to implicate you in this any further, and sooner or later someone is going to drop by and question you about your American houseguests. Besides, they need to get back to the States ASAP. It's better all the way around."

"You'll use my helicopter, of course."

Yes, they would need her chopper. The Piper had mysteriously disappeared during the night. Juliana's doing. She handled things. Efficiently. Quietly.

"Be very careful," he said, concerned about leaving her, more concerned about staying. Either way, he was making her a target. "There may be reprisals."

"I know you, Gabe. No one will be able to trace what happened down there to you, let alone to me."

He nodded. Squeezed her shoulder. "I'll let them know they need to get ready to go."

She rose when he did; her hand on his arm stopped him from leaving the room.

"Please don't be a stranger." Her eyes pleaded with a sincerity that damn near broke what was left of his heart. "You're all I have left of them."

She should hate him. She should hate life. Her husband was dead. Her daughter was dead. And Gabe should have saved them both.

And yet Juliana loved him.

He nodded, knowing that a stranger was all he could ever be. But when she moved against him, nestled her head against his chest, he couldn't keep his arms from winding around her. Holding her close. Rocking her, providing the only comfort he could give.

"Go with God, Gabriel," she whispered and let him go.

Gab worked his jaw until it ached. He and God weren't exactly on the best of terms these days. A mutual agreement. A rift that he wasn't certain could ever be healed.

Buenos Aires, later that day

Jenna held back, wanting to be the last one off the helicopter. It was a helluva a step up from the Piper, that was for certain. Plush and roomy, quiet and smooth. The Bell 427 had room for eight and a chopper pilot who knew how to get the most out of the air miles. He'd delivered them to Buenos Aires in record time.

Still, she was damn glad to be setting her feet on terra firma again—even if it was in the form of an asphalt tarmac, well away from the main terminals at the international airport.

"Angelina Foundation" was painted in bold black lettering on the side of the small chopper hangar. "Angelina" was also painted on the side of the chopper.

She'd been wanting to ask Jones about it all during the flight. But there was something about him today. Something even darker and fiercer than usual and, conversely, something profoundly heartbreaking about him. Ever since they'd landed the Piper at Juliana's villa, he'd been a different person.

Deep feelings. Huge emotions. He had them. And Juliana had set them off.

Jenna wouldn't have figured it. Not of Jones. Not of the man who had made it his mission to badger and berate her from the moment he'd set eyes on her.

"Today, McMillan."

Jenna blinked, realized that none other than the big man himself was standing on the tarmac, looking up into the chopper, waiting for her to get out.

Moment of truth time. She had some things to say to him. Things that weren't going to be easy.

"Sorry." She scrambled out of her seat belt, walked bent at the waist, keeping her head low, toward the cockpit door.

"Daydreaming about all the awards you're going to receive for the story about your big adventure?

There was more disgust than question in his tone.

She breathed deep, let it out. Accepted his hand and let him help her to the ground. It was huge and hard and scarred. She wondered what other scars he carried.

Told herself to forget it. She'd never see the man again. And why that thought brought a little pang of regret, she had no idea.

The air smelled like ocean and jet fuel and the South American summer. Heat waves shimmered over the asphalt as they walked toward the open hangar door, fifty yards away where Amy and Dallas waited for them.

"About that." She stopped. Squinted against the sun and looked up at him.

"About what?"

"The story. There isn't going to be one."

He stared, his expression unchanged. Distrustful.

"Some things . . . are just better left alone." She offered a tight smile. When he said nothing, she used one of his tried and true taunts on him. "This is the part where you're supposed to show appreciation."

His hand on her arm stopped her when she would have walked away. A hard grip. Almost angry. "Why? Why would you do that?" Almost demanding. His distrust revving up several degrees.

"What is it with you?" she demanded, mad as hell suddenly. She jerked her arm, tried to break his grasp. His fingers tightened like steel bands.

"Why can't you just accept a gift when it's offered to you?"

"Because I've learned over time that there's always a catch. What's yours?"

"You're paranoid, you know that? Why can't you just accept what I tell you at face value? You don't seem to have any trouble accepting anything Juliana gives you."

For a moment, she thought he was going to hit her. Whatever nerve she'd touched, it was raw and bleeding and she'd riled it up big time.

"Look," she said, regretting bringing Juliana into it, but it was too late to take it back now. "I know you consider journalists an inferior life-form, but here's a news flash for you. I care. I care about what happens to people. I care when bad things happen to good people. Hell, call me crazy, but I even care when bad things happen to you. And I figure, if I write this story, no matter how much I try to cloak it in generalities and reference 'unidentified' sources, that there are others who might not accept that and come down here and start digging for more."

He considered her. "Others who don't have the moral integrity that, say, you do."

Bastard. He was mocking her.

"Yeah. Others liked that." Sarcasm dripped from each word.

She was good and pissed now. But she also had one other thing to say to him. So she drew a bracing breath. "Whatever you think of me, do know this. I'm sorry about Alvaro."

She stopped, swallowed hard. Whether it was delayed stress, fatigue, grief or all three, she didn't know, but she felt watery suddenly. And very, very responsible. "I'm . . . very, very sorry about Alvaro. He was a good man. I never knew . . . I never guessed that I was digging into something that would get him killed. That would get Raul killed. And those people. Those poor, poor people."

Tears filled her eyes as she thought of the victims

of MC6's special brand of torture. It was small consolation that they were no longer in pain. They'd had families. Futures—until the most vile of the vile had stolen everything.

"Just . . . forget it. Let go of my arm, okay?" She was done, finished, empty. She didn't want to fight him anymore.

For a long moment, he stood there. Looming over her like, hell, like some avenging angel. The sun glinting off the sheen of his thick brown hair, his broad shoulders casting a long, dark shadow. His mouth compressed, his jaw unyielding.

Maybe in another lifetime, she'd have wanted to get to know him. Know what he hid behind that warrior's face.

"Thank you," he said finally. "For killing the story. I appreciate it."

She saw something in him then that she hadn't seen before. Humility.

It stunned her. Almost dizzied her with the rush of emotions that small glimpse into his inner self revealed.

It didn't mean she liked him. He was still a badass with a bad attitude.

But then he did the damnedest thing. He touched a hand to her hair, pulled her close and kissed her.

Like he meant it.

Like he enjoyed it.

Which was pretty amazing in itself, because she enjoyed it too.

Then he let her go.

"Because I've been wondering if that mouth was

good for anything but sass, that's why," he said, answering the question that was still forming in her befuddled head.

Why did you do that?

Then he left her there, standing in the sun, staring at his broad back as he headed for the hangar.

She touched her fingers to her lips. Felt the burn. Then she snapped out of it.

"Well?" she yelled. *Was it good for something else?*

He kept on walking. Lifted his right hand. Wobbled it back and forth: *So-so.*

Smart-ass. He was the ultimate smart-ass.

Yet, for some reason, she was smiling and had no idea of why when she followed him out of the sun.

The busy terminal buzzed with life around them as Dallas and Amy waited for their flight to West Palm while Jenna would head to Wyoming.

"I need to go home," she'd said as she and Amy had hugged and cried and said their good-byes with heartfelt promises to keep in touch.

The only one left to say good-bye to was Jones.

"Guess this is the end of the line." Dallas balanced on his crutches and extended his hand.

The big man took it. "Take care of that leg."

They shook—a world of meaning in their firm grips: *Thanks. Well done.*

Dallas couldn't help but grin, shake his head. "I hope to hell I don't see you again, because if I do, it can only mean one of us is in deep shit."

Jones actually smiled. "You can guard my back anytime."

The supreme compliment. One warrior to another.

Dallas nodded. "Same goes." Then he held back and waited while Amy said her good-byes.

She hadn't managed to say a word before Jones preempted her. "No thank yous, okay? I didn't help you, remember? I made sure you didn't interfere."

Amy smiled, nodded. "It was important," she said, holding Jones' dark gaze. "What we did. What you helped me do."

"Yeah. It was important. And for the record, you can guard my back anytime, too."

She went up on her toes, flung her arms around his neck. Jones, Dallas was amused to see, didn't quite know what to do about it.

He hesitated, then patted her back . . . like he thought he might break her or something.

"And I *do* thank you," she whispered in his ear. "Stay safe, okay?"

Jones nodded, set her away. Then turned his hard gaze on Jenna.

This ought to be interesting, Dallas thought as Amy walked to his side and slipped her arm around his waist.

"McMillan," Jones said, his voice as stiff as his shoulders.

"Jones," Jenna said, matching his tone and bearing.

And then she kissed him. Moved right in, slapped her palms around his ears, pulled his head down and laid one on him.

Dallas didn't know whether to laugh or get the hell out of the way. There was bound to be fallout.

But there wasn't.

Jenna let him go, licked her lips and stood back. Then she seemed to consider.

"So-so," she said with a hand wobble, turned and with a whispered good-bye to Amy, headed for the terminal.

And damned if Jones didn't just stand there, a half-assed grin on his face.

CHAPTER TWENTY-FIVE

Offices of E.D.E.N. Securities, Inc., early the next morning

Next time you bound off to parts unknown trying to fulfill a death wish, you'd better, by God, take us with you." Ethan hid his concern behind a dark scowl.

Dallas had known he'd get plenty of flack from his brothers and sister. So he decided to get it over with straight off. They'd flown through the night, landed at West Palm International around seven A.M.

He'd been whipped—Amy too—but they'd both agreed to face the music before they crashed.

He hadn't been wrong either. He'd been getting the third degree complete with liberal doses of grief ever since he'd hobbled into the office on his crutches an hour ago.

"You must be slowing down," Nolan said with a grunt and a nod toward the crutches. "Age'll do that."

"Right. Kick a man when he's down," Dallas grumbled around a yawn. "Go ahead. I've still got one good leg. See what kind of damage you can do."

"They're always like this," Eve said in aside to

Amy, who was listening to the brothers whale on each other. "You get used to it after a while. What you don't get used to is seeing them banged up. Mom's gonna have a cow."

"Mom doesn't need to know," Dallas warned with a sharp look in Eve's direction.

Eve snorted. "Yeah. She probably won't even notice the crutches."

"I sprained my ankle, okay? Stepped in a hole."

Eve rolled her eyes. "It's your story, you can tell it any way you want to."

It was all a ruse, of course. The gentle jabs, the trash talk. All a cover. There had been huge relief in their eyes when Dallas had walked into the office with Amy. And there had been quiet, stunned concern when Dallas had told them what had happened in Argentina.

"Look, I'd love to hang around and take more of this abuse," Dallas said, "but I need some shut-eye. So does Amy."

"You need to check in with the folks," Eve reminded him.

"I will. Later. Give 'em a call for me, okay? Let them know their baby boy is back and just fine."

"Hey—I'm the baby, old man, and don't you forget it." Nolan pointed his bottle of root beer at Dallas for emphasis. "I get a lot of miles off that coveted position and I'm not giving it up. Not even to a cripple."

"Good-bye," Dallas said, grinning over his brother's smart-ass sense of humor. "I'm outta here."

It was the clamp of a hand on his shoulder from

Nolan, the hug—longer than necessary—from Eve, and the long, thoughtful look from Ethan that told the real tale.

They'd been worried. They were still worried. And they were here. Whenever he needed them. Whatever he needed them for.

He sensed the same familial attitude toward Amy as they each hugged her in turn and said quiet good-byes. Because that's just the way they were. Open. Giving. Accepting.

"You're so lucky," Amy said as they walked outside, the keys to Ethan's SUV in Dallas' hand. "So lucky to have them."

"Yeah," he said. "I am."

Amy woke up to soft light and silence.

She was alone in Dallas' bed. The sheets where he'd slept beside her were cool.

She laid there for long moments. Let the cobwebs clear. Appreciated the clean sheets and sense of safety before turning her head to glance at the clock on his night stand.

5:38. She thought. Calculated. They'd left the E.D.E.N. offices around nine this morning. Arrived at Dallas' townhouse by ten. And they'd both crashed. That meant she'd slept almost eight hours. The first solid eight hours of sleep she'd had in longer than she could remember.

Yawning, rubbing sleep from her eyes, she wandered out of the bedroom.

"Hey," Dallas said from the kitchen. He was

dressed in a body-hugging green t-shirt and tan cargo pants. The bandage on his arm was covered by the sleeve of his shirt. His hair was combed and he'd shaved. Except for the bare feet and the crutches, he looked like a spit and polished marine. And he looked beautiful.

She knew every inch of skin, sinew and muscle beneath those clothes. Knew his scars, knew his most sensitive places, knew what made him weak, what made him strong.

Just like she knew what made her strong.

He did.

"Hey." She smiled and eased onto a barstool as he slid a mug of coffee across the counter to her. "Thanks."

She sipped, savored. "Umm. Good. I could get used to this."

Dallas stilled, stiffened, then turned back to the coffee pot, filled his mug.

He said nothing, but Amy read his body language loud and clear: *Don't. Don't get used to it.*

The rich, mellow cocoon she'd felt envelop her let go like a bursting bubble. And in a heartbeat, she went from warm and happy and secure to cold and confused and exposed.

Don't get used to it.

"I called out for pizza," he said, moving carefully around the kitchen on his crutches. "Hope you're hungry."

She had been. She'd been starved. But she'd suddenly lost her appetite.

"How's your leg?" she managed because she had

to say something. Something other than, *Don't do this. Don't shut me out. Don't turn me away.*

"It's fine. Be glad when I can ditch these things, though."

Like he'd be glad when he could ditch her.

Oh, God.

She could deal with the pain. She'd dealt with a lot of pain in her life. And she wouldn't make it hard for him. What she couldn't do was stay here any longer and suffer through all this polite distance.

"Can I use your phone? I lost mine somewhere along the way."

He frowned, shrugged. "Sure."

She lifted the phone book off the counter and took it with her into his bedroom. Found out there was a flight for JFK leaving in two hours and called a cab.

Then she gathered her things in silence and walked back into the kitchen. He was leaning against the counter, arms crossed over his chest, looking grim.

Because he doesn't know how to let me down without hurting me.

She was determined that he wouldn't have to.

"Good news," she said, pasting on a happy face. "There's a flight to New York leaving in two hours. But that means I have to hustle because it's going to be tight."

A muscle in his jaw twitched. He unfolded his arms, braced his palms behind him on the counter. "You don't have to leave so soon."

She nodded. "Yeah. I do." And fought tears. "I need to see my mom. See how she's doing, you know?"

And she needed . . . she needed so badly to get out here before she broke down and begged.

"Look . . . I'm probably going to get a little sloppy here. Never have been too good with good-byes. Guess that's why I just sort of skipped out before."

She stopped, swallowed, drew a bracing breath. "Thank you, Dallas. Thank you for everything. God. That sounds so lame. But I don't know what else to say. You . . . what you did for me. The risks you took. Well. I don't know how to repay you."

But she did know. She'd repay him by making this easy for him. By getting out of his hair.

He closed his eyes. Shook his head. "Amy—"

"No. You don't have to say anything. In fact, please don't. It's okay. I'll be okay. I'll be good. Great, in fact." She bobbed her head up and down, hoped to hell her fake smile hadn't turned into a grimace that mirrored her pain.

"Really," she added for emphasis as he stood there looking miserable and guilty and grim.

Finally he nodded. "I'll take you to the airport."

No resistance. None. The final nail in her coffin.

"Not necessary." She shouldered her backpack. "I called it cab. It should be here any minute."

He gathered his crutches, tucked them under his arms and walked over to her. Searched her face.

"I'm sorry."

Sorry he didn't love her. Sorry he couldn't ask her to stay. Sorry, sorry, sorry.

"It's okay. It's really okay."

Because she couldn't stop herself, she lifted her hand. Touched his face one last time.

"Gotta go," she said and quickly backed away.

Then she rushed for the door, swung it open and left him without looking back.

Fast. Cutting. Clean. It was the only way to survive leaving Dallas Garrett.

And she would survive.

"Airport," she said when the cab pulled up and she climbed inside.

She always survived.

Dallas sat in his living room in the dark. The scent of cold pizza permeated the air. The full box sat untouched on the coffee table.

The silence was suffocating. The tick of a clock. The hum of his climate control system. The total absence of Amy.

He wondered if she'd made it back to New York yet. Wondered if she was crying now.

He propped his chin on his fist. She was in love with him. He knew that. Just as he knew she'd get over it. That she'd get on with her life now.

It was the one thing he felt good about. He'd played a part in closing a chapter that had threatened and tormented and tortured her.

Now she was free to move on.

He pictured her face. The ivory skin. The dusting of freckles that was so sexy and sweet. Those blue, blue eyes that spoke to him. Blue eyes misted with tears as she'd bravely let him go.

Because she had wanted to make it easy for him.

Because she thought he didn't love her.

He slumped back in his overstuffed chair.

Alone in the dark. In the quiet.

And he had only himself to blame.

Three weeks later

Well, what do you know, déjà vu all over again."

Dallas glared at Nolan across the expanse of his walnut desk at E.D.E.N.

His brother stood in his office doorway. Arms crossed over his chest, shoulder leaning against the frame, the ever-present bottle of root beer in his hand.

"If you're referring to your irritating habit of sticking your unwanted nose into my business— yeah. It's starting to feel a helluva a lot like *Groundhog Day.*"

Undaunted, Nolan pushed away from the door. Eased a hip on the corner of Dallas' desk and picked up a paperweight in the shape of a dolphin—a gift from his mother.

"I was thinking more in terms of you getting squirrelly on us again."

"Squirrelly." Dallas repeated, not wanting to be sucked into this discussion but knowing it was unavoidable.

"Yeah. You know." Nolan set down the paperweight. "Pissed at the world in general. Moody. Miserable," he added with meaning.

He was miserable. And he knew he was making everyone around him miserable, too.

But he'd made his decision. It was the right one. At least it was the right one for Amy.

He missed her like hell. Wondered how she was. What she was doing. If she was okay. A hundred times in the past three weeks he'd picked up the phone, stared at the number he'd gotten from directory assistance and put the phone down without dialing.

It was best. For her, it was best.

And his well-intended family needed to accept that.

"Two words," Dallas said, holding his brother's gaze. "Butt out."

"Yeah, I thought you'd say that, but it's not going to happen."

Dallas heaved out a long breath, leaned back in his chair and laced his fingers behind his head. "I have work to do."

"Actually, you don't. We cleared your schedule."

"What are you talking about?"

"He's talking about this," Eve said, walking into the room with Ethan right behind her.

"What is this—a fucking intervention?"

"Close enough." Eve slapped a sheet of paper on his desk.

"Christ. Can't a man work in peace?" he sputtered, leaned forward and snatched up the paper. It was an e-ticket. One-way to New York.

"Like she said," Ethan answered. "You don't have any work today. Not for the next week, as a matter of fact."

"Now get your ass to New York. Go get your woman," Nolan said. "You let her go once, bro. We're not going to let you make the same mistake again."

"And straighten out your attitude while you're there, okay?" Eve said sweetly.

He looked from the ticket to them, to the window. Fought a temptation so great it made his gut hurt.

"Go to her," Eve said softly. "You're good for her, Dallas. And she's good for you. Whatever is keeping you from accepting that is wrong thinking."

"Flight leaves at three," Ethan said. "Be on it."

And then they left him.

Alone.

To think.

And to make the biggest decision of his life.

CHAPTER TWENTY-SIX

Upstate New York

It had been almost a month since they'd left Argentina, yet some nights, when Amy left work at Winter Haven, she expected to walk out to a sea of green grass, a hot summer night and blue surf. But it was still the thick of winter in New York and the chill that settled in her bones as the artic cold hit her full in the face snapped her back to reality like a slap.

It was a black, moonless night. A front had moved in during the afternoon, dropped two fresh inches of snow on top of the existing six and promised at least two more before it was all over.

Thick fat flakes, as dense as fog, drifted down, settling on her shoulders, dusting her hair. She burrowed deeper into her muffler, dug her car keys out of her pocket and unlocked the door.

The little Honda wasn't much. But she could afford it and it ran well, even in the coldest of weather. She climbed inside, slipped the key in the ignition and fired it up. She set the heater to full defrost, dug under the seat for her ice scraper and headed back out to clear the windows of snow.

Five minutes later, she pulled out of the employee parking lot, her wipers fighting valiantly to keep her windshield clear. Then she drove. And she didn't let herself think about a night not so long ago when, on this very road, she'd taken a life to save her own.

Thirty minutes after that, after a slow and careful drive on snow-packed roads, she pulled into her parking space at her apartment building in town.

She shut off the motor. A fresh film of snow immediately covered her windshield. She was thinking of hot chocolate to cut the chill as she gathered her purse and opened the door. Hot chocolate on a cold, snowy night. More than a treat: a comfort. To cut the loneliness. To replace the warmth of a certain man.

She missed him so much. Didn't realize it was possible to miss someone so much. To ache heart deep with missing him. To long foolishly for a happily ever after.

But that was the stuff of fairy tales. And her life had never been that.

Her boots sank into a good four inches of snow when she stepped outside. She turned to lock her doors and heard his voice. Soft. Warm. Here.

"Hey."

She stopped cold, her fingers frozen on her key.

Then she spun around.

And there he was.

Dallas.

"Hey," he said again, a tentative smile tilting up one corner of his mouth.

All she could manage to do was to stare, incredulous, yet desperate to believe her eyes weren't playing tricks.

But it *was* Dallas.

Dark, dangerous, beautiful, huddled against the cold in a lightweight jacket. His hands stuffed in his pants pockets. The jacket collar tugged up around his ears to stall the cold.

His breath puffed out in foggy clouds; snow covered his thick dark hair. And under the scant glow from the streetlight on the corner, his blue gaze was locked on hers, a small smile crinkling the corners of his eyes.

"What . . . well . . . um. You're a long way from home," she finally said. It was a chore to squeeze the words out around the tightening in her throat.

Her heart pounded, her ears rang and more than the cold had her trembling.

"What I want to know," he said, hunching his shoulders and suppressing a shudder, "is why anyone would want to subject themselves to this deep freeze. Pretty as hell, yeah. But, damn, is it cold."

She still couldn't say anything. He obviously knew it.

"Don't suppose you'd have a hot cup of coffee for a cold man?" He lifted a thick dark eyebrow. Hopeful. Even a little hesitant.

"Um . . . sure. Yes. Of course. L-look at you. You have to be freezing."

"In a word," he admitted, and took her arm when she started walking toward her apartment door in halting steps—warning her foolish, foolish heart not

to hope that he was here for any other reason than to
check on her.

Amy left him in her tiny living room while she hung
up her coat and headed for the kitchen, hiking up the
thermostat on her way.

"It'll warm up in a few minutes," she said over her
shoulder, then rattled around in her cupboards for the
coffee and filters.

Her hands were shaking as she filled the glass pot
with tap water. Shaking hard.

She set the pot on the counter. Lowered her head.
Drew a deep breath. Tried to settle herself down.

But she was so rattled. So . . . overcome with the
joy of seeing him. Over the idea that he'd come all this
way. To see her. Surely . . . please God, let it mean
something.

Tears leaked from her eyes. Damnable, hot heavy
tears of hope and dread and . . . God. She blinked
them back. She had to get ahold of herself.

"Amy."

She actually flinched. Stiffened when she felt his
hands cup her shoulders. Felt the warmth of his body
behind her seeping into her back. Couldn't stop the
tears this time as he turned her around to face him.

She couldn't look at him. She couldn't let him see
what he did to her. Couldn't let him . . .

Kiss her.

But she did. Her lips trembled as he tipped her
face up to his with a curled finger under her chin and

lowered his mouth to hers. All gentleness. Apology. Regret.

"I never should have let you go," he whispered and kissed the corner of her mouth. Nuzzled his nose along her cheek, wiping her tears with his thumbs. "I'm sorry."

A sob wracked her body as she threw her arms around his neck and clung. Just clung and cried while he wrapped her tight and held her.

"You're shivering," he whispered against her hair.

She choked out a laugh. "Look who's talking."

She felt his smile against her hair. "How about we skip the coffee and go warm each other up?"

"Yeah," she said, finally meeting his eyes and seeing everything she needed to see there. "How about we do that?"

She was a wonder of fluid grace, of greedy taking, delicious giving. The first time, she damn near burned him alive, a frenzied and furious need to feed a fire that demanded quenching.

The next time, they took each other slowly. With reverence. With lush, lazy strokes, with long languid kisses. The kind that said we have tonight. And we have many, many tomorrows.

Dallas eased up on an elbow beside her. Watched her beautiful face as she rested. Her pale skin glowed almost iridescent in the tiny room in the double bed. Her silver gold hair fanned around her face on the pillow. A smile of utter contentment lit her face.

Mine, he thought. She had to be his. Had *been* his from the first time he'd seen her, wild with terror and needing him on Jolo.

And finally, finally he understood. Now he had to make her understand. He owed her that. He owed her the opportunity to know exactly what she was getting into. Then she could decide if she still wanted to take him on.

He could count the times on one hand when he'd been this scared. His first parachute jump. The first time he'd come face-to-face with a man whose only focus was to kill him. When Amy had run out into a hail of gunfire to retrieve the M-60. He'd thought he'd lost her then.

Could still lose her now.

He brushed a fall of hair back from her temple. "You awake?"

She yawned, then stretched like a cat and squirmed deeper into the mattress. "Do I have to be?"

He grinned in spite of the way his heart was beating against his ribs. "Yeah. I think you do."

She opened her eyes. Blinked. Gazed up at him. "Am I going to want to hear this?"

There was that uncertainty again. There was the doubt. He hated that he was the cause of it. But there wasn't any other way.

"I love you," he said to assuage her concerns and because he simply needed to say it . . . just say it. Finally.

Her eyes glittered in the dim light. "I know," she said. "I've always known."

He smiled tightly. "That would be why women are the superior sex. They're a lot smarter then us mere men. Took me a long time to figure it out."

"So why do I get the feeling that this is a problem?"

He ran his hand down the length of her arm. Laced her fingers with his. Brought them to his mouth. Kissed her fingertips.

"Once upon a time," he began, smiling with her when he launched into an impromptu fairy tale, "there was a little boy who wanted to grow up and save the world. If you were to ask his family, they would all say the same thing about him."

"That he was wonderful?"

He grunted. "That he was focused, rigid, controlling in everything he did. That all of his life he required perfection. That meant he needed to be perfect too. And that any woman who wanted to spend her life with him needed to be perfect."

"Oh." The delight left her eyes and the worry returned.

"But when the boy became a man," he went on, finally getting to the tough part, "something happened to make his perfect life not so perfect anymore.

"He went to war," he said, stopped and shook his head. "He went to war. It's what he'd trained to do. What he wanted to do in the name of his country, for the sake of his family, for all the reasons that make a man with a purpose a patriot."

He stopped. Looked into the darkness toward the other side of the room. Looked back down at her; a concerned frown pinched her brows.

"Good men died in that war. Men he was responsible for. Men who left mothers and sisters and babies and wives. Men who didn't come home. Men who died in pieces on a cold mountain pass in a godforsaken country that's still at war."

"And they haunt you," she whispered.

Only then did he realize he'd fallen silent.

He swallowed. Nodded. "They haunt me."

"We all have ghosts, Dallas."

"Yeah. It seems we do. Only—I wasn't supposed to, see? None of that was supposed to affect me. Me and my perfectly planned out life.

"I have holes, Amy," he admitted as she waited in silence. "Big black holes that I fall into . . . for days sometimes. Holes I can't dig my way out of. Sometimes, I don't even want to. I just want to stay there, curled up, cocooned, separated from what's real and what's keeping me from facing the memories that hit me like . . . like—"

"Like a shot from a cannon," she finished for him.

"Yeah. Like that. You have them too, don't you?"

She nodded. "I haven't been diagnosed. But I've done a lot of reading since—well, since what happened to me on Jolo. PSTD. The medical condition of the decade."

He lay back down beside her, gathered her close. "So, you have before you an imperfect man. A man who doesn't know if he can keep himself together, let alone help another wounded soul through her own kind of hell.

"Christ," he muttered, frustrated and unsure, "you need someone you can count on to be there for you.

Not someone who will bring you down when you need to be shored up."

She was quiet for a long time. Then she placed her hand over his heart. It was small and warm and so very, very welcome there. "You know what I think about perfect people, Dallas? I think they don't exist. I think they're a trick of light and mirrors and shadows. And I don't think I could live with or love a man who had a misguided goal of perfection."

She turned in his arms, pressed her forehead to his and met his eyes. "I like a man with scars. I like a man who looks in the mirror and sees himself for who he is. For what he is. An imperfect person in an imperfect world.

"In fact," she touched her lips to his, achingly tender, incredibly sweet. "I love a man like that."

Easy. She made what he'd been making so hard, so easy. Relief was huge and sweet and humbling.

He smiled against her mouth, nipped her lower lip. "Well, it just so happens that I know where you can pick up a slightly used, fairly imperfect man who fits that description."

"Really? He doesn't have any warts, now does he? Because I draw the line at warts."

He laughed, rolled her under him and pinned her to the mattress. "No warts. Lotta scars, though."

"Ah," she said, threading her hands through his hair. "Bonus points. I think maybe we can make a deal here."

"Yeah," he said, smiling into the face he wanted to see on his pillow every morning for the rest of his life. "Here's the deal. I get to marry you. You get to become a Garrett—although, considering what you're marrying into, I'm not certain that's much of an incentive."

"They love you."

"They made me come here," he admitted, "so I guess they aren't so bad."

"No," she agreed. "They aren't so bad. And neither are you. We'll be fine, Dallas. We'll be good."

"We'll be great," he promised, for the first time believing it as he slipped easily inside of her.

EPILOGUE

Three months later, West Palm Beach

She loves it here." Amy stood in the shade of the covered pavilion watching her mother. Karen Walker's wheelchair had been rolled to the edge of the grass where she sat staring out over a small lake where sandhill cranes and snowy white egrets waded along the bank. The sun was warm on her face and she actually had a little color on her cheeks.

"I know it's hard for you to see it," she said, glancing up at Dallas, who stood with his arm slung possessively over her shoulder, "but I can tell."

She wound her arm around his waist as he hugged her. "I'm glad. I was afraid the move might be hard on her."

That was another thing she loved about this man who would soon be her husband. He looked at all sides of every situation. And more than likely, he had a solution to every problem.

Amy never could have afforded this beautiful facility for her mother's care. Winter Haven had been a state-run institution, her mother's expenses covered by federal and state funding. Mary's House was a brand-new, state-of-the-art mental health facility built and funded by Darin Kincaid. Darin, Amy had learned, was Nolan's father-in-law.

"The story behind Mary's House is long and sad," Dallas had told her when he'd shown her the brochures with its beautiful color photos of the building, the private rooms and the extravagantly appointed grounds.

"Dallas, I can't afford this."

"You can. Because it's not going to cost you a penny."

She'd been speechless.

"Someday I'll tell you the details, but the bottom line is Kincaid wanted to right an old wrong and the best way he knew how to do it was to provide for people like your mother who need safe haven, need special care, and don't have the means of paying."

Even now, two months after they'd moved her mother from Winter Haven in New York to Mary's Place in West Palm, Amy still had difficulty grasping the opulence—both materially and emotionally.

Today, it was the emotional abundance that touched her the deepest.

"Here you go, Karen," she heard Susan Garrett say as she joined Amy's mother by her chair and handed her a cool glass of ice tea.

It was her mother's birthday today. That, according to Dallas' mother, made it a special family celebration.

All day long, Amy had been fighting back tears. Joyful tears. Grateful tears. I-can't-believe-my-good-fortune tears as one by one the Garrett clan had shown up at Mary's House for a birthday party slash potluck slash picnic.

Susan Garrett had made all the arrangements. She'd reserved the outside pavilion for the gathering and made all the phone calls. Wes, their dad, was busy bouncing Nolan's little guy on his knee and, as usual, the Garrett "children" were giving each other ten kinds of grief.

Amy watched it all in a daze. A little in awe of Jillian, Nolan's wife. She was a big-time news personality in West Palm—and she made, according to Nolan, "a killer bowl of potato chips."

Jillian, evidently didn't cook. Nolan didn't seem to care.

Ethan and Darcy were there. So were Eve and her husband, Mac, whose dark good looks and quick smile could compete with the Garrett men, any day.

Even Manny and his new wife Lily and their son Adam joined the party, with Jason Wilson and his wife in tow.

"Is that . . . that can't be . . ." Amy stuttered when she saw the woman at Jason's side. "She looks like . . . like that famous rock star."

"Sweet Baby Jane?" Dallas asked with a grin.

"It's not, is it?"

He popped an olive into his mouth. " 'Fraid so."

"Dallas. You didn't tell me."

He grinned down on her. "Tell you what?"

"Well . . . that there was going to be a celebrity here."

He grunted. "Don't let Janey hear you say that. Far be it from me to dispute her, but she considers us the closest thing to normal in her life—and she loves just being a person when she's with us."

Amy relaxed a little. Grinned. "Normal is a bit of a stretch," she agreed.

"I warned you."

He had. He'd warned her that his family was loud and boisterous and irreverent when they all got together during their down time.

They were all that and more. And Amy loved it. Loved the idea of belonging to a family almost as much as she loved Dallas.

She glanced back at her mother, touched a hand to her heart when she saw Nolan's little boy on her lap and Wes kneeling beside them, supporting the little guy's weight.

"She's smiling," Amy said, swallowing back tears.

"Like you said," Dallas turned her in his arms and kissed her forehead. "She's happy here."

"She's happy," Amy said, not caring that there were tears running down her face, "because of you. You and your wonderful not-so-normal family. I love them. I love them all."

"See, now that's what I call a very nice coincidence. Because they all love you too," he added gently.

"Thank you." She snuggled up against him. "Just thank you."

"Don't thank me yet, sweetheart. The ugly family secret is about to come out."

She leaned back. He'd linked his hands together at the small of her back and held her hips close to his. "You have an ugly secret?"

His eyes danced. "Should have told you before, huh?"

"Depends. What's the secret?"

He hooked a thumb over his shoulder.

She peeked around him.

Eve was dragging something that looked like a . . . "Is that a croquet set?"

"Game on!" Eve shouted. "And I pity the fool who thinks they can beat me on this fine, fine day."

"Jenna says hi." Amy dropped down on the sofa beside Dallas the next evening.

He looked up from the newspaper. "How is she?"

"Good. I think. Kind of subdued. She asked if we'd heard anything from Gabe."

"That's not likely to ever happen."

"I wonder about him, sometimes, too. If he's okay. If Reed and Lang made out okay."

Dallas folded the paper, set it on the coffee table and turned to her. "You don't have to worry about those three. They know how to handle themselves."

She leaned back into him when he lifted his arm in invitation. "I wonder how Juliana fits into that puzzle."

"Amazing woman."

Amy nodded against his shoulder. "Sad, though. Beneath her gracious welcome, I thought she seemed a little sad."

"Everyone has secrets," he agreed and kissed her temple.

"And ghosts," she added.

They'd been addressing their ghosts. They were down to monthly visits now, but both Dallas and Amy had been seeing someone to help them deal with the PSTD.

It was slow. But it was coming along. She didn't figure they'd ever be fully free of their past. In truth, she didn't want to be. She never would have met Dallas if it hadn't been for what had happened to her on Jolo. And what had happened to her . . . it was part of who she was now.

But the man beside her—he was the biggest part.

She turned in his arms. Kissed him with feeling.

When she pulled away, they were both smiling.

"You thinking what I'm thinking?" he asked in a deep, sexy bedroom voice.

"Yeah." She ran a finger suggestively down his chest. "Let's do it. Let's go get the croquet set. I need to practice."

He groaned, wounded to the bone. "Eve has turned you into a monster."

"But, I'm your monster, right? And you wouldn't have me any other way."

"Scars and all," he said, running his thumb tenderly along the crescent-shaped scar on her temple. "Scars and all."

Dear Reader,

It has been a joy introducing you to the amazing men and women of E.D.E.N., Inc. during the course of the Bodyguards series. And judging from the many responses I've received, you have enjoyed reading about Nolan and Jillian, Eve and Mac, Ethan and Darcy, Jase and Janey, Manny and Lily, and Dallas and Amy as much as I've enjoyed telling their stories.

It's always hard to say good-bye to old friends—and truly, the Garretts and their extended family have become my friends—as I hope they've become yours. So let's not say good-bye, okay? Let's just say so long for now, wish them well and hope that we may someday see them again.

If you like the E.D.E.N. series, I promise I have several more similar stories in mind. Gabe and Jenna, for instance. They're both calling to me. Both have a story to be told—Gabe's dark and deep and Jenna's feisty and fun. And as obnoxious as he was, there was something about Johnny Duane Reed that made me smile and wonder about the heart and true nature of the man who lived behind that sexy grin. Not to mention Sam Lang. The quiet man. How many secrets must he harbor? I wonder what it's going to take to pry them out of him. . . .

I love hearing from you and make all efforts to answer all my mail, so don't hesitate to contact to me via my website: www.cindygerard.com.

All my best until next time,
Cindy